Praise for the *Arthur Quinn* books

'A brilliant creation … fast-paced and thrilling' – Eoin Colfer, author of *Artemis Fowl*

'A clever blend of fantasy and the every day. It's like Harry Potter, Dublin style' – *Irish Examiner*

'One of the most exciting adventure stories published in Ireland in the last few years' – *Irish Independent*

'An absolute rip-roaring

'A gripping supernatural

'Norse myth, Irish hist~~ory~~ ~~and contemporary Dublin~~ blend convincingly' – *The Irish Times*

'A mystical world of mythological characters comes alive, time stops, the unimaginable occurs, and the excitement is full blast from beginning to end' – *VOYA, Voices of Youth Advocates*

'An action-packed suspense mystery' – *School Librarian Journal*

'It's like a ride on the back of the Fenris Wolf itself, breathlessly exciting … perfect for everyone who enjoyed *Avengers Assemble*.' – Alexander Gordon Smith, *Inis Magazine*

'A fantastic, riveting read and one you will enjoy over and over. Bring on the third book!!!' – Mary Esther Judy, *The Bookbag*

ARTHUR QUINN

AND
HELL'S KEEPER

BOOK 3
THE FATHER OF LIES CHRONICLES

ALAN EARLY

MERCIER PRESS
IRISH PUBLISHER – IRISH STORY

MERCIER PRESS
Cork
www.mercierpress.ie

© Alan Early, 2013

ISBN: 978 1 78117 158 5

10 9 8 7 6 5 4 3 2 1

A CIP record for this title is available from the British Library

Printed and bound in the EU.

To Paul, Dee, Lou, Ruairí and Tag,

for your names and so much more.

PROLOGUE

Neil Conifrey felt a surge of relief when he saw the turn off the main road up ahead. It had been a long journey from Dublin and the snail's pace of the Friday rush-hour traffic had only made it longer. Kurt and Susanna had squabbled in the back for most of the two-hour-plus drive, while Joanna – Neil's wife – sat staunchly silent in the passenger seat, massaging away a particularly painful migraine. Now, as they approached the turn-off, the bickering finally came to an end. Neil glanced in the rear-view mirror at his two kids. Kurt was sixteen and had definitely inherited genes from Joanna's side of the family. With the cleft in his chin and the slightly bulging eyes, he was the spitting image of Joanna's older brother. He even shared his uncle's dark five o'clock shadow. Ten-year-old Susanna, on the other hand, took after Neil with her mop of wiry brown hair and poor eyesight.

He focused back on his driving as he turned up the laneway towards the holiday home. Despite the harsh winter they'd just emerged from, the gravel track was overgrown with brambles and bushes already. Usually he didn't have to trim back the growth until their annual visit over the May Bank Holiday, but by the looks of it he'd have to do some work on it this weekend.

Bad weather had forced them to remain in Dublin over Christmas. Normally they were glad to get out of the city to visit Joanna's parents in Leitrim, but the snow and ice had put a stop to that. Now – to celebrate Joanna's birthday – Neil had taken the family to their holiday home a few miles outside Mullingar. He thought it would be a much-needed break from the hustle and bustle of the city – although, judging by the way it had begun, he figured he'd have gotten more rest back in Dublin.

The house itself was secluded at the end of the laneway, overlooking a small hillside. It was a compact bungalow, painted a cheery yellow and of a clean, modern design. The sun had set a couple of hours before and, as Neil parked the car, he was surprised to see light pouring from one of the windows.

'Did anyone leave a light on last time we were here?'

he asked, pulling up the handbrake. He turned to his children, irritated.

'No,' Kurt answered sullenly, looking out of his window.

'Wasn't me,' said Susanna. 'Honest.'

Neil turned to Joanna, raising a quizzical eyebrow.

'Don't look at me like that,' she warned him. 'You probably left it on. You always do at home.' He unhooked his seat belt, unwilling to admit that she was more than likely right. He did have a habit of forgetting to turn off the house lights at night or any time he was going out.

They bustled out of the car. Joanna leaned back against the bonnet, inhaling the cool air deeply, glad to be out of the stuffy vehicle. She was holding a bag of basic groceries they'd picked up in a petrol station en route. Susanna ran off to inspect the apple tree she had planted the previous spring. As Neil heaved their one suitcase out of the car boot, Kurt was waving his mobile phone in the air, trying to catch some reception.

'I have no bars,' he complained. 'Dad, there are no bars.'

'Of course there aren't,' Neil said, pulling the wheeled case towards the front door. 'There weren't any when we came here last year or the summer before that or the spring before that. And there won't be any if we come here in May. But isn't it nice to be away from the pitfalls of modern society for a few days?'

Kurt chose not to answer, sighed and thrust the phone back in his pocket petulantly. Neil smiled to himself, took the house keys out of his pocket and tried to find the right one before his son could voice another complaint. Even after coming here all these years, he still couldn't work out the previous owners' key-coding system.

'No apples,' said Susanna sadly, crossing back from the small front garden.

'They'll grow in the autumn, Suzie,' said her mother. 'Don't worry. As soon as your dad gets the door open, we'll put on some nice hot chocolate. How does that sound?'

As if on cue, Neil managed to turn the correct key in the door with a click.

'All aboard!' he exclaimed as he went in – an old joke he'd used countless times before, which they all rolled their eyes at now.

Considering the house had spent some months uninhabited, Neil had expected it to be almost arctic inside, but he was bewildered to find that it was actually quite warm. As he put down the case, the family all piled past him into the kitchen – to where he'd apparently left the light glowing on their last visit. None of the rest of them seemed to notice the warmth in the house, or, if they did, they didn't think it strange. He watched through the door as Joanna turned the stove on and his children rooted through the cupboard for supplies. He made his way slowly towards them, keeping his ears alert for … well, he didn't know what for. He didn't want to think about it, really. The back of his hand felt a radiator as he passed; it was hot to the touch.

'Any marshmallows?' Joanna was asking as she heaped spoonfuls of chocolate powder into a saucepan of simmering milk.

'Just a few,' Kurt replied, retrieving a near-empty bag of marshmallows.

'We'll put some more on the shopping list for tomorrow.'

'Joanna,' said Neil.

'Hmm?' She didn't turn, just kept stirring the chocolate.

'Joanna,' he said again, more urgently this time.

'What is it?' she asked irritably, swivelling towards him.

'Did you put that there?' He pointed to the breakfast table. The calendar from the wall had been left on it, open to the month of February. The first three weeks' worth of days had been crossed off – right up to today. A rough-edged X the colour of rust marked off each day. It looked like it had been scrawled with a fingertip in ink. Or …

'Is that blood?' Kurt spluttered, staring at the calendar.

'Hello there!' said a voice behind them. Neil spun to

find himself facing a tall man. He had platinum-blond hair, cropped close to his skull. His beard was trimmed into what he'd often heard Joanna refer to as 'fashionable stubble'. His eyes were a shockingly pale blue and they darted from one member of the Conifrey family to the next. He was wearing pinstriped trousers, a matching waistcoat, shirt and tie. There was no sign of the blazer that would complete the three-piece ensemble. Over it all, he wore a frilly pink apron that had 'Kiss the Cook' scrawled across it in cartoony text and a print of a naked, muscled chest underneath it. He was grinning at them, exposing a row of flawless white teeth.

'Is that hot chocolate?' he asked, slamming the door behind him. 'I do love hot chocolate.'

'Wh– … who are you?'

Without warning, the man leapt forward. He thrust a hand against Neil's chest and pushed him backwards. Joanna cried out as Neil flew through the air, crashed into the kitchen units and slumped to the ground.

'Who am I?' cackled the blond-haired man shrilly. 'I am Loki, the Father of Lies,' he said, strolling nonchalantly further into the kitchen. 'And we're all going to have such fun together!'

PART ONE

CHAPTER ONE

'We should go to the cinema tomorrow.'

'Is there anything good on?'

'There's that new one about the gangster who moves to a small town. It's meant to be OK.'

'Ugh, no. How about the new one in the "Blue Moon" series? It's got vampires.'

'And also romance. And that Robert Mattinson guy. So, no thanks!'

'We can decide when we get there. I'll ask my mum to drive us into Tralee. You up for it, Arthur?'

Arthur Quinn was in another world, kicking an empty Coke can in front of him as he shuffled along the pavement heading home from school. He should have been as excited as his friends for the weekend ahead, but he just couldn't get that 'Friday feeling'. His brown hair, naturally shaggy, was starting to become unruly again after a tight haircut only a month previously. Freckles covered his nose and high cheekbones. His right eye was a deep blue, punctuated by flecks of apple green, while his left eye was covered in a dark leather eye-patch. It was permanently bloodshot now and the once-blue iris had turned an ugly crimson. A line of scar-tissue peeked out from either side of the patch, tracing where a chunk of rock from an exploding tower had taken the vision there. The can tumbled off the path and kept rolling along the rain gutter.

'Arthur?'

'Hmm?' He picked the can off the road and dropped it into a nearby bin, then turned to his friends. Paul, Louise and Dave were all staring at him quizzically. 'Sorry, did you say something?'

'I asked if you wanted to come to the cinema tomorrow,' Paul repeated irritably. He was tall and lanky, in the middle of his first teenage growth spurt. The eldest of the group, he'd just turned thirteen a few weeks earlier, although Arthur hadn't been around to join in the celebrations. He'd still been living in Dublin then. Last October, Arthur's father, Joe, had been offered a job in the capital city, working on the excavation for the upcoming Dublin Metro train. When the work had been postponed indefinitely a month ago, Joe had made the decision to move home to Kerry. They'd been back in the quiet village of Farranfore less than a week, but already Arthur was missing his Dublin friends. It wasn't that he didn't like Paul, Louise or Dave. On the contrary, he still valued their friendship greatly. But he and his Dublin mates had been through so much together in such a short time. Only they could really understand how he felt now and the fears that he had.

'Oh. Uh … no thanks.'

'Oh come on, Arthur! It'll be fun,' Louise urged. She was almost as tall as Paul, with black hair and olive skin that were a result of genes from her Italian mother.

'It's been a long week and I just want to rest,' Arthur lied. Granted, it had been a long week, but he didn't feel like resting. He'd had enough of that in the hospital after the explosion. He'd caused the explosion himself, three weeks ago, in order to stop the evil trickster god Loki's latest plan. Arthur had had to do it and he still believed that losing the sight in one eye was a better option than what the god had had in mind for him. Loki had been trying to transform everyone in Ireland into wolves, an unstoppable army to help him conquer the world.

A millennium before, the trickster god had created three terrible children with the ultimate aim of destroying the world. The other gods were enraged by his actions and bound him under Dublin for eternity, disposing of his children in various ways. However, when construction on the Metro began, Loki was freed and set about finding and releasing his evil brood. Arthur – with the help of his friends and an army of dead Vikings that had been buried to guard it – managed to defeat and kill the first child, the World Serpent. Then Loki went to find his second child – a wolf-man called Fenrir. Fenrir was supposed to have created an army of wolves for Loki to enslave humanity with, but, after spending a thousand years living in this world, he had grown to respect – and even like – the human race. He had disobeyed the Father of Lies' orders and went as far as hiding Loki's third child in case the god returned. Only Fenrir knew the whereabouts of Loki's daughter – Hell's Keeper, as she was known.

But after the explosion at the tower, Fenrir had gone missing …

The only thing Arthur wanted to do this weekend was chat to his Dublin friends online. He was desperately looking forward to finding out if they'd had any luck in finding Fenrir with Ash's GPS since he'd left them the Sunday before.

'Don't worry, Mad-Eye Moody,' said Dave. 'We won't go to a 3D film!' He pointed to Arthur's eye-patch and burst out laughing. Despite the dull pain he still felt there, Arthur couldn't help but join in. Dave was short for his age. Actually, if he had been nine, he would still have been short for his age. He was tubby, moved slowly and had greasy hair. In other words, perfect fodder for bullies. His one saving grace – and the one thing that kept bullies at bay – was the witty one-liners he was known for.

A car-horn honked. Arthur looked around to see his dad behind the wheel, waving to him.

'See you three Monday,' Arthur shouted to them as he ran to the car. He was secretly pleased that his dad had shown up when he did; it meant that he wouldn't have to field any more questions about why he didn't want to go to the cinema. He guessed his old friends wouldn't be too impressed that he was blowing them off for his new friends in Dublin. Buckling himself into the passenger seat, he said hi to Joe.

'Good day at school?' Joe enquired as they drove through the quiet market town. His hair was starting to thin and he was going grey at the temples, but apart from that, and the bags that sometimes appeared under his eyes, he showed no other signs of aging. Upon quitting the job in Dublin, he'd been fortunate enough to return to his previous career as a freelance engineering consultant. The work wasn't as regular as in the city – which meant that he had much more time to do errands and hang out with Arthur.

Arthur's mother had always liked the freedom the job had given Joe. It meant that they could book weekends away at short notice or that she could rely on him to pick up Arthur from school. But then, less than a year earlier, she'd suddenly become sick. She'd deteriorated very quickly, getting weaker with each passing day. Arthur still missed her and thought of her constantly. He reached for the golden ribbon tied around his right wrist. It had been hers and she'd worn it always, so when she died he had taken it as a constant reminder of her.

They passed through the quiet village and into the countryside. It was an overcast February day outside, mild and dry for this time of year. As they waited at a crossroads for a tractor to turn, Arthur gazed with fascination at a robin by the ditch in the road. It was pecking at a scrap of sandwich someone – probably a farmer – had dropped earlier. Just then, a crow swooped down out of nowhere. It grabbed the crust in its strong beak and soared away, leaving the robin hungry. Joe pulled away before Arthur had a chance to throw out some of his leftovers from lunch.

Their house was a large two-storey building covered in a sandstone facing. Each of the four front-facing rooms had a bay window. There was an expansive lawn in the front – always kept neatly mowed and with a cosy rockery in one corner – and a long, unkempt field in the back. Joe kept meaning to get some animals to keep in the meadow – a couple of goats or sheep, he used to say – but he never got around to it.

He parked and unlocked the front door. Arthur dropped his schoolbag on the hardwood floor and loped upstairs.

'Dinner in an hour!' Joe shouted after him as he bounded into his bedroom and collapsed on the bed. He sighed and looked around the room, thinking of Ash and the others in Dublin.

This is home, this is home, he kept telling himself. But then, why didn't it feel like it?

In a time before the writing of history, in Asgard, the realm of the gods, the great rainbow Bifrost is a bridge between the worlds. Seven colours shimmer and shift across the magical structure. It changes position – travelling to where a god most needs use of the bridge – and leads from any point in Asgard to any point in Midgard, the world of man.

The sun is at its highest point in the clear azure sky. It is noon and, though the air is hot, Loki feels comfortable in his heavy brown tunic. Such is the magic of the place. Bifrost rises before him then dips over a hillside and into Midgard. He sits on a boulder, watching the fluctuating colours and resting before his journey. He has a small feast laid out before him on the rocky terrain, comprising seven types of cheese, nine wines from the nine worlds and more meat, mead, bread, pâté and sweets than one could count. He is filling his belly now with a swan leg, savouring the rich flavour as meat juices seep down his bearded chin. He smirks as he chews, thinking of all he has achieved in such a short time.

Two days ago, the gods shamed him. They sat and laughed as an ugly giantess abused him, stitching his mouth shut. He stormed out of Odin All-Father's great dining hall then, vowing vengeance on them all. He rose the following morning and created the World Serpent, sending it to the world of man to wreak devastation. Next, he transformed an injured and pitiful beast into the Fenris Wolf – a wolf who could change himself into a man – and charged him with building an army of men with similar powers, with which he would rule. And now, finally, he will create his third – and most powerful – child.

He glugs some mead and throws the now-empty horn aside. It cracks in two and golden, syrupy droplets spill out. He stands, stretching his back and neck with a crack, then turns towards Bifrost. Suddenly he breaks into a run, faster than any man's legs could carry him. He sprints up the bridge and, even though it appears to be nothing more than a translucent rainbow, his footing is solid.

As he reaches the apex of Bifrost, he leaps into the air, landing on his backside with a thump. Then he slides down the other side of the bridge, arms splayed out joyously and screaming '*Wheee!*' all the way down. The sky grows darker as he descends, until his feet land in Midgard. It is night in this part of the world of man and the village he has arrived in is totally silent. All are asleep here, for which Loki is thankful. If anyone had been awake and seen the rainbow in the middle of the night, they might have raised their weapons against him. And though he could easily have dealt with them, he doesn't want the inconvenience.

The village is called Roskilde and many worshippers of the gods reside here. What a suitable place to steal from Odin, Loki thinks as he walks between the low huts. They are constructed from wood, with straw and earth roofs. A narrow hole has been left in the centre of each roof to allow smoke from the cooking fire within to escape. His footfalls make no sound on the twigs or pebbles scattered about and, apart from some heavy snoring from a few huts, the only sound to be heard is the light lapping of the nearby river and a couple of longboats knocking gently against the wooden quay.

He stands stock-still in the centre of the village, closes his eyes and listens. Slowly he turns his head, searching for a particular sound. And then–

'There!' he hisses to himself, following the direction of the noise. It had been a whimper, tinny and in the distance, but distinct nonetheless. A baby's whimper.

He arrives at the hut where the sound came from, and enters noiselessly. Although it is pitch black inside, he can see perfectly. A man and woman sleep soundly on one bed-roll. Straw has been gathered in a pile for the mattress with some deerhide laid over it. The couple are snuggled together underneath a warm bearskin. Loki looks down at them pitilessly. They don't even stir at his arrival in their house, but continue to dream peacefully.

The baby lies next to them. She is wrapped first in tight swaddling and then in another piece of the velvety bearskin. The fur blanket is so thick around the babe that she has no need of bed-roll straw like her parents. Her eyes are wide open, staring up at Loki, and she whimpers again – this time Loki can sense her fear – spittle bubbling out at the side of her lips. It's intoxicating. She's clearly terrified, more scared than she's ever been in her short life, too frightened to cry for her mother and father. A third whimpering sound is all she can manage.

He leans down and picks her up, cradling her in his arms. Then he swivels and leaves the house.

'You will be my most terrible child,' he whispers to her as he strides back through Roskilde. 'I will give you a part of myself. For generations to come, people will whisper your name around campfires and in the dark of night. You, Hel, will be the thing they fear the most.'

The baby girl finally starts to cry – a high-pitched shriek that pierces everyone's dreams in the village, waking them. But by now it is too late. Loki steps onto Bifrost and the two of them are gone. The anguished cries of the child's parents rend the night, while the wails of the lost babe echo throughout Roskilde. And that sound echoes through all of Midgard for all of time. The sound of a taken baby. The sound of Hel herself.

CHAPTER TWO

Arthur's eyes shot open. The sound of the baby's cries faded slowly inside his head. He felt a wetness on his cheek and when he touched it he was shocked to find tears seeping out of his good eye. He sat up in bed and pulled the pendant from around his neck. It had come into his possession months ago, when he'd found it in a tunnel underneath the city of Dublin. It was round, roughly twice the size of a two-euro coin and seemed to be made of bronze. An image was hammered onto the face of the pendant. It depicted a tall, wide tree with bare branches intertwining on top. A snake was coiled around the trunk, strangling it. The pendant protected Arthur from Loki – the trickster god couldn't touch it without being blasted away – and it was glowing green now as it always did whenever something happened in connection with Loki.

Arthur wiped the drying tears from his face and threw his blanket off. He put the pendant back around his neck, got out of bed and knelt on the carpeted floor. He reached under the bed, brushing aside the old *Beano* annuals he had piled there before finding what he was looking for. His hand gripped the handle and pulled out the war hammer.

He'd found the hammer underneath Dublin, near where he'd found the pendant. The head of it was forged from iron and ancient letters and symbols were embossed into the gleaming metal – runes that even the pendant wouldn't allow Arthur to read. The handle itself was a simple piece of timber – barely long enough for an adult's grip – wrapped in fine rope for extra traction. It felt lighter in Arthur's grasp than it had any right to, as if it was made just for him. He'd held other war hammers and they didn't suit him. But this one was different – it had belonged to the god and warrior Thor, who'd died battling the World Serpent. The hammer wasn't radiating like the pendant, but it was giving off a low warmth.

'Ready for battle,' Arthur murmured, clutching the handle tightly. It had played an integral part in defeating Loki before and he knew it would do so again. It was the only weapon he knew of powerful enough to hurt the god, and it had already saved his life more than once. He slid it back under the bed, confident that it would come to him when he most needed it.

With the dream or vision or prophecy or whatever-it-was still fresh in his mind's eye, Arthur knew he'd have to let his friends in Dublin know what he'd seen. He always dreamed of Asgard when Loki was up to something.

He had barely been in contact with anyone from Dublin since he and Joe had moved last Sunday. Part of him had expected Ash, his best friend, to email or text. But the other part of him realised that she was still hurt by his leaving. On Wednesday evening, he'd had a text from Ellie Lavender, one of their other friends, suggesting that they should all have a video chat at lunchtime on Saturday. Well it was only after eight o'clock now, but he couldn't wait any longer. He picked up his mobile phone from the bedside locker – about to call Ellie to have her bring forward the video chat – when it rang.

A JPEG of Ash filled the screen along with the text 'Incoming Call'. He held the phone at arm's length, unsure how to proceed. Then, on the fourth ring, he pressed the 'Answer' key and put the phone to his ear.

'Hi,' he said.

'Hey,' Ash's voice came through the tinny speaker. 'We all need to talk.'

'I know. Ellie arranged a video chat for twelve-ish. Didn't she mention it?'

'She did but I mean we all need to talk now.'

'Why? What's happened?' Had Loki done something to her? Or Max or Ellie or any of them?

'We had a dream. We had *the* dream.'

'What? Who?'

'All of us.'

'Huh? Max and the Lavenders too?'

'No, Arthur. You don't get it. All of us. My parents, the Lavenders' granddad, everyone.'

Loki bit his fingertip with a sharp canine, breaking the skin. A pearl of blood formed on the tip: a perfect, glistening orb. He pressed his finger to the calendar and drew an X across the day's date. As he dragged his fingertip across the paper, the wound stung. When he was finished, for a couple of seconds the fingertip was encased in a bright green light, and when the light faded it was healed. He looked down at the calendar. Just over a week to go until the next full moon. The full moon – fundamental to the source of Fenrir's power – would help him find the wolf.

'Good morning, Wolf-father,' said a voice at the door behind him. The girl was wearing her black hair loose for a change and it hung sleekly down by her shoulders. When Loki had brought her here she'd been wearing an antique frilly dress from the early twentieth century, made grubby and stinking after the explosion. Now she was wearing a pair of denim jeans and a black fleece hoodie that he'd found for her amongst the teenage boy's spare clothes. Her name was Drysi and she was the first person that Fenrir had turned into a wolf, a thousand years ago. This, technically, made her Fenrir's daughter and Loki's granddaughter. She certainly had more sense than Fenrir, Loki thought, and had remained by his side since his return, unlike her turncoat father.

She rolled into the kitchen in the wheelchair they'd been lucky to find in the attic. Neil had left it there for when his frail mother-in-law came to stay for a couple of weeks every summer. Unlike the bamboo contraption Drysi had been used to, this was simpler to manoeuvre and she was able to move around the house with ease. She'd lost the use of her legs a hundred years ago, during the 1916 Rising, when a roof had collapsed on her. But she believed to this day that Loki, when the world was finally his, would restore her ability to walk.

'Good morning, Drysi,' Loki said. 'Did you sleep well?'

Drysi went to the fridge, where she raided the bag of food the Conifrey family had arrived with the night before.

'I slept well,' she told him, before adding spitefully, 'but I suspect our guests didn't.'

'Oh no?'

'No.' She smirked as she carried just enough bread and butter for herself to the table; Loki never needed to eat and only did so out of habit, but she had appetites just like any other living being. 'By the way, they were making a bit of a racket when I passed the living room just now.'

'Is that so?' said Loki. He kicked his chair back and strode down the hallway towards the living room. He paused just outside and knocked on the door.

'Room service!' he called in a high-pitched falsetto before bursting in.

The room, like the rest of the house, was quite modern. Not much more than a blank canvas with a few touches from the family here and there: framed photographs, DVDs, old magazines and books. The Conifrey family were sitting in the centre of the floor on a plush cream rug. Each of them had their arms tied behind their backs, their legs bound together with black duct tape and a strip of the same tape across their mouth. They were positioned back to back, with more layers of tape wrapped around them, keeping them all tightly in place. Despite this,

Loki could still hear the sounds of snivelling from the girl child.

'What's going on?' he demanded. He dropped down in front of her and ripped the tape off the girl's lips, with no regard for the stinging pain that followed. She whimpered more.

'Quit your whining,' warned Loki, 'and tell me what's wrong!'

'I ... I had a nightmare,' the girl, Susanna, said, avoiding his eyes.

'So?'

'You were in it.'

'Oh *really*?' He seemed pleased at that and he sat back, crossing his arms eagerly. 'Tell me more.'

'You ... you took a baby.'

As she said this, the rest of the family turned their heads towards her, their eyes wide. Loki noticed their reaction. He moved around and pulled the tape from the man's mouth, taking some unshaven facial hair with it. The man couldn't help but yelp in pain.

'Why did you look so surprised just now?'

'Please,' said Neil. 'Please, for the love of God, let us go.'

'Answer me!'

'Just let my family go,' he pleaded further, ignoring Loki's demand. 'Please just–'

He was cut off when the trickster god slapped him hard across the face.

'Enough! Answer my question,' said Loki, struggling to remain calm and keep his anger in check. 'Why were you so shocked when she told me about her nightmare?'

'Because I had the same one,' Neil told him, his voice weak.

'What happened in it?'

'You were in some other world. And then you travelled on a rainbow. To … to a small village. It was a long time ago, I think. At least it looked that way. You stole a baby.'

'Hel,' uttered Loki, leaning away from the man in quiet awe.

'Yes! That's right. That's what you called her.'

'Did you all have this dream?' Loki looked at the rest of the family. They nodded slowly, their eyes filled with fear.

'What does it mean?' asked Drysi from the doorway.

Loki stared at the floor, deep in thought. Drysi repeated her question.

'I don't know,' Loki answered eventually, getting to his feet and striding briskly past the girl out the door. 'But it can't be good.'

'The exact same dream,' Arthur muttered, still amazed.

'Yup,' said Ellie's voice from his laptop speakers.

After the call with Ash, he'd promised that he'd video chat with them all in half an hour. He had just needed time to have a quick shower and get dressed. He had also wanted to ask Joe about the dream. His dad had been reading a newspaper when he'd gone downstairs to the kitchen.

'Dad,' he had said, somewhat coyly.

'Yes, son?' Joe didn't look up from the paper.

'Did you have a weird nightmare last night?'

'I did as it happens.' He peered over the edge of the broadsheet at Arthur quizzically. 'Why do you ask?'

'I got up to use the bathroom at one stage during the night,' he lied, 'and I heard you moaning.'

'Oh.' Joe seemed to buy it, setting the paper down. 'It was such an odd dream.'

'What happened in it?'

'There was some guy ... this crazy-looking man ...' His eyes met Arthur's again. 'And he stole a baby. I felt like I *was* that baby in a weird way ... like I was the one being taken. It was really horrible.'

After that Arthur had gone back to his room to shower and dress. He was sitting at the computer now, watching the faces of his friends on-screen. One half of the monitor showed the video link-up of Ash and Max Barry. Ash – short for Ashling – was the same age as Arthur and was one of the first friends he'd made when he moved to Dublin. Her wavy auburn hair was tied up in a ponytail, the way she usually wore it. She and Arthur shared a lot of the same interests: similar music, books and films. But, unlike Arthur, she was really into electronics. She could spend hours by herself poring over circuit boards and program coding. In fact, she'd been the one that set up this three-way video chat.

Next to her was Max who, at eight, was Ash's little brother. He had the same shade of hair as the rest of the Barry family, but it sat on top of his head in tight curls. He had an excitable demeanour and almost continuously rattled on about football, the one great love of his life.

So far Ash and Max had managed to keep their involvement in foiling Loki's schemes secret from their older sister, Stace, and their parents. Arthur firmly believed that this was the best course of action. The more people who got involved with Loki, the more likely they would be hurt by him.

On the other side of the screen were the Lavenders. At eleven years old, Ellie Lavender was the world's youngest paranormal investigator. She had a slight frame, which made her seem younger, and her straight black hair was cut into a bob that ended just above her shoulders. Since Arthur had known her she had always worn an oversized adult trench coat. Whenever her parents were off travelling the world, as they had been for the last few months, her mother lent Ellie her coat to wear. Right now they were in Greece. With her knowledge of world mythologies, her abnormally high IQ and her photographic memory, Ellie had all the skills necessary for a great detective. She had even managed to recall Arthur's face after Loki had wiped everyone's knowledge of the World Serpent's attack on Dublin. When she'd seen him on TV the year before, his face had been so familiar that her suspicions had been aroused and she'd decided to investigate him. Now she was as wrapped up in Loki's devious plans as the rest of them.

Xander Lavender, or Ex as he preferred to be known, was the polar opposite of his sister. He was a year older than the rest of them but seemed to have been rushed through adolescence. He was as tall and broad as an average man and even had a few wisps of facial hair on his chin. His hair was shaved tightly to his round skull, giving him a fierce appearance. While Ellie was chatty and intelligent, Ex was quiet and brooding. He rarely spoke and when he did it was short and to the point.

Ellie was just finishing her account of the dream in close detail once more.

'But you mean everyone?' Arthur said, aghast. 'Everyone in the world?'

'That's what the news is reporting. It looks like most of the world had exactly the same Dream with a capital D.'

'I still can't believe it,' Ash said. 'It seemed so real.'

'Are these just like the dreams you always get, Arthur?' Ellie asked.

'It was definitely another one of the Asgard dreams,' Arthur said, 'or visions. Whatever you want to call them.'

'What can it mean?' That was Max. After having the dream for himself and witnessing the baby-napping, he seemed quieter, more subdued than usual. He'd experienced some bad nightmares after Loki's first scheme and Arthur hoped they wouldn't start up again.

'Haven't a clue, Max. Although every time I had one of the dreams before, they usually told me something that would help me defeat Loki. So maybe …'

'Maybe it's someone reaching out to us?' Ellie finished for him. 'Someone wants to help humanity? To beat Loki?'

'Possibly. Who knows … but tell me, what else has been going on? How are the army?' he asked, referring to the surviving members of the Viking army who had helped them fight the World Serpent. After the monster was defeated, the army had remained alive, so they were now living in the Viking Experience in Dublin, hiding in plain sight. Although 'alive' wasn't quite the right way to describe them, Arthur thought. Sure, they could move and think, but their skin had shrunk and discoloured like an Egyptian mummy's, their hair was gone and Arthur hadn't a clue if their hearts were still beating. They weren't dead but they weren't quite alive either.

'They're fine,' Ash said. 'We visited them on Thursday after school. Eirik seems to miss you.' The soldiers couldn't talk – their vocal chords had long since withered away – but they could communicate to some extent by grunting, and Eirik was the most proficient at this.

'What about the webcam? Find anything?'

Ash had been held captive by Loki for a short time and she had struck up a friendship with Fenrir, who had also been a prisoner. And now he had a webcam that belonged to her. The webcam was wireless and GPS-enabled, so if it was still out there she should be able to track it down.

'Nothing,' she said, frustrated. 'It might have been destroyed. Or maybe Fenrir's already gone. Maybe Loki has him.'

'I hope not. Because if Loki finds Fenrir before we do, I have a sneaking suspicion that all hope of stopping him is gone.'

CHAPTER THREE

Within twenty-four hours, every news agency on earth was broadcasting reports of the mysterious Dream. It was such a huge story that journalists the world over decided to capitalise the 'D' to emphasise the importance. The Dream – which hardly varied at all from one account to another – appeared to focus primarily on the inhabitants of Western Europe, as it hit when most of the populations in these time zones were asleep. Despite this, reports were also coming in from every other continent that the Dream had spread there also. People who had dozed off for an afternoon nap in the Americas, to those who'd slept in or worked night-shifts in Australasia, all testified to having had the same dream. Enthusiastic reporters visiting the town of Roskilde, Denmark, helped to fill the twenty-four-hour rolling news channels. There was no doubt that this had been the village featured in the Dream. Most Dreamers were even able to name the town itself – as if it was somewhere they'd actually been to – and historians confirmed that the descriptions of the Viking-era village matched how they believed Roskilde looked a thousand years ago.

No one could identify the baby that had been stolen all those centuries ago. No one could explain the Dream. No one came forward with any helpful information. And no one felt quite safe going to sleep the following night.

But sleep came and days and nights passed without any further incidents. Some people reported that they'd had another one, claiming that their nightmares of going to work without any clothes on, or of finding that they were back in school on the day of an important exam which they hadn't studied for, were in fact prophecies of the End of Days. News coverage continued to pore over the Dream, while analysts and psychologists searched the vision for metaphors. They prattled on for hours about the obvious symbolism behind the rainbow or how the whole Dream was really an allegory for the Iraq War. They were all so busy looking into the various hidden meanings that they couldn't see the wood for the trees. In fact, some historians who suggested that the rainbow was similar to the Norse legend of Bifrost were actually laughed off the air.

Only Arthur and his friends knew the truth, but they weren't planning on letting anyone in on the secret any time soon. They'd spent most of the weekend working to find Fenrir. Ash had managed to hack into a security database that had access to all exterior CCTV cameras in the country. They took turns staring at chunks of grainy footage from the day of the explosion, hoping to catch a glimpse of the wolf-man and where he'd disappeared to. All to no avail.

By Monday morning, Arthur was feeling downbeat and distraught, and his right eye was tired from the hours spent examining the pixellated videos. He went to school to find the whole place abuzz with excited chatter about the Dream. Paul, Louise and Dave were eager to hear his take on it. After discussing it at length with Ash and the others, he didn't feel like rehashing it all again so he just gave them brief one-word answers. They soon realised he didn't want to talk and left him with his thoughts. He barely even noticed when they kept their distance for the rest of the week.

He walked home by himself every day. He'd begun the week by half-running home, hoping that some news of Fenrir awaited him there. By the end of the week – and with no further developments – he just strolled home slowly. Alone and dejected.

On Friday, as he left school behind him for the weekend, Arthur visited his mother.

Although he hadn't been to the cemetery in months, he could still find the way to his mother's grave without any trouble. The route would always be imprinted on his mind and he manoeuvred through the narrow, grassy pathways with ease. The grave itself had crisp, white gravel scattered over the top and a low limestone edging around it. A red lantern sat in the centre of the grave. The tiny LED bulb inside it was glowing faintly. Thanks to the small solar panel attached to the top, it would stay lit for years. The gravestone was black marble with green veins creeping through its pristine surface. It reflected the rolling clouds from the sky above. His mother's name was chiselled out in neat Roman text: 'Rhona Hilda Quinn, Beloved Mother and Wife'. Below that were her dates of birth and of death, and above these, in an oval frame embedded in the stone, was a portrait of her from a few years ago. Her eyes were a pale green and she had fair, strawberry-blonde hair which curled inward at the jawline, framing her face nicely. Like Arthur, she had high cheekbones and her skin was sprinkled with freckles.

'Hi, Mum,' he said to the open air. This was the first time he'd attempted to talk to her. After the funeral, Joe had suggested that Arthur speak or pray to his mother. It would help the healing process, he'd said. But Arthur had always felt too stupid talking like that. She was gone and she couldn't hear him, end of. But now it didn't feel as uncomfortable as he'd anticipated. In fact, it kind of felt right.

'I'm sorry I didn't come and see you sooner,' he went on. 'We moved back a couple of weeks ago. I know it's no excuse but I've been busy.'

Some crows cawed overhead, drawing his attention. When they passed, he turned back to the grave.

'I guess, wherever you are, you've seen what's happened to me. Loki and everything. You probably know where Fenrir is now, right?'

He didn't expect an answer but part of him still hoped for one.

'Help me, Mum. Help me find him. Please.'

The wind picked up, stirring some fallen leaves across the grave. Apart from that, all was silent. Without another word, Arthur turned and left.

The moon was full in the black sky on the night Loki and Drysi finally left the Conifrey holiday home behind them. On their way out the door, the girl took one last glance at the restrained family in the living room. They were all gagged once more and looked to her with pleading eyes. It had been just over a week since they'd been taken hostage, but it felt like so much longer. Drysi had fed them once a day on dry ham sandwiches and water, and their faces were drawn and haggard from hunger and exhaustion.

'Should we let them go?' she asked Loki as he strode out the door.

'Of course not,' he spat.

Drysi couldn't help but flinch. The bite in his words said she should have known better.

Loki, who had been standing on the threshold and gazing at the white disc of the moon, turned back to her. 'Apologies,' he said. 'I shouldn't have been so sharp. But think, my child: we don't want them running to the police now, do we?'

'No, Wolf-father,' she said in a low voice, still hurting from the way he had spoken.

The sky was clear and she could see stars and constellations twinkling above. There was a security light that they usually switched on to see in the dark. There was no need of it tonight, however. The moon lit up everything around her. The Conifrey family car was still parked where they'd left it a week ago. Drysi could even make out the crags and craters on the moon's broad face.

Loki looked down at her. 'Excellent. Let's go.' He took hold of the wheelchair's handles and pushed. He hadn't been very talkative since the Conifreys had had the Dream. In fact, he'd been positively grumpy. If he wasn't glued to the calendar, counting off the days, he was glued to the portable TV in the kitchen, watching the news about the Dream. He seemed worried about the whole affair but Drysi couldn't understand why. It was only a dream. As he wheeled her away from the bungalow and over the hill behind it, she decided it was time to broach the subject.

'Wolf-father?'

'Yes?'

'About the Dream?'

'Yes?'

'Have you … thought more about it?' She knew he had but didn't want to show him she knew he was bothered by it. It was always a bad idea to make Loki angry.

'Of course.'

'And?'

'And …' He stopped pushing her suddenly. She strained her neck around to get a better look at him. He was staring at the moon once more. The light cast half of his face in whiteness and the other half in shadow. 'And,' he continued eventually, 'I think that someone is helping Arthur.'

'The gods?'

'Someone.' The way in which he said it told her he was done talking about the Dream. He started off again, pushing the wheelchair down into the wide valley away from the holiday home. Luckily for them both, the ground wasn't too rocky and the grass was short and dry, so it didn't get caught in the wheels. It had probably been trimmed back by some of the sheep that Drysi had seen wandering over from a neighbouring farmer's meadow.

They reached the bottom of the hill and all was bright and airy there. No trees or houses shaded the light of the moon, which seemed even larger in the sky at this point, more intimidating.

'This will do,' said Loki.

'Here?' Drysi said, looking around her at the wide meadow. She turned to Loki hopefully. 'Will we really find my father?'

'Do you doubt me?'

'No, Wolf-father, of course not! But I was wondering … how will we find him?'

'The moon links you all. All the wolves. You were born in the light of the moon. And you especially, Drysi, have a close bond with your father.'

'He's a traitor,' Drysi reminded him.

'I don't mean that kind of bond. I mean a sort of telepathic bond.' He leaned down closer so he was face to face with her. 'You just need to harness it.'

With that, he gripped the girl by the shoulders and lifted her out of the wheelchair. She felt safe in his arms, clutched tightly in his grasp. He carried her away from the chair like that, with her legs hanging down below her. It was an awkward way to lift someone, but it did not bother the god. He moved her gracefully and with ease. Then he laid her on the ground.

The grass was cold beneath her back and she tried to sit up, but Loki pushed her back calmly.

'Lie down,' he said. 'Relax.'

'What should I–'

'Shh.' He bit his fingertip, bringing blood instantly. Drysi had seen him do this countless times since they'd been in the house, so she wasn't shocked. What did surprise her was when he leant down and traced the blood on her forehead. He drew an oval with a circle inside it, a third eye right above her other two.

'Close your eyes and think of Fenrir,' he whispered.

Drysi did as he said and pictured her father in her mind. She saw him as she had seen him for the first time. When she was just a little girl, running through the fields. She hadn't been scared when the great man with the bushy black hair and beard had called to her. She'd gone willingly to him. And then he had turned her into this wolf-girl.

She saw the thousand years she and Fenrir had spent together, recruiting more wolves as time passed. She saw him tell her about Loki and the wonderful power that he held. She saw Fenrir changing, becoming more human, more forgiving and empathetic, more loving. She saw him grow to like the humans. She saw her father decide not to make an army for Loki. And finally she saw him rescue her from a collapsed tower, saving her life.

'Open your eye.' Loki's voice sounded far away.

Drysi's eyes blinked open. The moon was brighter than she imagined and she had to squint up at Loki.

'No,' he said. 'I told you to open your eye.'

'They are open.'

'Open this one.' He tapped the middle of her forehead where he'd scrawled with blood.

'But how?'

'Concentrate.'

'I'm trying–'

'Open it!'

Drysi bent all her will on the eye Loki had drawn on her forehead and suddenly she felt a strange sensation. It wasn't as if she could see through this third eye – it certainly wasn't like looking – but rather as if the whole world had opened up before her. She could feel the world and she could sense its inhabitants.

And all she had to do was focus on her target – just sniff him out like stalking prey on one of her hunts – and she would find him.

'Father …' she uttered.

Beep, beep, beep.

'Ugh,' moaned Ash, turning over in her bed to knock off the alarm. It couldn't be Monday morning already. She forced her eyelids to open as much as they could and took in the time on the bedside clock: 7.30 – time to get up.

She rolled onto her back and braced herself for the day and week ahead. They'd spent all weekend like they had the previous one: scouring the Internet and CCTV footage for any sign of Fenrir. And all weekend they'd come up with nothing. Absolutely nothing. So far they'd spent two weekends in a row, and any spare time they found in between, working on the secret project. She wondered how much longer they could go on like this with no results.

With a sigh, she threw the duvet back and climbed out of bed. Her laptop was on, the fan whirring away. Since the hunt for Fenrir had begun, she hadn't switched it off once. She had a program constantly running in the background, searching for her webcam's signal. She knew the battery she'd put in it wouldn't die for up to two years, so as soon as the webcam came into contact with any Wi-Fi signal her program would pick it up. Of course, like the CCTV videos, this had provided zero results.

She headed for the bathroom, but Stace had beaten her to it and she could hear her showering inside. Her older sister had a habit of taking too long in the bathroom, especially if she was in the middle of a nice hot shower. Ash banged her fist on the door.

'Stace!' she called. 'Hurry up!'

'All right, all right! I'll be out in a minute!' a voice replied through the sound of the rushing water.

Ash sighed again and went back to her bedroom. She was usually a morning person and eager to get the day started. But today, after the disappointing weekend, she just wasn't in a good mood.

She took a quick glance at the laptop – still nothing.

Not that she expected it to be any different. Then she looked out the window. The red Toyota was still parked on the street outside – as it had been parked on and off for the past couple of weeks. She couldn't see the occupant from this vantage point but knew who it was nonetheless.

Detective Morrissey. He was a Garda who'd been investigating some of the destruction caused by Loki, and Ash had first noticed his car the day after Arthur left for Kerry. When he was still there on the second day, she'd decided to investigate further.

'Detective Morrissey?' she had said, tapping on his window as she went to school.

The man had rolled down the window and smiled wryly at her. 'Good morning, Ashling.'

'What are you doing here?'

'I'm on surveillance.'

'Surveillance?' Ash peered at the estate around her. 'Surveillance of who?'

'You.'

'Me?' Ash was taken aback. 'Why?'

'Simply put, I don't believe the story you or any of your friends spun me after the museum raid. I think you had something to do with it. Or, at the very least, you know who was behind it. Plus, the anonymous tip that led us to the stolen artefacts seemed to be in a child's voice – and it took us to the same lake that you almost drowned in a few months ago. Then there was the suspicious injury to Arthur Quinn around the same time. Something just doesn't quite add up about you all.'

'You can't just sit here, though,' she said, 'spying on me!'

'Oh, I can, Ashling. Because I'm pretty certain that if I'm patient you'll slip up and take me right to the mastermind.'

Since then, he'd been keeping Ash's estate under tight surveillance – his own secret project. He parked in the street during his off-time, watching her and her friends' comings and goings. Sometimes he even followed their bus to school and waited until they disappeared inside before driving off. She, Max and the Lavenders had decided not to mention the Garda's presence to Arthur. It couldn't do any good and would just make him worry. Anyway, he was powerless to change the situation. Ash wished they could just tell the Garda the truth, but she agreed with Arthur. The less people who knew about Loki, the better. She just hoped that Morrissey would give up soon and leave them alone.

Beep, beep, beep.

I didn't think I hit 'Snooze', she thought to herself, going to turn off the alarm properly. But as she got closer to it, she realised the sound wasn't coming from her clock. She turned slowly on the spot towards the beeping noise … towards her laptop.

A map of Ireland filled the monitor and a red dot was blinking just off the Dublin coast. With each beep, the dot moved a pixel closer to the shoreline. The location of the webcam!

She grabbed her phone from the bedside locker and hit the first speed-dial.

'Arthur!' she said excitedly as soon as he answered. 'You'll never guess what just happened!'

CHAPTER FOUR

'Where is it?' Arthur exclaimed when Ash had told him about the webcam signal.

'Just off the Dublin coast and it's moving in all the time,' she said into the phone, studying the computer screen. 'I obviously couldn't find it before because it was out of range of any phone or Wi-Fi signal.'

'That's assuming it is Fenrir and that he didn't dump the webcam weeks ago.'

'I don't think he would. Even if he didn't know how important it was, he seemed so nice that he'd want to take care of it for me until he could return it. Plus, if he did get rid of it, how is it at sea and moving inland?'

'Maybe someone else took it ...' He trailed off. 'But you're right, it's our only lead.'

'What now?'

Arthur looked at his watch. It was ten to eight; a train for Dublin stopped in Farranfore at five past, he knew. He could hear Joe bustling about downstairs, simultaneously preparing breakfast and making some sandwiches for his lunch. There was no way he'd agree to let Arthur take the day off school, but this was too important a chance to let pass.

'I'll get the train to Dublin,' he decided quickly.

'And mitch school? Why don't you stay there and we'll go and find him – me, Ellie and Ex?'

'No!' he said sternly. 'It's too dangerous for you. Wait for me.'

'Too dangerous how?'

'Because if you know where Fenrir is, there's a good chance Loki will too. You have nothing to protect you. I have the pendant, I have the hammer. If Loki shows up they're our only chance against him.'

'OK,' she conceded. 'You're right, I guess.'

'If I'm going, I better go now or I'll miss the train. I'll be in Dublin around lunchtime. Can you meet me in Heuston Station and we'll go from there together? And pick up the others on the way?'

'Shouldn't we take the Vikings?'

'Just Eirik. We may need the element of surprise and I don't think a hundred dead Vikings will help that. Plus

Eirik can blend in better than the rest.'

'Sounds like a plan. But are you go–?'

Arthur hung up before she could finish her question. He didn't like to be rude but he really hadn't much time to spare if he intended to catch the 8:05 train. Luckily he was already showered and dressed, so he didn't have to waste precious minutes doing that. He tipped his backpack over his bed, emptying out the contents. Books, stationery and pens all toppled out. He grabbed a T-shirt, hoodie and jeans from his wardrobe and a pair of Converse runners from the end of his bed and stuffed them into the bag. He figured a young boy in a school uniform would attract too much unwanted attention on the train, so he could change in the toilet once he boarded. He took some savings he had stashed in a worn sock in his bedside locker – it wasn't much but should be enough to get him to and from Dublin. And finally he squeezed the hammer into the already full-to-bursting schoolbag.

He put on a coat, swung the bag over one shoulder and crept downstairs. He stepped lightly, praying that Joe wouldn't hear him.

'Morning, you!'

Damn! thought Arthur, walking in to the kitchen where his dad was laying slices of cheese across buttery chunks of crusty bread.

'Morning.'

'Where are you off to so early?' He usually didn't leave for school till half eight.

'I'm meeting the guys,' he said, making it up as he spoke. 'We're collecting some leaves for an art project.' He was getting good at lying to Joe. Worryingly good.

'OK. Don't forget your lunch.' Joe nodded at the two sandwiches already made and wrapped in tinfoil. 'See ya later.'

Arthur grabbed the tinfoil pack, turned to go, then stopped and looked back at his father. He felt a pang of guilt in the pit of his stomach.

'Dad?'

'Hmm?'

'Love you.'

Joe looked up in surprise. 'Love you too, son. What's gotten into you?'

'Nothing. I just … nothing. See you later.'

A clear morning awaited him outside, but dark clouds threatened on the horizon. It was a mile from their house to the village. Usually it took him about fifteen minutes to walk it. But with just under ten minutes till the train left, he'd have to run. He waited until he was out of sight of the kitchen window before setting off down the road at a sprint. The hammer made the run awkward, as the bag hopped up and down against his back, thumping into him painfully. He made it to the station, panting and with shaky, quivering legs, just as the train pulled in to the platform.

'Return to Dublin, please!' he asked breathlessly at the ticket booth, shoving some money at the woman behind the Perspex window and keeping his good eye glued to the train in case it started to pull off without him. The woman gazed at him suspiciously before hitting some keys on a machine in front of her that spat out the ticket. He grabbed it more urgently than he'd meant to and leapt onto the train just as the electronic doors started beeping to warn passengers that they were closing. He leant back against the wall of the train, still out of breath, and watched as Farranfore fell behind him. He was finally on his way: to Dublin, to Fenrir.

The fishing boat that cruised into Dublin Harbour was just like all the others. It was a trawler, mostly painted white, with a blue undercarriage. The paint was peeling in several places, showing patches of green and brown rust underneath. It was smaller than many of the other boats and would only take a three- or four-person crew to man it properly. The net was drawn in as it navigated into the port, but it was dripping wet and had obviously been used recently. The captain – the sole crew member of the vessel – steered the boat into a dock. When it was close enough, he grasped a couple of thick, coarse ropes and leapt onto dry land. Then he secured the ropes onto the mooring with a couple of tight clove hitch knots, tugging on them one last time to ensure the vessel wasn't going anywhere before turning and heading away from the water. The name painted in navy cursive letters on each side read *Drysi*.

Fenrir walked through the port, passing fellow fishermen, longshoremen, customs officers and even a few members of the US Navy on his way. None of them gave him a second glance. Though he was as broad and lofty as he'd ever been, his build wasn't that unusual for a seafaring man. In fact, his slim waist and wide, strong shoulders made him the perfect candidate for a life at sea. He'd shaved off his thick beard and made a point of maintaining his appearance that way over the past month, so his jawline was smooth now, with only a faint five o'clock shadow. And he'd cut his hair short too. He hadn't risked going to a barber's so had had to do it himself, looking in the mirror and chopping clumps of black hair away with a pair of blunted kitchen scissors. It wasn't exactly what he'd call fashionable, but at least it would disguise him from anyone on the lookout for a man with long hair and a beard. He wore a small red beanie hat over the ragged hair, along with boots, a pair of jeans, a checked fleece shirt and a waterproof waxed jacket.

After escaping from Loki's clutches during the mayhem of the explosion, he'd made his way straight to the boat. As soon as the battle at the tower had ended and the dust was settling, Fenrir had felt a strange mixture of relief and regret. If Loki had been angry when he'd first found him weeks earlier, there would be no end to the torture the god would inflict on him for actually standing against him. And so, getting to a new hiding place had been first on his agenda. He had seen the other wolves scattering in the aftermath of the battle and, though he liked many of them, he didn't intend to invite them along. It would be much easier to hide one person than many. Off he had gone, by himself, through the dark of the night.

He'd kept the boat docked in Dublin Harbour for years and no one – not even Drysi – knew about it. Despite limiting the wolves' chances to leave the seclusion of the tower for decades, he had snuck off several times by himself for fishing trips over the years. It was as close as he could safely get to the thrill of the hunt. He'd spent the past month on the boat, just out of range of any phone or television signal. He hadn't even bothered putting on the radio, cherishing the silence. He'd spent his days fishing, reading and simply looking at the water lapping at the side of the vessel, and he spent his nights worrying and wondering if this would all blow over soon and praying that Loki wouldn't find him this time.

His peace had been disrupted the previous night when Drysi had visited him in his sleep.

'Father,' she had said, her face filling his mind. Her eyes were shut but a third one in the middle of her forehead was staring at him. It was disconcerting.

'Drysi,' he could hear himself respond in his head.

'Father, where are you?' She seemed concerned.

'I'm sleeping.'

'I know. But where?'

'Why do you want to know that?'

'Meet me, Father.'

'But … Loki …'

'He … he abandoned me, Father. It was terrible; he called me a useless cripple and left me by the side of the road. And the things he did to people! The things I saw!' She squeezed tears out of her closed eyes while her third one just kept staring.

'I'm so sorry, Drysi.'

'Meet me. Tomorrow.'

He hesitated, not quite sure what to believe or what to think.

'Please, Father,' Drysi pleaded. 'I miss you so much.'

And eventually he said the thing that he most wanted to say, even if he wasn't certain it was the thing he should say.

'All right.' His voice broke slightly. 'I'll meet you.'

And here he was, on his way to meet his daughter. A part of him – a cold and logical part – screamed that this was all too simple, that Drysi had lied to him before and would do so again. This part of him was wary and on edge – the wolf ready to bolt at the first click of a hunter's gun. And this small part of him had taken the precaution of slipping a flick-knife into his pocket. But another, bigger part of him – the man and the father – desperately yearned to believe Drysi, wanted her to be his good, loving daughter once more. This part of him wanted them to live together in a world where Loki was gone – dead or defeated, it didn't matter: just gone. And this part of him, this foolish but hopeful part, refused to consider for a second that he was walking into a trap.

'The train's late,' Ash said, checking the time on the little dashboard clock.

'It's not late,' contradicted Ellie. 'That clock is fast.'

They were sitting in a 1960s pastel-blue Volkswagen Beetle. It belonged to the Lavenders' parents. Ex had no problem 'borrowing' it from under the nose of their grandfather, who took care of them while their parents were away. He'd been getting very forgetful over the past few years and spent most of his days dozing in the drawing-room armchair, which had attained a deep granddad-shaped groove in the padding. Even though he was far too young to legally have a driver's licence, Ex was more than capable behind the wheel and no one paid him a second glance as they sat parked outside Heuston Station.

When Arthur had hung up on Ash that morning, she'd instantly called Ellie with her findings and told her of his plan to meet up.

'There's just one problem,' Ash had said when she'd explained everything.

'What's that?'

'I have to shake off Detective Morrissey. He's outside right now. If I head directly for the train station he'll realise something is going on.'

'Hmm ... I have an idea.'

They went to school as normal. Ash and Max took the bus and met Ellie and Ex outside the busy Belmont School. They smiled and chatted, laughing nonchalantly.

'Can you see him?' Ash asked with a big false grin on her face.

'He's parked a hundred yards away,' answered Ex, who was also wearing a strained smile. Anyone who saw them would think he was looking at Ash, but in reality he was staring right past her at Morrissey's red Toyota. As Ash had expected, the Garda had followed them.

'We'll go into class,' said Ellie, just as pleasantly as the other two, 'and stay until morning break. Then we'll sneak off. He can't wait for us all day.'

'Won't Miss Keegan be looking for us then?' Ash pointed out, thinking of their soon-to-be worried teacher.

'Of course. But I'd rather have *her* searching for us than Morrissey.'

'Remember, Max,' warned Ash, 'you can't tell anyone where we've gone.'

'Can't I come, though?'

'No. It'll be easier to get away with less of us going. You have to stay.'

The school bell rang, beckoning them all inside.

'Just keep schtum,' Ellie reminded him as they followed everyone into the school.

Although they had only intended on spending the first two hours of the day in class, time seemed to drag. Miss Keegan's lessons – which usually managed to be both fun and informative – felt like torture today. Ash found herself peeking at her phone every couple of minutes – either to check the time or to see if there was any further movement on the webcam signal. An hour into the class, the signal stopped moving just on the coastline of the city. At the docks, Ash realised. She glanced at Ellie and Ex; they, too, seemed distracted. Ex was tapping his fingers on the desk impatiently while his sister kept pulling back her sleeve to look at the time. Luckily no one else in the class seemed to pick up on the tension emanating from them.

Eventually the bell rang for morning break. The class thronged out excitedly, none more pleased than Ash, Ellie and Ex. From the front schoolyard, where the balls and Frisbees were soaring through the air, they could see the main road. A few cars were parked there but they saw no sign of Detective Morrissey's red Toyota. They stood by the south-facing school wall, waiting anxiously. Then, when the bell rang to announce the end of break-time, they took their chance and sprinted off school property. During the hustle and bustle following break, no one saw them go.

Ex had driven that morning and left the Beetle in a car park half a mile from the school. Ash saw the sense in parking it so far away: Detective Morrissey had seen Ash with the Lavenders and might know their car, so it was best to keep it out of sight. The three of them piled in and Ex sped off towards the city centre.

With just a little time to spare before Arthur's train was due, they'd stopped in Smithfield, parking by the Viking Experience. Ash had got out of the car and told the others to wait. She'd walked to the high-walled enclosure in the middle of the cobblestoned Smithfield Square. Murals of Viking life adorned each wall. It was the off-season so the park was closed now, but it was due to reopen in mid-March – in just a few days. She went straight to a fire escape in one of the side walls and banged the secret knock on the door. The youngest Viking, who'd been only seventeen or eighteen when he'd died, opened the door. Like the other dead warriors, he was tall with a slim, muscular physique. Unlike the others, his skin hadn't receded as much but it was still quite brown and leathery. If he was going out in public, he usually covered it with layers of flesh-tone foundation. He was wearing a T-shirt and some jeans – being reanimated corpses, the Vikings didn't feel the cold – that he had borrowed from the costume room. He looked at Ash with quizzical sunken eyes.

'Eirik,' she said, 'we need you. There's no time for make-up.'

He nodded, then disappeared into the complex, re-appearing a moment later wearing a baseball cap pulled down low over his face and carrying a long-sword. It was rusted slightly but could still do a good amount of damage, especially with Eirik wielding it. He got into the passenger seat while the smaller pair of Ellie and Ash sat in the back. Then Ex sped off towards Heuston Station, where they were waiting now.

'Look – there he is!' said Ellie, pointing at Arthur coming out of the building. He didn't have to look around for too long before spotting the blue Beetle – it was hard to miss.

'Hi,' he said, climbing into the back next to Ash. 'Where are we headed?'

'To Dublin Harbour,' Ash said, showing him the GPS display on her smartphone.

Clontarf had once been a village north of Dublin city. Fenrir could still see it in his mind's eye as it had been: just a row of little huts. Even though it had been swallowed up by the city spread years before, it still retained some of its former charm. He had been the one to suggest the café to meet in. The Bridge Café was the one place he'd visited every time he had gone fishing. That all seemed like another lifetime now. The café was exactly as he remembered it. It was situated just on the corner of Vernon Avenue, a little blue-faced building with one wide window and a wooden painted sign overhead. He'd once heard the term 'greasy spoon' used to describe a café or restaurant that tended to be a bit rough around the edges and specialised in quick, fried food, and he thought it was a very fitting description for The Bridge. Inside, the walls were covered in tongue-and-groove panelling and painted bright yellow, and waxy chequered tablecloths were draped over the tables, which were packed too tightly into the small space. There was a counter at the back of the café with crisps, cakes and sandwiches on display and an open stainless-steel kitchen behind. Everything was covered in a fine layer of grease. Fenrir loved the place.

Drysi was already there when he entered. She was sitting at the small round table nearest the window, with a glass of juice in front of her. She looked up when he entered, a little bell tinkling over the door. The café was busy and every other table was occupied. She smiled at him shyly.

'Hello, Father.'

'Drysi,' he said, taking the seat opposite her. 'How are you?'

'I'm good. Thank you for coming.'

'Of course I came. You're my daughter. I love you. I always hoped I'd see you again. And …' He hesitated, the god's name stuck in his throat. 'And Loki?'

'He's gone,' was all Drysi said, looking down with what seemed to be genuine loss in her eyes. Fenrir reached out and laid a hand over one of hers. That hopeful part of him was winning over the logical side. His daughter was his once more.

'Gone,' he said.

She looked up at him with tears glistening in her eyes.

'He was awful, Father. So … so … awful!'

'It's all right, Drysi. You're safe with me now. We'll go away – away from all of this nonsense – just you and me.'

'But where?'

Just then, a waitress came over. She was a squat and tubby woman, with crimson, curly hair. She was wearing a pair of thick glasses on her nose and had another pair on a gold chain around her neck. The apron she wore matched the tablecloths and she had a little notepad in hand, ready to take Fenrir's order.

'Just a coffee, please,' he said and waited until she returned to the kitchen to continue talking. He faced

Drysi once more. 'You have a new wheelchair,' he noticed. 'And new clothes.'

'We found them in an abandoned house. When I was still with him. He got sick of me soon after. He said–' She stopped, choking on her words. 'I was lucky, I guess. Lucky to get away.'

'You were. Last night, you spoke to me in a dream. You've never been able to do that before. How did you do it?'

'I don't know, Father. I think I just needed to find you so much that you appeared in my dream. I hoped and prayed it was real.'

'And it was.'

'Yes.'

The waitress returned with the mug of coffee. When she saw that the little jug of milk on the table was dry, she took it and promised to fill it up.

'I have a boat by the dock – we can leave now if you're ready,' Fenrir told Drysi as the waitress walked off.

'No, we can't, Father. Not yet, anyway.'

'What? Why?'

'Loki was looking for Hel. It became an obsession. He'll do anything to find her and if he does then it won't matter where we go. It'll never be far enough.' She leaned forward over the tabletop and whispered conspiratorially.

'You said you knew where Hel was. We need to get to her before Loki does.'

'But—'

'Please, Father. I've seen what Loki can do. I've seen the terrible things he does to humans. We have to stop him ever doing it again.'

'Drysi, I'm not sure—'

'We're the only ones that can put an end to it, Father,' she said, pleading now. 'If we don't, think of all the people Loki will kill using Hel's power. Think of what he'll do to the world.'

Fenrir looked away from her, ashamed of himself. She was right. What kind of craven coward had he become? How could he think of just running away? But she didn't understand. She didn't know the full truth.

'You don't need to worry, Drysi,' he said, meeting her gaze once more.

'Of course I do! Hel—'

'Hel is of no danger to anyone.'

'What! What do you mean? Where is she, Father? Where is Hel?'

And Fenrir told her. He told her the truth about Hel. He told her exactly where he'd hidden Hel all those years ago and exactly why she could never help Loki. When he was done, the waitress returned with the jug of milk.

'Will you have anything else?'

'No thanks,' Drysi replied, the corners of her lips slowly turning up in a satisfied grin. 'I've got all I need.'

'Is that a fact?' the waitress said, suddenly with Loki's voice. She turned to smirk at Fenrir but he was staring with disbelief at Drysi.

I should have known, a voice screamed inside his head. *I should have known!*

He kicked back his chair and before it could hit the floor he had the flick-knife out and ready. But as he swung his arm towards the Loki-waitress, the steel of the blade turned bright red. Heat coursed through the handle, scorching the palm of his hand enough to make him drop it. By the time it landed on the ground, the blade had completely melted, resembling flowing magma, and flames licked all along the wooden handle.

Before he could turn to run, the heel of the waitress' hand had connected with the underside of his chin. He soared backwards in an arc, smashing through the window and landing with a heavy thud on the ground outside.

CHAPTER FIVE

'We're getting close now,' Ash said with her eyes fixed firmly on the phone screen.

Ex had parked the Beetle in a spot marked 'Staff Only' a few minutes ago. They had gotten out of the car and followed Ash along the docks, moving ever closer to the blinking dot on the little screen. Eirik had left the sword in the car, deciding at the last minute that it would draw too much unwanted attention. Luckily for them, a huge freighter was coming in further down the harbour and most of the staff were too preoccupied with that to wonder why four kids and a suspicious-looking adult were wandering around the docks.

The phone started beeping frantically. Ash hit the touchscreen to silence it, then looked up at the trawler they'd arrived at.

'Here we are,' she said.

'You sure it's the right one?' Arthur asked. He didn't want to have come the whole way here only to get on someone else's boat.

'It's definitely it,' Ellie said. 'See the name on the side. *Drysi*. He named it after his daughter.'

Arthur nodded in agreement. He was still impressed by how Ellie noticed the smallest of details long before the rest of them.

'Hello?' he called out, stepping closer to the boat. 'Anybody home?'

When no response came, he looked back at his friends and shrugged his shoulders. 'Guess we should take a look around,' he said, then took a short running jump onto the deck of the trawler. It swayed forwards underneath him as he landed. The rest looked at each other doubtfully and then, seeing no other option, followed him on board.

'Anyone here?' Arthur called again, moving towards the stack. A few steps there led down into the hull. He took them and found himself face to face with a door with a round window in it. He peered through the smudged glass and could just about make the features of the lower deck: a single unmade bunk, a kitchenette with a table big enough for one person to sit at and a narrow door left open into a tight-fitting bathroom. He shook the handle but the door was firmly locked.

He turned around and had just reached the top of the stairs again when suddenly a huge man landed on the deck of the boat. The vessel bobbed violently up and down in the water with the force of the impact.

'What—?' the man cried in surprise.

Ash turned towards him. 'Fenrir, it's me,' she said in a soothing voice.

'Ash.' Fenrir's face was flushed and he was out of breath. 'What are you doing here?'

'We've come looking for you.' She pointed out the others. 'You remember Ellie and Ex? And that's Eirik. And you've met Arthur. We've come to ask you about Hel.'

At the mention of the name, Fenrir turned away, shaking his head and thinking how lucky he had been to get away from Loki at the café. As soon as he'd been thrown through the window, he had scrambled to his feet. Loki's laughter rang in his ears as he fled. He couldn't fight his father again. Not a second time. Fenrir was powerful but he would never be a match for the god. And he valued his own life too much to try to prove otherwise.

'No, no, no,' he said, shaking his head violently. 'You'll all have to go. I'm leaving now.'

'Fenrir, please,' begged Ash.

'I said no. You can get off or stay, I don't care. But I'm pulling out of this dock in the next minute either way. I just hope you can all swim back to land.' He pushed past Arthur down the stairs and unlocked the door, then ran back to the tiller and started to switch on the engine.

'Mister Fenrir, sir,' Arthur said, taking a tentative step towards the man. 'We stopped the Jormungand; we stopped Hati's Bite. If you don't help us, we have no chance of stopping Loki this time. Ash says that you know how good humanity can be. Well, please think of that. Think what Loki will destroy if we don't stop him. You don't have to come with us but, please, just tell us about the girl, what happened to her.'

His plea seemed to get through to Fenrir. He stopped what he was doing and turned to look Arthur in the eye.

'War wound?' he asked, pointing to the eye-patch.

Arthur nodded. 'Loki.'

Fenrir nodded back, as if he had expected that answer.

'You fought well,' he said, 'on the tower. You fought well but Loki … Loki is …'

He sighed then looked out at the sea. Apart from the giant freighter making its way slowly into the docks, the water was still. Dark storm clouds hung on the horizon. 'There used to be an island out there. Clontarf Island. We lived on it for a while.' He paused for a moment, lost in the memory. 'The island's gone now. It sank beneath the waves.' He nodded reluctantly. 'OK. You have five minutes to ask any questions you have.' He crossed back past them, went down to the lower deck and sat at the table. They all clambered inside; it was quite a squeeze so Eirik waited by the door.

'I'm not sure I should tell you anything,' Fenrir warned them. 'I've already said too much today. But ask your questions – I suppose I can't do any more harm than I already have.'

'Tell us all you can about Hel,' said Arthur.

'Where to begin?' he mused to himself. 'After the Father of Lies had created myself and my brother, the World Serpent, he abducted a child … a baby girl.'

He looked out through the porthole, picturing the little girl he had never had the chance to meet.

'He took the girl from a Viking village back to Asgard. And he gave her … I don't know quite how to put it. He gave her a part of himself. He made her half god. He gave her a power that every god has but no god wants to use.'

'What was it?' asked Arthur.

'All the gods have the power to create,' Fenrir said, 'but they also have the power to destroy. They can wipe something out of existence as easily as they can create it. No god will do that, though. It's just not in their nature.

Gods create out of ego. They want worshippers and followers. They want people to fight wars over them and tell tales about them for centuries to come. They want to show off the landscapes they create to each other: the wildest beasts and the most delicate flowers.

'Loki is different, however. Odin has always been the best at creation but Loki … Loki was never very good at it – just look at the abominations he made, myself included. So his ego cries out for something else: destruction. If he can't be better than the other gods, then he'll just destroy everything. But destruction takes a lot out of gods. Every time they destroy something, they destroy a part of themselves. Eventually they could destroy one thing too many and end up wiping themselves out of existence. Loki is smart though. He saw a way around this. And so he gave this power of destruction, this power of undoing creation, to the girl he called Hel.'

'Why didn't the gods stop him?'

'They tried to. They tried to find the girl but they couldn't. The power coursed through her and she grew. Within a couple of days, she'd reached her teenage years. The gods were looking for a baby the whole time, not a girl near grown.'

'You told me before that she freed you,' prompted Ash. 'How?'

'The gods found me and bound me. They tricked me. They played on my pride and I let them bind me with a ribbon. I thought I could escape easily, but it was a magical ribbon called Gleipnir, forged by all manner of strangeness. So I just let them tie me up and then I couldn't get out. No matter how hard I tried, the ribbon held me in place. The gods left me, confident that I would be there for millennia to come.

'But then, the next day, Hel found me. She had followed the gods to the island. I could smell Loki's magic in her blood and I knew she was there to help me. She used her destructive power on the ribbon. It was almost too strong, even for her. Gleipnir was created from dark blood magic. It was designed never to be broken. Hel used all her power to tear the ribbon in just one place and it fell apart around me. She had freed me, but in doing so she had drained so much of her own power that she almost killed herself. She fell into a deep, deep coma as a result.

'I managed to escape Asgard. And I took the sleeping Hel with me to Dublin. I made some more wolves and formed a family for myself in Ireland, a community of sorts. And all the while, Hel was unconscious. She was asleep for almost a thousand years, and all that time I hid her from everyone, including the rest of the wolves. Even Drysi. And in that time, I grew to see humanity for what it was. I experienced the love, the friendship, the creativity. All the goodness of the human heart. So I vowed never to do Loki's bidding again and to protect Hel from him.'

He looked back at them, and as he did so the bright daylight through the porthole showed his face in high contrast. His gaze fell on Arthur, who was staring up at him and absentmindedly fiddling with the ribbon tied around his wrist.

'What are you doing?' he asked him.

'Nothing,' said Arthur, dropping his fingers from it. 'It's a nervous tic. Sorry. It was my mother's; she used to do it too.'

Fenrir stared for a moment at the ribbon and when he finally continued his expression was sad.

'Things changed about eighteen, twenty years ago. Hel woke up. I could sense Loki's dark magic flowing through her, rousing her, and I knew he had created her for something terrible. I didn't want the part of her that was Loki's gift to take over, to destroy the world that I had grown fond of. But I could also sense something else: the soul of the child she once was. I wanted that soul to have the life she should have had, the life she deserved. It was like there were two personalities inside the one woman: the one that Loki created called Hel and the innocent, stolen girl whose name I didn't know.

'So I came up with a way of trapping the part of Loki, the bad part, inside her. Using magic I'd learned over the centuries, I wiped her memories of all the misfortune that had befallen her. I ensnared the Hel personality within the body, leaving only the human girl who had been taken. I gave her a new name and helped her start a new, happy, human life.'

His eyes were shining with tears now and his voice was starting to shake.

'And Arthur, oh Arthur, I'm so sorry,' he said. 'I'm so very sorry.'

'For what?'

'For what I'm about to tell you. If what I think is right, I'm so sorry.'

He looked down, as if in shame.

'I gave her two names,' Fenrir continued after collecting his thoughts. 'The first was of Celtic origin, meaning "powerful". The second was Viking and it meant "hidden". I thought it was very suitable. So I called her … I called her … Rhona Hilda.'

Arthur felt as if the wind had been knocked out of him. He rocked backwards, his heart pumping furiously.

'It … it can't be,' he stuttered.

'I'm so sorry, Arthur.'

'What?' urged Ash. 'What does it mean?'

'He's saying,' Arthur said. 'He's saying that ... that Hel ... Hel was my mother.'

CHAPTER SIX

There was a mass intake of breath in the cramped cabin, all eyes flitting between Arthur and Fenrir. The words hung in the air for a moment between them all, the awful realisation of Hel's true identity.

'But ... how?' Ellie eventually asked the question on everyone's minds. 'Arthur's mother is ...'

'Dead,' Arthur murmured.

Fenrir looked at Ellie then back at Arthur, whose face had turned a pallid colour.

'Sit down, boy,' he advised. 'You've had quite a shock.'

'Just answer her,' said Arthur, sitting on the edge of the bed. Fenrir's suggestion had been spot-on: his legs had felt like they were going to collapse under him.

'I only realised the truth seconds ago myself,' said the man. 'To understand for yourself, you need to know how

I trapped the evil part of her – the Hel part. That's the key to everything.'

'Get to the point!' Arthur wasn't feeling very courteous right now.

'OK. When I saw that she was waking up, I knew that the evil part of her would take over. I knew she wouldn't have a chance of a normal life. I couldn't take the evil out of her; Loki had put it there to begin with and the magic was too strong. But I could trap it, bind it. I just needed something to hold Hel in place. And I had just the thing – Gleipnir. The magical ribbon the gods had used to bind me, the ribbon that was never supposed to break. I still had it after all those years. It was said that it could bind anything, so I harnessed that power and tied it around Rhona's wrist. I couldn't work out how to bind the ends together like Odin had done, so I used a simple knot, but it seemed to be enough. The magic in the ribbon meant that it shrank to fit perfectly. And, though she never fully understood why, I warned her never to take it off. She forgot about me but remembered my last words to her. I think deep down she knew there was something about her that was different, but she sensed it was not a part she wanted to unleash. Except that you took it off her wrist, didn't you, Arthur? That's how I worked it out just now – when I saw the ribbon on your wrist. To protect her identity, I tried to forget Rhona too, but I always hoped she'd have a normal life, a family. And you'd be just the right age.'

The boy looked down at the ribbon around his own wrist. He remembered the day his mother had died and how he'd untied the golden piece of silk from her arm. Something to remember her by. Tears welled up in his good eye as he stroked the fabric.

'She was my mum and she died,' he said in a low voice, not daring to look up. 'It was a year ago. And I took the ribbon. I didn't know.'

'Of course you didn't know.' Fenrir was on his feet now, moving next to Arthur. He laid a heavy hand on the boy's shoulder. 'But I don't think she died, Arthur.'

'She did! She started getting weaker and weaker. For no reason. She only survived a fortnight.'

'No, Arthur, she didn't.' Fenrir sat down next to him. 'If what you're saying is true – if she just suddenly faded away a year ago – then I'm certain she didn't die.'

'But–'

'The evil part of your mother – Hel – could probably sense Loki's growing power in Dublin. She must have realised that the god would soon be free. But she knew that Rhona would never take off the ribbon, leaving her trapped and helpless to reach Loki. So she needed to get someone else to take it off. Hel knew this would never happen while Rhona was alive – Rhona wouldn't allow it. So Hel did the only thing she could think of: she made Rhona think she was dying. Whatever she did, it convinced everyone around her that Rhona was seriously ill and that she died. It was a long shot – her only shot, really – but Hel's plan worked. When she was gone, you took off the ribbon, setting Hel free. But you couldn't have known what this would do.'

Arthur thought of his mother's grave back home in Farranfore. He thought of the gravestone with the little framed picture. 'We buried her, though. How could she survive underground?'

'She's half god. Loki survived a thousand years underground; Hel can definitely survive a few years.'

'If she's so powerful, then why hasn't she freed herself from the grave?' Ash pointed out. 'Just wipe the coffin and earth from existence? Or why allow herself to be buried in the first place?'

'Quite simply, she isn't powerful enough. She's been asleep for so long she needs Loki's presence to restore her fully. It was the same with the Jormungand. Even I felt stronger when Loki turned up.'

'I don't understand,' Arthur said, suddenly loud. 'Who's alive? My mother or Hel?'

'Both. Two personalities are trapped in the one body,

86

like two sides of the same coin: that of the original child, human and good, and that created by Loki, godly and evil. Rhona had been in charge for twenty years. But with the ribbon removed, right now Hel is ruling the coin. She's much stronger than Rhona and as soon as Loki releases her she will suppress your mother's personality and be completely in charge.'

Arthur looked deep into Fenrir's gold-coloured eyes. 'You have to help us,' he pleaded.

The wolf-man got up, shaking his head, and walked away. 'I can't,' he said. 'I won't face him again. I just need to get away.'

'Get away to where?' piped up Ellie. 'If Loki wins, there'll be nowhere to hide.'

Fenrir looked at her with sad eyes.

'I don't care,' he said. 'I've lived long enough. There's no point in fighting a hopeless battle. I just want to spend my remaining days in peace.'

'But—'

'You have no idea the unimaginable pain he can inflict on me. I won't do it. Besides, there is nothing I can do against Hel. Only Arthur has a chance of stopping her.' He turned to the boy. 'The only way that I know of to defeat her is if Rhona can regain control of the body. And you're the only one who might be able to get through to Rhona, to give her the strength to do this.' He stood in the doorway, shoulders hunched stubbornly. 'But you need to go now. Loki and Drysi are probably already on their way to find Hel. They tricked me into telling them who she is.'

No one spoke on the way back to the car. They'd left Fenrir on his boat, realising that he'd told them all he could. Despite final pleas from Ash and Ellie, he had refused to change his mind about helping them. So, reluctantly, they left.

As they walked back to the Beetle, Ellie said quietly, 'It's up to us.'

Silent nods between the rest of them indicated they were all in agreement. Only Arthur didn't nod. Now they knew where Hel was, they had to assume that Loki was headed there too. They just had to reach her before he did. No discussion was required; they all knew what had to be done, even if they didn't know how to do it. Ex turned on the ignition and they set off once more.

When they were nearly out of the city and Ex had to figure out which motorway to head for, he broke the silence.

'Where is your home exactly, Arthur?'

'Farranfore, Kerry,' he replied monotonously from the backseat. 'But there's no point in going. Loki will get there before us. We've lost.'

'We haven't lost,' said Ash, trying to sound more cheerful than she felt and break through the wall of despair that seemed to have enclosed Arthur since he had learned the truth. 'Not yet. We can still reach there first.'

'No, we can't,' he said, turning to look out the window. 'We haven't a chance.'

He watched the city speed past, blurring into rolling green countryside. There was so much to take in from what Fenrir had said that his mind was as confused as the view through the window, shooting from one rapid thought to another. My mum was dead. My mum is not dead. My mum is a half god called Hel. My mum is a stolen baby called Rhona. Fenrir won't help. Loki has won. Loki can't win. Loki must be stopped. But we can't stop him. We'll never stop him. There's no one who can help us now. There's no one who'll believe us. Loki will win. Loki's my … in a weird way, Loki's my grandfather.

Arthur had never known anything about his mother's parents. All through his childhood he'd often visited his grandparents on Joe's side of the family – and still did. But Rhona's extended family had been a constant mystery. He and Joe knew that Rhona always became uncomfortable when they broached the subject and so they never really talked about it. When Arthur had asked his dad about them, Joe had explained that there hadn't even been any of her relations at their wedding. Any time Joe had ever pushed her about her family, she had just simply shut down, staring into the middle distance with glassy eyes. She didn't want to talk about it – that much was clear – and Joe, assuming that she'd had a traumatic childhood, eventually stopped asking. Now Arthur knew why she'd been so reticent. She would hardly have wanted to admit that she couldn't remember her family at all, or maybe a part of her mind was simply trained not to think of them.

The light in the sky was dimming, turning a gradient of oranges and reds. He looked down at the ribbon around his right wrist. Fenrir had called it 'Gleipnir'. A creation of great power and dark magic, designed never to be destroyed or broken. The one thing that had kept Hel at bay all those years, the one thing that could hold the Fenris Wolf, the one thing that had done damage to Hel before. For the past year, he'd worn it around his own wrist, not realising what a great gift it was. Could it help her again, he wondered, touching the soft silk.

'How are you feeling?' Ash, who was sitting beside him, asked softly. Ellie was squeezed at the far side of her, staring at a GPS map on her iPad, while Eirik was in the front with Ex, gazing with wonder at the vehicles speeding along the motorway.

'I won't lie. I've been better,' said Arthur.

She reached over and took his hand away from the ribbon, intertwining her fingers through his to give it a reassuring squeeze. She held onto his hand as she spoke.

'I don't know what to say, Arthur.'

'You don't have to say anything.'

'But I want to.' A single tear rolled down her cheek as she looked at him. She wanted to say something to comfort him, to put his mind at ease. She'd like to tell him that she was sure they'd stop Loki or that his mother would overpower the Hel part of her. She desperately wanted to whisper to him that, no matter what happened tonight, she'd be there for him because she cared for him. A lot. But none of the words would come. Instead, she told him a story.

'Before I started school,' she began, speaking in a low voice so that none of the others would hear her, 'we lived next door to this girl called Clare Pond. Clare was my age and we were best friends from the time we could walk. Anyway, Clare's dad was a teacher in some posh private school so when we were old enough, she went there and I went to Belmont. After that, Clare didn't talk to me any more, especially when she was with her new friends. I could hear them laughing at me when they thought I couldn't. I was hurt and surprised and didn't understand what I'd done wrong.'

She stopped, suddenly caught up with emotion and surprised that the story still had such an effect on her.

'Sorry,' she said. 'I've never told this story to anyone before. Anyway, about a year after that, Clare moved away. Then I ran into her out of the blue last summer in town. She seemed really pleased to see me and even said sorry for how she'd been before. She regretted it, she said.' Ash looked at Arthur's confused expression. 'I don't really know why I'm telling you this. I guess what I'm trying to say – probably not very well – is that there are two sides to most people. And, eventually, most of them make the right choice. I'm sure your mom will too.'

'Thanks, Ash,' Arthur replied, squeezing her hand back. 'I just keep thinking about when I was young and how amazing my mum was, like there wasn't a bad bone in her body. When I was about six, I fell off my bike at my house. I grazed my knee. It wasn't that bad but at the time I thought it was. I just kept screaming for my mammy. She ran out. And she started crying herself when she saw how upset I was. She picked me up, held me close and carried me inside. Then she cleaned my knee, put a Band

Aid on it and wrapped me up in a big hug.'

He looked Ash straight in the eyes. 'She told me she would always be there for me, always keep me safe. I just can't imagine how she could be like that and have something like Hel inside her.'

Ash squeezed his hand again, unsure of what to say. At that moment her phone rang. They all looked at her with wide, worried eyes – even Eirik and Ex in the front – as she pulled it out of her pocket.

'It's Mom,' she said, reading the display. She hesitated, her finger hovering over the touchscreen.

'Answer it,' said Ellie.

'I can't.' She pushed it into Ellie's hands. 'You do it.'

'What? What am I supposed to say?' She gave it back quickly. The ringtone seemed to get louder with each second. 'You answer it.'

Ash looked down at the phone again.

'No,' she said. 'She must know by now that we mitched school. She'll want to know where I am.'

'Make something up,' Arthur told her. 'Say you're at Ellie and Ex's.'

Ash shook her head. 'She'll hear the car engine. It's not exactly subtle.'

'It doesn't look like she's going to give up,' Ex said, as the sound continued. 'Just answer the phone.'

'I can't … I don't know what to …' She looked around at them uncertainly. 'What am I supposed to tell her … I–'

Before she knew what he was doing, Eirik reached back, plucked the phone from her grasp, screwed down his window and threw it out. The ringing sound was cut off the instant it hit the ground.

'Well …' said Ellie after a moment of silence. 'That was one way of dealing with it.'

Garda Eddie McKean was on traffic duty but Garda Eddie McKean hated traffic duty. It meant sitting in a squad car that either got too cold or too hot, parked in a lonely lay-by and aiming a speedometer gun at the vehicles whizzing past on the motorway. His wrist muscles invariably grew weary of holding up the gun and his eyesight started to blur from staring at the read-out monitor for so long. Every time a car or bus or truck went by within the speed limit, the gun would beep once. But the rare times that something was going too fast, his squad car would be filled with an irritating chirping sound that lasted ten or twelve seconds.

He was just starting to believe that this afternoon was a

bust when something drew his attention to the motorway. A small, dark shape flew through the air and landed right on the grassy verge. Whatever it was, it was thrown from the window of a passing blue Volkswagen Beetle.

Garda Eddie McKean wasn't a fan of litterers to begin with, but it wasn't the sight of the broken phone a few yards from his car that got his blood up on this occasion. It was the sight of the Beetle itself.

He looked down at the handful of faxes that had come through on the wire not an hour previously. Sure enough, right on top of the pile was the order to pursue a 1960s pastel-blue VW Beetle. The note read: 'Pursue but do not detain until suspects have reached final location, at which point contact Detective P. Morrissey in Pearse Street Station.'

Garda Eddie McKean smiled to himself – some action at last – dropped the speed gun on the pile of faxes, straightened his cap, revved the engine and shot off.

'Incoming!' said Ex anxiously from the driver's seat.

'Huh?' asked Ellie.

'Incoming! Behind us!'

All but Ex turned to look through the rear windscreen.

The motorway consisted of three lanes on each side of the road, and most of the cars were doing the top speed limit of 120 kph. At this time of the evening – an hour or so before rush hour truly began – there were only a few vehicles on either side of the thoroughfare. They could see three cars coming up behind them, at various distances. But Ash knew that it was the one furthest away that Ex had spotted. The squad car was still about half a kilometre away.

'How long has it been following?' asked Ellie.

'Not long,' Ex told her. 'Since Eirik dumped the phone.'

The Viking grunted softly and shrugged apologetically.

'It's not his fault,' said Ash. 'I bet it's Detective Morrissey's doing.' The words spilled out before she could stop them.

'What?' cried Arthur. 'Why?'

'He's been keeping a close eye on me over the past few weeks.'

He turned on her, annoyed. 'You didn't tell me that!'

'We didn't want to worry you and we thought we'd lost him.'

'Well, I'm worried now,' he said, gazing back through the windscreen.

'OK, OK, I'm sorry. He must have had the cops

watching out for us when he worked out we'd left school. The car isn't very inconspicuous. But what do we do now?'

'If we get caught, the best-case scenario is that he brings us straight home,' said Ellie.

'That can't happen,' said Arthur. 'We don't have the time.'

'So …?' prompted Ex, waiting for orders.

Arthur looked over his shoulder at the squad car one last time.

'We have to lose him,' he said.

'Evasive measures, Ex,' said Ellie.

'Evasive measures,' said Ex, the ghost of a smile creeping across his lips.

He pressed harder on the accelerator and wound from one lane to another and then back again, squeezed between two cars. As soon as he could, Ex pumped the speed even more and swerved in front of a huge articulated truck, giving them momentary cover from the pursuing Garda.

Garda Eddie McKean had just confirmed that the licence plate on the Beetle matched the registration on the fax when the little blue car sped up. He growled to himself, realising they'd spotted him, and leaned over the steering wheel. Time to change tactics. In all his years in uniform no one had gotten away from him and he didn't intend to break that record now.

He hit a switch under the dash and stamped his foot on the accelerator.

'Oh great,' Ellie said sarcastically as the squad car's sirens started crying and the blue lights on top flashed brightly. 'And there's the cherry on top!' She swivelled in her seat to look back at her brother. 'Ex, be more evasive than that!'

He stamped his foot further down on the accelerator. The Beetle revved, struggling to reach the speeds Ex was attempting to push it to. Meanwhile, the Garda was in the middle lane, gradually closing the gap between them. He overtook a car in the inside lane and was rapidly catching up to the next car in his lane – a white Nissan. Arthur could see the driver: an elderly woman hunched over the wheel and squinting over her hands. She was just staring straight ahead, taking her time, and didn't notice the squad car coming up behind her. A massively long lorry rumbled along next to her in the right-hand lane, which meant that the Garda was stuck behind the slow elderly driver and the truck was preventing him overtaking. Suddenly, the squad car accelerated more and moved into the left-hand lane. But as it did, the woman steered her car to the left, heading for a turn-off. She didn't bother signalling and didn't hear the furious horn-honks of the Garda as he had to break suddenly to avoid a crash. He fell behind and, for a brief moment, Arthur hoped it would stay that way. But once the Nissan was off the motorway, the squad car sped up once more, moving rapidly towards them.

Meanwhile, Garda Eddie McKean could feel his face reddening with anger. This was not turning out to be his evening.

'Faster, Ex!' urged Arthur. 'He's right behind us! Go faster!'

'I'm going as fast as I can,' Ex muttered through gritted teeth. 'This is an old car. We'll never outrun him.'

The squad car came up alongside them on the right-hand side. Arthur could see the Garda inside gesticulating frantically at them with one arm. Although Arthur couldn't hear what he was shouting, he knew it was 'Pull over now!' Spittle flew out of the Garda's mouth and Arthur even noticed a blue vein pop out on his forehead, throbbing rapidly.

But before McKean could overtake them – and force them to stop the car – Ex swerved suddenly to the right.

The Garda just managed to avoid the Beetle, braking and falling behind it. He punched his fist on the wheel and the horn blared angrily. He pushed the car into gear and accelerated again. He was coming up on their left-hand side now, gesturing wildly through the window at Ellie. The blue light lit up her face rhythmically.

'What do we do?' she said, staring back at the Garda with wide eyes.

'We can't stop,' answered Arthur. 'Whatever happens, we have to get to Farranfore.'

'But he's going to keep going until he catches us,' said Ash. 'He'll radio for help if we don't stop.'

'*Grnk!*' grunted Eirik from the passenger seat. '*Nwk qus gwnkl!*'

The others looked at each other, none of them understanding what he'd been trying to say. When he saw the looks of confusion, he rolled his eyes in an exaggerated manner. He reached out to Arthur and took his hand.

'Ar-khur,' he said before letting go. Then, without any warning, he unhooked his seat belt, flung open the passenger door and leaped out of the speeding car.

A shocked silence filled the Beetle as Eirik sailed towards the squad car. Ex swerved in his surprise but quickly brought the car back under control, the momentum causing the door to slam shut. As the others watched, Eirik landed with a thump on the bonnet of the Garda's car. He gripped it, digging his fingers under the small lip around the edge. Garda Eddie McKean cried out at the appearance of a centuries-old Viking on the hood of his car. He veered to the left and straight onto the grassy slope at the side of the motorway. Mud and earth sprayed into the air as Eirik was thrown off the car onto his back. The car itself came to a crunching halt as the bonnet hit the bottom of the incline at speed.

As Ex sped further away from the crash site, the others looked out through the back window. The front end of the squad car was embedded in the earth and the back wheels were spinning uselessly in mid-air. Eirik had managed to get into a sitting position and was triumphantly watching them go while Garda Eddie McKean struggled out of the car, staring helplessly after the rapidly dwindling Beetle. He kicked his driver's door furiously and turned to apprehend Eirik, but the Viking was disappearing into the thick woodland beyond the embankment.

'That was close,' sighed Ash, as she settled back into her seat.

Arthur nodded. 'Tell me about it!'

They arrived in Farranfore just before eight o'clock. After they had left the Garda's smoking squad car in their wake, the rest of the drive to Kerry went smoothly enough. Arthur had been worried that the traffic cop would alert more Gardaí to the Beetle's presence, so they had gotten off the motorway quickly and used the back roads. It had taken a little longer, but they had not been spotted by any other cops. When they got to Farranfore, Arthur directed Ex to the village cemetery.

It was a strange feeling to be back in the town with Ash, Ellie and Ex in tow. And especially on this mission. Joe would be getting worried that Arthur wasn't home from school. Arthur knew he should call and put his mind at ease, but they hadn't time. Plus, knowing what he now knew about his mother, he couldn't face Joe until some resolution had been reached. If only I'd stayed here today and let Ash find Fenrir, Arthur thought, then maybe I'd have had a better chance of reaching Hel first. As it was now, he seriously doubted they were in time.

Ex parked outside the stone-walled entrance to the graveyard and they all got out of the car. The sky was a deep crimson, reflecting the lights of the town, and not even the moon, hiding behind the thickest cloud, broke the monotony.

'Let me go alone,' Arthur told them.

'What if something happens to you?' asked Ash.

'Well, if it does you can help then. But, please, for now I need to do this by myself.'

'Are you sure?'

'I am,' he said and slung the backpack with the hammer still in it over his shoulder. He wasn't sure whether or not Loki could sense the magic of the hammer, but he wanted to try to keep whatever element of surprise he could. Then, as the sun vanished below the horizon, he went into the quiet graveyard by himself.

If it hadn't been for the nearby streetlights of the village, the cemetery would have been pitch black. As it was, he could see adequately in the gloom and he followed the familiar path through the graves. A mist had settled a foot above the ground and wispy fingers of fog caressed the gravestones. When he was close enough to see his mother's resting place, he could make out a figure sitting on the tombstone. She had her back to him and was hunched over slightly, her outline lit from below by the red eternal lantern. His feet crunched across gravel and dried grass as he moved ever closer, keeping his eye fixed on the figure.

'Hello?' he called out, but got no reply; the figure didn't so much as shudder. He could see now that she was wearing a long navy-blue dress. He recalled seeing it once before: they'd buried his mother in it. As he kept walking, his hands started to shake. He put them in his pockets to stop them, but it was no use so he took them out again. He could feel the warmth of the pendant on his chest and knew that it would be glowing green, ready to protect him from Loki, but that wasn't much comfort. All he wanted was to run away from this place and never look back. But he had to keep going.

He stopped by the edge of his mother's open grave. A deep hole looked down into an empty coffin and the lid was lying next to the grave itself, snapped jaggedly in two.

'Mum?'

The woman on the gravestone lifted her head and slowly slid from her seat, deliberately turning to face him. Her movements were jerky, like she wasn't used to controlling her limbs; it was a disturbing sight – lacking in humanity – and Arthur felt fear rise in his throat. Her hair was as he'd remembered it: strawberry-blonde, curling inwards around the jaw. But the rest of her was completely different. Her eyes were golden, as Fenrir's had been, but were glowing and shone in the darkness. Her face was contorted, her high cheekbones and narrow chin exaggerated and drawn. Deep wrinkles indented her entire face, marking out her forehead and mouth lines.

Even in the red of the eternal lamp, her complexion seemed wrong, as if the skin itself would be a pallid, sickly green colour under normal light. Either way, there was no radiance in it and no love in her expression. This was not his mother. This was Hel.

'Hello, Arthur,' she said. Even her voice was different: deeper and scratchier somehow.

'Let my mum go.'

'I am your mum.'

'No you're not. You're an abomination.'

'Now, now, Arthur!' scolded a voice from behind him. 'That's not a nice thing to say to mummy dearest, is it?' Loki appeared from the darkness, pushing Drysi in her wheelchair. As he strolled forward, he hummed an old song that Arthur vaguely recognised: 'Tie a Yellow Ribbon Round the Ole Oak Tree'. The god probably thought it suited the situation in some sick way. He stopped at Hel's side and tilted his head quizzically at Arthur.

'Aren't you going to say hello to your dearest grandpapa?' asked Loki. 'And by "dearest grandpapa" I clearly mean me! I always knew there was something special about you, something drawing us together. And now I know what.' He patted his pockets absentmindedly. 'I wish I had some Werther's Originals to give you. That's what granddaddies do, right?'

'You'll never be my grandfather, Loki. No matter what you think.'

'Do you know what, Arthur? I believe, for the first time, I'm in agreement with you.' He laughed suddenly. Drysi and Hel joined in.

'Set my mother free,' Arthur said.

'Or what?' Loki stopped cackling and looked straight at him.

'I've stopped you before. I'll stop you again.'

'I don't think you quite see the gravity of the situation.' He looked past Arthur. 'Oh look – here comes the cavalry!'

Arthur looked over his shoulder to see Ash, Ellie and Ex stumbling through the graveyard towards him.

'I told you to wait,' he hissed at them.

'Oh, the more the merrier I always say!' cried Loki, clapping his hands in delight. 'You're all just in time for the final show.' He turned to the woman standing by the gravestone. 'Hel, dearest, would you be so kind as to deal with Arthur?'

'Of course, Father.' She pointed a long, crooked finger at him.

'What are you doing?' Arthur asked, taking a step back.

'Just erasing the mistake of your existence,' she said nonchalantly.

106

He turned to run for cover, but it was too late. Lightning shot out of her hand, slamming into his back. His friends rushed forward as green bolts of energy pulsed around him frantically.

'Arthur!' cried Ash, reaching for his hand. He tried to grab hold of her but her hand didn't seem to be solid and passed through his own. No – he realised with apprehension – it's my hand that's not solid! He looked down at the rest of his body and watched it fade as the pulses rushed through him.

He looked up one last time into Ash's face. Tears were spilling from her eyes.

And with that, Arthur Quinn blinked out of existence.

PART TWO

CHAPTER SEVEN

In Asgard, the realm of the gods, there is a tree. Though at first glance it is just like any other tree, anyone who dares to look at it would know that this is *not* like any other tree. The branches – which once flourished with greenery and fruits and berries of every sort – are now bare. Only withered berries and bone-dry leaves cling to the once-strong twigs. The trunk stands straight and upright, though the bark is falling off in thick clumps here and there. The tree overlooks a precipice situated by a river that flows over the edge into a waterfall. Three great roots extend from the trunk and into the river, soaking up the water. These are gnarled, with fungi sprouting all over and dark-green sap oozing into the waterfall. It is called Yggdrasill, the tree of life, but now it is clearly diseased and dying.

The river crashes over the edge of the cliff, plummeting into the pool below in a white foam. The pool is known as the Well of Urd. It has no bottom and is ever-deepening, as it contains all the knowledge that was ever known, that will be known and that could be known. The green waters ripple out from the foaming waterfall but, aside from that, all is still at the well.

This part of Asgard is frequently battered with torrential wind and rain, but on this day the weather has been stilled. It is impossible to tell the time of day, as the sky above is a deep blood-red and black clouds shift past the horizon. It is even difficult to tell if the flaming crimson disc in the sky is the sun or a burning moon or even an exploding star. No gods dare to roam the land on this day and no animals attempt to hunt their prey. All is eerily silent and motionless in the world of the gods, as if the very realm itself is waiting, anticipating ...

Suddenly there is a movement. A female figure steps out of the waterfall, followed closely by a second and a third. They stay standing in the middle of the crashing water and their features are obscured by the foam and rushing river. They are tall and slender, dressed in flimsy gowns that cling to their perfect forms. Their long hair is slicked down against their skulls in the water. Their faces – if they have any at all – are just vague indentations behind the waterfall, hinting at hollows for eyes. They are turned at an angle and it's somehow obvious that they are looking past the edge of the well at the boy on the ground.

The ground is hard and dusty beneath the boy, a threatening shade of red reflecting that of the sky. He is on his side, unconscious, and he is wearing a pair of denim jeans, a T-shirt and a hoodie. A schoolbag is on his back and a leather patch covers his left eye. The Norns can sense a great power emanating from the backpack but also from the boy. A ribbon is tied around his right wrist and somehow – despite the lack of a breeze – the ends of the ribbon sway in the air. A faint golden light shimmers and pulses from it, then fades as the ribbon falls still by his hand once more.

Arthur Quinn wakes in Asgard. He sits up and, although the red landscape and sky are alien to him, he knows instantly where he is. He's been here many times before, in his dreams. In the visions he always saw the realm of the gods through someone else's eyes. But now, he is seeing it with his own.

'Welcome, Arthur Quinn,' says one of the figures standing in the well. He looks up at them and guesses that the woman in the centre has spoken.

'Uh, hi,' he says, getting to his feet. He is surprised by how steady he is on them.

'Do you know where you are?'

'Asgard.'

'That is correct.'

He takes a few steps towards the pool.

'But how did I get here? Last thing I remember was–'

'We will tell you that in time, Arthur Quinn,' the woman cuts him off. 'But first, do you know who we are? What we are?'

He nods, moving even closer to take a look into the depths of the pool. There is just darkness beyond; it really is as bottomless as the legends say, he thinks.

'Yes,' he says, turning back to the figures in the waterfall. 'I know who you are. You're the Norns of Asgard. You can read the knowledge in the well and you'll tell me about the present, the future and my fate.'

'That is correct.'

'So tell me then – am I dead?'

'Perhaps my sister Verdandi can elucidate on that,' says the Norn in the centre. She turns to the sister on her right and Verdandi steps forward.

'You are not dead,' she tells him. 'Loki and Hel tried to erase you from existence. But they failed.'

'How did they fail? And why did I end up here?' Arthur is thrilled beyond belief that he is still alive, but his thoughts quickly turn to his friends and family back in Midgard, the world of man. Without him they are powerless against Loki. He needs to get back, and quickly, to save them.

'They failed because they forgot about Gleipnir,' explains Verdandi. Arthur glances at the ribbon on his wrist.

'Gleipnir?' he repeats.

'The ribbon cannot be destroyed. Hel tried that before and failed. And it kept you bound to reality. She could not pluck you from existence while you were wearing Gleipnir.'

'OK. But why am I here?'

Verdandi turns to her sister on the far left. 'Skuld,' she says, 'mayhap you can tell Arthur Quinn more?'

Skuld studies the flowing waters of the well, reading Arthur's future. Eventually, she looks back at him and speaks.

'Although Hel failed to completely destroy you, she did succeed in one aspect.'

'What?'

'She created a world where Arthur Quinn never existed.'

'A world where …' He finds that he can't finish the thought.

'Each time a world is created, a delicate balance is struck. Think of your world as an arch. And Hel and Loki have just removed the keystone. Your world is crumbling,

Arthur. And if it falls, then all of creation will be destroyed with it.'

'All of creation …?'

'Look at the tree above you, Arthur.' He does as she bids and looks at the tree at the top of the waterfall. It looks very different from the last time he saw it in a vision, when it had been covered in bright-green leaves and was ripe with fruit.

'That tree is Yggdrasill,' she tells him. 'The tree of life. It brought you here so that you would understand, for you to see what is at risk. Its roots are anchored in each of the worlds. If one world ceases to be, they all will. Disease from Midgard has spread into the tree already. If the tree dies, then there is no hope for any of us: gods, men or giants. Ragnarok.'

'The end of the world,' he mutters, remembering the Vikings explaining that word to him before.

'The end of creation itself,' corrects the Norn.

'I have this.' He holds up his wrist to show off Gleipnir. 'If it saved me, can't we use it to save the world somehow?'

'Not even Gleipnir is powerful enough for that. But my sister Urd may tell you more.' She looks at the Norn in the centre, the wisest of the three, who can read fate. When Urd is done gazing into the whirling waters, she looks back at Arthur.

'The only way to save Yggdrasill and the known worlds is to restore balance. And the only way to restore balance is to defeat Loki. You must return to Midgard now, Arthur Quinn,' she says. 'Only you can stop the Father of Lies. Only you can save creation. Only you.'

'People keep telling me that!' he cries in desperation. 'Be honest with me for once. Tell me why it has to be me!'

'I can't, Arthur Quinn. No man, nor beast, nor god should know too much of his fate.'

'But you've told me nothing!' he shouts in anger. 'At least tell me how I kill him!'

'To kill a god is a terrible thing. You kill a part of yourself in doing so.'

'Then how am I supposed to stop him?'

The Norn pauses; for the first time in her long existence, she is stuck for words.

'Like All-Father Odin, you have a damaged eye and, like him, you will learn to see the truth through it,' she says finally.

He turns from the Norns and walks a few steps away, simmering in anger.

'Send me home,' he says with his back to them.

'Arthur,' warns Urd, 'you must know that the world will not be as you left it.'

'Send me home!'

'Close your eye. When you open it again, you will be in Dublin.'

Arthur turns for one last look at the Norns but he finds himself all alone. Only the waterfall rushes into the well and the figures have disappeared. He reaches under his T-shirt and grips his pendant tightly, then looks at the tree at the edge of the cliff. As he does, a branch breaks off Yggdrasill. He shuts his eye and–

–opened it again. He was falling through a green sky towards a great expanse of dark water.

'*Aargh!*' he screamed, as the air rushed past his ears. Not again, was all he could think as he plunged head first into the cold water.

CHAPTER EIGHT

Before he had a chance to hold his breath Arthur swallowed a mouthful of water. He went to spit it out but quickly realised that if he did he'd only ingest more water. It wasn't as cold as he'd thought it would be and, even though he'd shut his eye before impact, he'd caught glimpses of dark shapes underneath the surface. His clothes were instantly soaked through and became heavy, dragging him downwards – and the stuffed backpack wasn't doing him any favours either. Despite all that, he managed to turn around and kick his legs against something solid in the murk. He thrust himself back towards the surface, pulling with his arms and kicking with all his might, and a moment later broke through, gasping in as much oxygen as his lungs could take.

Gloomy clouds filled the sky for as far as he could

see. They were a deep green colour and rolled over the landscape at a frightening rate, threatening heavy rainstorms. Frantic bolts of electricity shot through them here and there: spiderwebs wriggling across the billowing haze or sparking inside it, highlighting how dense the cover was. Yet the sun was still up there somewhere, hidden behind the clouds, and the surrounding air was warm. In fact, not just warm: it was hot, dry and humid; Joe would have called it 'muggy'. A few years previously they'd taken a holiday in Spain. It had been the height of an unnaturally scorching summer and one evening, as they returned to the hotel from the beach, the day had felt just like this. Dark clouds had appeared in the sky and, within minutes, they had found themselves in the middle of a tropical thunderstorm. Afterwards, Joe had said that that weather had been unusual even for Spain. If that was the case, then it was very strange for Ireland.

The water Arthur was floating in stretched away in front of him. It was odd. The Norns had promised to send him back to Dublin, but now he seemed to be in a lake and he couldn't think of any lakes in Dublin. The water was still, reflecting the shifting cloud formations from above. Through the murk below, he could see some dark forms but couldn't make out what they were. Arthur looked to his side and the sight made him gasp. More shocking than the amount of water – even more terrifying than the green and stormy sky – were the buildings he could see rising out of the flood. On either side, grey Georgian-era structures peeped out of the water. In some cases he could only see the slanted peaks of the roofs; in others he could see the top few storeys. Many of the windows had been smashed in and water had flowed into the buildings themselves. He suddenly realised what the dark shapes underneath him had been and he dipped his head below the surface of the water for a second look.

They were cars and statues and park-benches and bins – all remnants of the street below. He could now even make out the first and second floors of the buildings, enveloped by the great flood. He took his head back out. He was more breathless now than he'd been the first time. But now it had nothing to do with being under water; now it was down to the shock and dread he felt at the realisation that was slowly forming in his mind. He knew where he was. He'd been here before countless times. Except the street hadn't been flooded as it was now. He waved his arm through the surface of the water in front of him, rotating gently on the spot. He was sure he knew the place; he just needed confirmation, although his stomach clenched in horror at the thought of it. He stopped turning.

The Dublin Spire loomed out of the water before him, towering above everything else in O'Connell Street. It had been erected at the turn of the century, a monument to celebrate the millennium and the city itself. It resembled a needle in design – shining steel that tapered to a fine point four hundred feet in the air – and it was the tallest structure in Dublin. Only a few months ago, Arthur had defeated the World Serpent and Loki here at the Spire itself. And now the bottom thirty or forty feet of it were submerged under the water along with every other building on O'Connell Street, the main thoroughfare of the city. As Arthur took in the sunken street around him, he realised that it wasn't just here that was flooded. The water extended down the cross-streets, around the corner at O'Connell Bridge, up the hill at Parnell Square. Everywhere. The entire city was under water. Without Arthur to stop him, it looked like Loki had already won.

For a while, Arthur floated aimlessly, trying to take in what had happened. The Norns must have sent him back too late. That was it. How was he expected to fix it now? Well, one thing was for certain: he couldn't stay in the water forever. He had landed near the shopping district of Henry Street so he decided to doggy-paddle down that way. Here, everything was in much the same state as he'd found O'Connell Street. Only the higher buildings were tall enough to rise out of the water and, of those that did, windows had been smashed in, signs hung crookedly and electrics flashed and sparked inside the ruined properties. Some of the shops, Arthur guessed from the signs of struggle and overturned merchandise inside, had been looted. The only sound he heard as he swam down the street was a siren whining agitatedly in the distance.

He could faintly see the bright sphere of the sun through the clouds, looking like a silver coin at the bottom of a muddy pond. Although the presence of the green, electrified clouds was worrying, he was glad that the sun couldn't penetrate them to add to the stifling warmth of the air. If it had he doubted that he'd have the energy to keep afloat, let alone swim. He had to stop and rest several times as he swam the length of the street. His backpack was weighing him down and making the going tough, but he didn't want to risk losing it and had no other way of carrying it. And because it was on his back, he couldn't take off his soaking hoodie, so had no choice but to keep struggling onwards.

Towards the end of the street, he came to a shop he recognised. 'Toyz Toyz Toyz' read the sign next to a mural of a pink teddy bear. A speech bubble coming out of its mouth – proclaiming 'Magic and Fun under One Roof!' – was hanging lopsided with a deep crack running down the middle. The paint on the teddy itself was cracking off, clearly weathered by incessant rain and heat. The biggest toy store in the city, it boasted three floors with any doll, action figure, board game, construction set or remote-control car that a child could possibly want. As in every other building on the street, the ground floor was completely submerged, along with half of the first floor. But from where Arthur was, the top floor seemed relatively untouched. Even the large second-storey window, which had a vinyl sticker of the trademarked bear on it, was still intact.

It seemed as good a place as any to go, so Arthur swam through one of the smashed first-floor windows. He was careful to avoid the sides where shards of glass remained fixed in the frame. There were spots of what looked like blood on some of the slivers, Arthur noticed grimly.

Swimming through the shop gave Arthur the creeps. It just felt wrong. The first floor had been home to the girls' section and every surface had been painted one shade of pink or another. A single fluorescent bulb buzzed overhead – crackling out sparks every few seconds – but it provided him with just enough light to see. Baby and

Barbie dolls floated in the water and were swept aside by the waves from his kicks. One of the doll's voice boxes was malfunctioning in the wet and kept repeating the same word over and over, only in a hoarse, staticky crackle: '*Mama! Mama! Mama! Mama!*' A shiver crept up his spine as he passed the yapping doll and he couldn't resist shoving it under the flood to silence it.

He made his way towards an escalator that stretched out of the water and led to the top floor. Like almost everything else in the store, its electrics had failed and the stairs were at rest now. He reached the escalator and stepped onto the nearest tread. He looked over the handrail but, seeing only darkness descending towards the ground floor, he turned and climbed the steps.

The top storey of the toy shop was just as he remembered it from his brief visit last October. Half of it was taken up with floor-to-ceiling shelves stuffed full of action figures, play-sets, transforming trucks and so on. The other half contained large toys for all ages: bikes, go-karts, swings and see-saws. Unlike downstairs, not a single light was working and he had to rely on the faint daylight coming through the large windows to see by. He let his bag slide off his back and then stripped off the hoodie gratefully, flinging it away. The floor was blessedly dry here and he collapsed onto the linoleum in an exhausted heap.

He lay on his back there for a whole half hour, although it barely felt like half a minute. He simply stared up at the dark light fixture in the ceiling, not thinking of Loki or the Norns or what had happened to the world. He concentrated on getting his strength back and he only realised that he'd been lying there for so long when he found that his clothes had dried in the stuffy heat of the shop.

His stomach rumbled and he found that he was suddenly starving. Of course, he hadn't eaten since the train that morning, which seemed like days ago. For all he knew, it had been days ago. He got to his feet as more hunger pains cramped his belly and he surveyed the shop. He didn't have to look long before he spotted his salvation. Just to the left of the escalators was a metal door marked 'Staff Only'. He grabbed the backpack, leaving the hoodie where it was, and went through the door.

Arthur found himself in a long corridor with cardboard boxes piled high on the right-hand side. A red emergency light glowed at the end of the hall. He walked beside the boxes, his fingers tapping off them as he went. He passed one door on his left which read 'Storeroom' and a second which read 'Office'. Both were locked. The third door, though, was the one he was most interested in. 'Canteen', the sign read in blocky black text. He breathed a sigh of relief when he turned the handle and the door opened.

The staff canteen was little more than a room with a basic kitchenette on one side and a breakfast table on the other side. Old newspapers, novels and copies of *Heat* magazine were piled on the table, alongside crusty-topped bottles of ketchup and brown sauce. A chocolate-bar wrapper lay next to the magazines but, when Arthur checked it, he found with dismay that the sweet goodness inside had all been eaten. He pulled open the two cupboards over the sink. One shelf contained a half-full box of Cornflakes, a jar of honey and a loaf of sliced bread overrun with blue mould. Beneath that were a bag of fun-sized chocolate bars and a tin of spaghetti. He found a bag of salt and vinegar crisps (his favourite) on another shelf, along with a packet of the type of curry-flavoured noodles that you just needed to add water to. There was nothing on the last shelf except cleaning products. It wasn't exactly a four-star meal, but it looked more appetising to him now than anything he'd ever had to eat before.

He yanked his school uniform out of his backpack, guessing he wouldn't be needing it any time soon, and stuffed all the food inside in its place. He even took the noodles, hoping he'd be able to find a working kettle somewhere to cook them. Then he went back to the main area of the toy store. He took out the packet of crisps and a chocolate bar and set about devouring them as he wandered down the quiet aisles of the shop.

As he munched, he remembered seeing Loki here for the first time all those months ago. He hadn't even known who or what Loki was at the time; he had just sensed that he was evil. Although, *I guess that's all I really needed to know*, he reminded himself.

He walked past the garden toys, looking at the trampolines and inflatable pools and swings, and then saw something that made him stop. An idea popped into his head. He stared at the stack of bright-yellow sandpits, wondering if it would work. *It will work*, he told himself. *It has to.*

Half an hour later and he was back on the water, putting his plan into action. He'd borrowed one of the sandpits, along with a pair of spades and a few other supplies. He thought of it as borrowing and really did intend to return everything once this was all over. At least that's what he told himself.

The idea had come to him when he'd seen the label attached to each sandpit. It showed two images: one of a couple of toddlers making sandcastles, the other of the same toddlers using the sandpit as a watertight pool. So, Arthur had reasoned, if the sandpit could be used as a paddling pool, did that mean it was watertight enough to be used as a boat?

He was sitting in the sandpit-boat right now and it seemed to be doing the trick. It was bobbing under the surface of the water more than a real boat would, but at least it was holding him afloat. He rowed out through the first-floor window, using one of the spades as an oar. He took the second one as a spare, just in case. Getting through the window was a tight squeeze but he managed it. Rowing was tough – especially since the round sandpit shape wasn't exactly hydrodynamic – but it was a lot easier than the swimming had been.

Arthur took one last look at the toy store, then turned and rowed for the Dublin estate he thought of as home.

The outer reaches of the city were in just as dire straits as the shopping district, if not more so. Whole houses were submerged, along with garden furniture, cars, bicycles and anything else that had been rooted to the ground when the floods came. Arthur could tell he was heading in the right direction, but it was surreal rowing through the familiar yet alien landscape. Once, the sandpit-boat brushed against something and almost got trapped. Arthur looked into the water to find out what was causing the obstruction. A tall, once-healthy oak tree was under the flood and he'd gotten wedged in the thick upper branches. He managed to get free and rowed on. Moments later, he passed a house whose rooftop was just above the waterline. He could see a ladder leaning against the house leading up to the roof. Clearly some people had taken residence on top of the building as the water rose. But they weren't there now. He shuddered to think of what might have happened to them.

An hour later, as he was pondering why he still hadn't seen any signs of life, he had his first indication that he wasn't alone. A scream sounded in the distance, forcing him to stop rowing. It was high-pitched and throaty, a terrible, forlorn sound. For a while, it echoed around him, seeming to bounce off the water itself. But then it faded and he was alone again. He didn't want to think about that scream, about the person who had made it or why they'd made it, but he couldn't help it. He gripped his spade-paddle tighter and rowed onwards. It was all he could think of doing: get home and decide where to go from there. Even if there was no home left, he had no other place to go.

The only other sound he heard on the rest of his

journey through the dead city was just as disconcerting. While he hadn't been able to pinpoint the location of the scream, he knew that this sound was coming from his left; he guessed towards the east. It started low then built gradually to a loud roar. It was the sound of engines, several of them at once. He couldn't tell what kind of engines they were but he supposed they must have been from some sort of motorboats. Then, just as gradually as the noise had built, it faded away.

It took him a while to find his bearings as he rowed through the streets in the general direction of home, but eventually he started noticing landmarks both under the water and looming above it to help guide him. Before he knew it, he was passing by his former school. Belmont had been a new construction and was a big, heavy design with sweeping curves and narrow lines. But now, like everything else, the lower half of the building was under water. All the windows had been smashed; even the glass roof had been destroyed. Graffiti covered the walls, screaming grief-laden messages. One read *Burn in Hell!* and beneath it someone else had sprayed *We're already in it!* Looking at the school, Arthur had the feeling that somebody had actively sought to defile the building. Why would anyone want to do that, he wondered, rowing past it.

It took him another forty minutes to reach the place

where he and Joe had lived for the past few months. Only the rooftops of the estate were visible above the water, as well as the very tops of the trees on the central green area. He went in for a closer look at his former house. He reached into his backpack and took out a couple of glow sticks he had 'borrowed' from the toy store. He snapped them and shook vigorously, as the instructions said, then dropped the pair of them into the water. Two circles of green radiance hit the walls of the house as the sticks fell. The windows and doors all looked tightly sealed and he could see a 'To Let' sign under the water in the front driveway. In a weird way, he felt the same as he had when arriving at the house last October, as if he was seeing it for the very first time. He remembered that evening, he remembered unpacking his things and putting up his posters, he remembered discovering the truth about Loki in the house, he remembered having his first fight with Ash there and he remembered leaving for the last time. He found himself welling up and there was a lump in his throat so he turned towards Ash's house.

The Barry household had been devastated. All that remained of it was the charred and scorched shell of the roof and the outer walls. He rowed towards it for a closer look. When he was close enough, he dropped two more glow sticks into the water. The windows and doors had blown out and the insides of the house appeared to have been vaporised. Whatever force had destroyed the house, it was so great that the windows in the houses next to it had been blown in. A fork of lightning sparked across the clouds overhead, bathing the murky and hollow house in momentary brightness, like a camera's flash. It was like staring into the gaping jaws of the Jormungand: empty and cold, a place of death. Whatever had happened here, it was clear that no one could have survived it. This he knew with great certainty. If anyone had been inside the house during the destruction, they had died. No doubt.

Just then, there was a sound behind him. Roaring engines, exactly like the ones he'd heard earlier. He turned in time to see a number of jet skis race into the estate. There were about ten of them, all painted black with luminous-green speed stripes. The sigil on each side depicted a tree with a serpent coiled around the trunk: the Jormungand. Each of the riders was togged out in black from head to toe, and they wore perfectly spherical and reflective black helmets that covered their heads and faces entirely. They came to a stop over where the green should have been, in a V-shaped formation, and the visors of the helmets turned in his direction. Arthur had seen people like this before.

They were Loki's raiders.

They were Loki's wolves.

CHAPTER NINE

The raider at the front of the formation stood up on his jet ski – one leg balanced on either support – and took off his helmet. He had a shaved head and a single bushy brow arched over a pair of squinting eyes. A scar cut through the centre of his lips, seeming to split his chin in two. He snarled at Arthur, gritting his teeth.

"Oo are you?' he growled at him. 'Wot're you doin' there?'

'Nothing,' Arthur started. 'I–'

'D'you escape from one of d'camps?'

'Camps? What camps?'

'Shurrup, you!' His face turned beetroot red. 'I'll ask d'questions here. Wot's your name then, one-eye?'

'Cyclops, maybe,' guffawed one of the others gleefully. The raiders had all now removed their helmets and were staring at Arthur.

'Actually,' said a third in a matter-of-fact tone, 'losin' an eye isn't a laughin' matter. A few years ago, I got in a brawl wiv dis bloke. 'E was my bruvver, come to think of it. And in d'heat of d'brawl, I popped 'is eye out wiv my thumb. It just came right out, so it did, made a sound like squeezing some of that bubble-wrap stuff. Anyway, after that, 'e 'ad terrible balance. 'E kept fallin' over and bumpin' into things and 'e looked like a right plonker … actually, now that I think of it, it is kinda funny!'

This set most of them off laughing. The scar-lipped one whipped around to growl at them and they promptly shut up. He faced Arthur again.

'Now,' he said. 'Wot's your name?'

'Ar–' He stopped. He suddenly had second thoughts about revealing his real name to some of Loki's wolves. 'Will,' he said. 'My name's Will.'

'Will,' grunted Scar-lip. 'Didja hear that, boys? He says his name's Will!' He broke out in heavy belly laughs, as did the others. 'Wot sort of a pansy-arsed name is Will? Very la-di-da! All right, boyo, you're coming wiv us.'

The others revved up their motors and slashed through the water towards him. Arthur didn't have time to try to escape, but even if he had, he doubted that he'd have been able to outrun the jet skis. The first raider to reach him grabbed him by the scruff of his neck, picking him straight up into the air and plopping him down on the seat behind him. One of the others took his backpack out of the sandpit-boat and put it into a trunk attached to his jet ski.

'Hold onto my waist tight,' warned Arthur's captor, before adding with a sneer, 'we wouldn't want you to drown.' He jammed his helmet back on his head and, with a roaring rev of the engines, they all zipped off, away from the burnt-out house. Arthur had one last look at the receding estate before it was gone.

Darkness started to fall as the jet skis raced through the dead city. The streetlights didn't come on as usual, so when it was almost too gloomy to see where they were going the raiders switched on high-beams. The lights cut through the blackness directly ahead of them but didn't reveal much on either side. No longer able to pick out familiar landmarks, Arthur soon lost track of the direction they were going in. The raider didn't say a word as they rode, although, even if he had, Arthur would have had trouble hearing him through the helmet and with the rush of air in his ears.

Eventually, they slowed down. The sun had long since set but the night air was still warm and clammy; not as bad as it had been during the day but still unnaturally hot for Ireland. Arthur looked at the sky above. The clouds were still shifting, sparking green in places, but without the sun to illuminate them they were a darker shade of ivy now. The moon was a blurred crescent through the clouds. Arthur peered past his captor at their new location. They were in front of an enormously high and long wall. The jet skis moved through a gap in the wall, past a 'Deliveries Entrance' sign and into a huge concrete structure. A steel landing platform stood at just the right level for the raiders to disembark. Concrete steps rose high into the darkness, punctuated along the stairwell with bright worklights. Several more raiders were milling around, going up and down the stairs or boarding their own jet skis and riding out.

Arthur's raider pulled the jet ski right up to the landing platform along with all the others, shut off the engine and stepped onto the metal dock. He yanked Arthur off the small vessel and shoved him towards the steps. With his captor right behind him and the raider who'd taken his bag in front of him, Arthur started up the staircase. He kept his eye fixed on the backpack, praying that no one would think to open it and discover his hammer inside. Voices and laughter bounced off the concrete the whole way up and Arthur had a sense that a lot more raiders were about than he had yet seen. Every so often they came to a landing with a door leading off to some other part of the structure. Wolf raiders poured in and out of these doors but he never got a good glimpse of the rooms beyond apart from a sense of harsh lighting and a cacophony of loud talking and clattering. The raider carrying his bag went through one of the doors on what Arthur counted as being the fourth floor. This room was darker than all the others they'd passed and much quieter. Arthur's captor pushed him towards an emergency door next to it, but Arthur just had time to see the other man come back out of the dim room without his belongings and head back down the steps.

The raider still with Arthur kicked the emergency door open, letting in the stifling night air with a whoosh.

'Down you go,' he ordered. When the boy didn't move, he gave him a harsh nudge forward. Arthur gasped when he saw where he was.

Croke Park was the largest sporting stadium in Dublin and the fourth largest in Europe. It was situated in the very heart of the city, less than a mile from O'Connell Street. Three tiers of seating circled the green pitch on three sides, while the fourth side was closed in with a smaller stand. High-powered floodlights beamed down from the edge of the roof, highlighting everything in glaring whiteness. Blue-plastic arena seating filled the stands entirely and some raiders were scattered about the

138

seats. A few were lounging back and relaxing; others were chatting or sipping beers. Some had even transformed into wolves and were chasing each other through the aisles of blue, playfully nipping at each other's tails.

'I said down you go!' the raider grunted once more, giving Arthur another sharp shove.

The view of the pitch was what had stopped Arthur in his tracks. It should have been under the flood like the ground outside the stadium, but this wasn't the case. Instead the playing field was full of people wearing dirty, mud-smeared rags. Some of them shuffled to and fro but most were just hunched or lying on the ground. The grass itself was gone, trampled into a sticky, muddy mess.

Steps led down the tier to the pitch, between rows of plastic seats. Before the raider could give him any more helpful encouragement, Arthur slowly started down, taking the steps one at a time because his legs felt suddenly unstable. As he went, some of the people below turned his way, giving him cursory glances, then looked away once more. A group of wolf raiders who were huddled in some nearby seats, watching the crowds, jeered him. They swore at him, calling him names and cackling loudly. One of them even threw an empty beer can at him. It clattered by his feet as he passed.

As he stepped onto the pitch, his foot slid out from

underneath him on the slippery muck and he landed with a thud on his back. Suddenly–

✦✦✦✦✦

–Yggdrasill, the tree of life, is being hammered by the rains of Asgard. Lightning strikes it, splitting a thick branch in two. And–

✦✦✦✦✦

Arthur blinked and found himself back in Croke Park. What was that, he wondered, still lying on the ground. He had managed to avoid hitting his head off the last concrete step, but the fall had hurt nonetheless. He lay still for a minute, stubbornly trying to block out the sounds of the laughing raiders in the stand. Then, just as he was about to get up, something tugged at his feet. He looked down the length of his body to see a grubby-cheeked boy aged about five pulling off his shoes. Before Arthur could stop him, he was off, weaving at a sprint through the mob and taking Arthur's favourite pair of Converse with him.

'Hey!' Arthur shouted after him. 'Get back here! They're –' He struggled to his feet, sliding even more now, and started to run after the boy, but the thief was lost in the crowds before he had taken more than a few steps. He sighed and looked down at his feet. His socks were already covered in mud and soaked through. Seeing no other choice, Arthur looked up and moved deeper into the huddled mass.

The things Arthur saw as he moved among the people on the pitch shocked and frightened him. The level of human despair he felt pouring from them was stifling and, much like a balloon, the tension threatened to burst at any minute. Judging by the raggedy, stained state of them, most appeared to be wearing the clothes they'd arrived in and Arthur guessed that they'd been here for weeks, if not months. The clothes were universally loose, as if the wearers hadn't had a decent meal for a long time. Their hair was greasy and their skin unwashed. Heavy bags hung under their tired-looking eyes and their ashen faces were drawn and ill-looking. They turned to him with want in their eyes, as if hoping that he might have some spare food or relief to offer them, but knowing that he wouldn't.

Many of the people were asleep already, especially the elderly captives. They lay on the ground itself, with only thin and uncomfortable layers of clothing or plastic bags between them and the slick mud. There was no cover from the night sky, no tents or huts to keep them dry when it rained. Arthur wondered what would happen whenever it did rain, as Croke Park didn't have a roof over the pitch. He was actually amazed that people could sleep at all with the bright floodlights glaring down, but he figured they must have gotten used to them by now. The stench throughout was pungent; even more so when he passed a line of Portaloos that clearly hadn't been emptied in days. Most people kept their voices to a low mumble, whispering together in small groups. Only the babies didn't seem to understand this protocol and cried loudly and wilfully. At one stage, Arthur heard angry shouting and turned towards the sound to see a pair of middle-aged men (both in dirty shirts and ties) fist-fighting over which of them owned a much-stained blazer. Eventually, one of the men knocked out the other with a fierce blow and triumphantly claimed the jacket.

As he continued to explore the camp, a numbness surged through him. He felt disconnected from the world, as if he was viewing himself on a cinema screen – just a character in a movie. A horror movie. He wondered if Joe was here somewhere, or the Barry family. He didn't know which fate would be worse: to have been killed in the house explosion or to end up at this camp. And what about the Lavenders? He hoped that in this world Ellie and Ex might be safe with their parents in some other country, away from the horror all around him. Although there was no way to be certain that the terrible things that had happened were restricted to Ireland.

Arthur wandered around for hours, feeling more lost and more lonely than he ever had in his life. The night didn't get any colder. More and more people fell asleep, but he couldn't. Not yet. He knew he wouldn't be able to drift off in this dreadful and strange environment. So he kept on walking, picking his way around the people back and forth across the pitch, just to keep moving. Anything to pass the time.

At one stage he remembered the hammer – and how it had come to him every time he was in mortal danger. He held his open palm in the direction of the door he'd come through, hoping to see the weapon crash through and soar straight into his grasp. But it didn't. He supposed he wasn't in mortal danger right now. Not really. He wasn't about to die. This place – whatever it was – was a place of slow, torturous death.

Arthur passed a small grouping by one of the pitch's goalposts. Between twenty and thirty people were laid out on the ground, lying on torn pieces of plastic sheeting in order to keep dry, arranged in a three-rowed grid system.

Most of them were asleep but some were awake, gazing up at the sky or at him as he walked past. The majority had eyes full of sadness but, as hard as those were to bear, Arthur preferred them to the second group, whose eyes were totally devoid of emotion. Those eyes told him that their owners had given up. A handful of people were moving through the lines of those lying down, bending to talk to them, checking their temperature with the backs of their hands, tending to their every need. It's a makeshift hospital, he realised as one woman on the ground hacked a throaty cough. They've made a hospital for the sickest people. Right here, under the goalposts.

'Hello, pet,' said a plump woman in her sixties. Despite her size, the skin was loose on her frame, evidence of just how unhealthy she was. She was holding the bottom half of a plastic bottle that had been cut in two, filled with water, and a small rag. This woman, Arthur realised, must be one of the nurses. She was the first person who had spoken to him since he'd got there. 'Can I help you at all?' she asked.

Arthur shook his head. He couldn't find the words to speak to her; he just didn't know what to say.

The nurse nodded slowly. 'OK, then. If you need any-thing, if you feel ill at all, just come on back. My name's Ann. If I'm not here, someone else will be.'

'Thanks,' he uttered, not knowing what else to say. The woman read his confused expression.

'You're new here, aren't you, pet?'

He nodded silently.

'Thought so. You can always tell. Who took your shoes?'

'Some kid.'

'Hmm. Be careful of your clothes, now, pet. They're currency around this place.'

'What do you mean?'

'Some of the guards will trade extra rations for items of clothing. And then they'll just rip up the clothes in front of your eyes.'

'Why would they do that?'

'Humiliation, I suppose. I'm guessing you weren't in one of the other camps either, were you, pet?'

'I was hiding … in my old home …'

'Oh. Well, one other piece of advice for you: don't cross the Wolfsguard. Some of them have terrible tempers.'

'The Wolfsguard?'

Nurse Ann pointed at the men in the stands. 'Those terrible men are the Wolfsguard, pet. They're Loki's police force. You've heard of Loki, right?'

'Yes … yes … I've heard of him. There must be a way out of here, though.'

'If there was, don't you think we'd all be gone? Although, I suppose it is difficult for a few hundred weak prisoners to just sneak out. No,' she added with finality, 'we're stuck here, I'm afraid.'

Lost for words, he started to move on again, but the woman reached out and took him by the arm.

'Hold on a second, pet,' she said. 'Wait there.' She hurried off, returning a few moments later. She held a ragged piece of plastic sheeting out to him. 'You'll need this to sleep on. I'd give you some shoes if I had any spare but I don't.'

'Thank you.' He took the sheet and turned to go once more. 'But I don't think I'll be able to sleep.'

'Oh,' Ann said knowingly, turning back to her charges, 'you'd be surprised, pet.'

CHAPTER TEN

The nurse had been right. Arthur was surprised the next morning when he found that he had managed to catch a few hours' sleep.

After the nurse had given him the sheeting, he'd wandered the muddy field for another while, gazing with ever-growing apprehension at the terrible sights around him. Eventually most of the camp grew quiet and all he had to look at was thousands of sleeping prisoners. He felt like an intruder – stepping over a snorer here, past a cuddling couple there. It was as if he was invading their privacy – although he supposed that no one had any real privacy in a place like this. It had been taken from them, along with their freedom. The only things they still had were their lives. That said, Arthur realised hopelessly while looking back in the direction of the makeshift hospital, it probably wasn't long before they started to lose those too.

His legs were soon aching from all the walking. He found an empty spot on the ground by the edge of the pitch. Only a handful of sleepers had chosen the perimeter to make their bed for the night and he quickly saw why. Most of the moisture and water had seeped to the declined verge around the camp and it was a soggier mess here than anywhere else. He didn't relish the thought of lying there, but since the rest of the pitch was tightly packed body-to-body, and since the Wolfsguard were on patrol keeping humans out of the tiered seating, he didn't have any other option.

Arthur laid the plastic sheeting over the ground. Brown water bubbled up through a couple of rips in the material but, aside from that, it seemed to be doing a fairly good job. He sat down on it, making more droplets of the coffee-coloured ooze drizzle through, then leaned his head back against an advertisement board that separated the pitch from the stand and thought of Ash, Joe and everyone else. He was still thinking of them when he woke up.

Somebody bumped into him, knocking him out of his dream-ravaged sleep. Although the sky was as gloomy and green as it had been the previous day, he still had to squint against the brightness, waiting for his eye to adjust. When it did, he took in the scene around him.

Nearly everyone was moving forward, heading towards the opposite corner to the hospital. They all wore determined, fixed gazes, staring straight ahead of them. What was most disconcerting was that almost no one spoke as they walked.

He pushed himself to his feet. His legs, he found, were still shaky, but not as weak as they had been the previous night. He picked up his sheeting (he thought of it as his now, he noticed with worry), shook off any excess clumps of sludge, folded it and stuffed it into his pocket.

'Excuse me,' he said to a passing man, who he guessed was in his early forties. 'Can you tell me where everyone's going?'

'Not been here long, have you?' replied the man, noting the relative cleanliness of Arthur's garb. 'It's breakfast-time. The Wolfsguard are never what you'd call generous, so you should make a move if you want to eat today.'

Arthur began to thank him for the advice but the man was already moving away, surging forward to get a good spot. He looked around, hoping to see a familiar face – even the plump woman from the hospital. Seeing no one he knew, he joined the breakfast throng.

He was astounded by how quickly swarms of people

squeezed into the corner where the guards would allocate the breakfast. It was anything but an orderly line; it was just a mob thrusting forward. Only the very old and very young stayed away, probably hoping that their friends and relatives would bring some food back to them. As he moved forward himself, he looked at their faces, their eyes hungry and their bellies rumbling. Arthur made a mental note to get enough food for himself and some of these weaker, famished folk.

A group of guards without helmets was coming out of one of the doors at the top of the lowest tier. One of them was wearing a tall chef's hat and matching apron, both stained liberally with food spillages. He was carrying a large pot with some indeterminable green-brown sludge sloshing over the rim as he walked. The others had black bin-bags or plastic crates full of half-eaten breakfast rolls, mouldy pizza slices and dried-up pieces of meat. The crowd surged forward frantically, waving tin bowls that Arthur recognised from the many camping trips he'd gone on with Joe. He was hustled along by the heaving horde, shoved to and fro as people jostled past him, so eager were they to get their ration of leftovers.

His legs collapsed unexpectedly. He couldn't tell whether he'd slipped or his limbs were still weak or – worse still – if someone had tripped him up. Either way, he got his hands out in front of him just in time to cushion his fall. He expected people would stop and help, but instead their feet pummelled the ground by his face as they ran around him, rushing forward impatiently. He attempted to stand up, but every time he got to his knees someone would knock him to the ground once more. Eventually he gave up, wrapping his arms around his head in the hopes of protecting his skull. Just then, someone grabbed the back of his mud-encrusted T-shirt and wrenched him backwards out of the flocking mob. He didn't even see who had pulled him out as he landed on the ground a few feet away with a thud; his saviour had disappeared into the crowd.

Arthur stepped away from the throng, relieved to be out of it, and watched as the chef guard poured the brown slop into a steel trough at the edge of the pitch, similar to one pigs would eat from. The mob grew more violent, jostling each other out of the way to get at the vile-looking 'food'. He was shocked to see that a couple of people had fainted and were being trampled underfoot; he'd been lucky to get away unhurt. Arthur turned away in distaste, but he could still hear the appalling sounds: pleading, screaming, sobbing.

The feeding frenzy lasted for almost an hour. The Wolfsguard amused themselves by flinging food high over the crowd and cackling as the starving prisoners rolled around in the mud, fighting for any scraps they could find. By the end, guards from all around the stadium had moved around to where the chef was standing, to watch the throng and join in the fun. When all the leftovers had been distributed, the crowd dispersed. Some of them were hobbling on injured limbs and some were still chewing what little food they'd caught. But none of them looked satisfied.

Arthur returned to his spot by the advertisement and sat down in the mud; he didn't bother with the sheeting this time, feeling too discouraged to care about this basic comfort. A woman was walking from person to person, handing out rations of the food she'd managed to catch. Arthur recognised her though it took him a moment to recall where from: it was Ann the nurse. She spotted him and squeezed through the crowds to him.

'There you are again, pet,' she said. The faint sun shining behind her head forced Arthur to squint up at her. 'Did you get anything?'

'No. I fell.'

'Well, in that case, here you go,' said Ann, picking a half-chewed crust from a slice of pizza out of the tin and offering it to Arthur. Mould was peppering one end of it and it felt hard and stale in Arthur's hand, but he was still grateful for it.

'Thanks.' He rolled it around in his palm. 'I'll save it for later.'

'Good idea. How'd you sleep, pet?'

'As well as can be expected.' His eyes strayed to where the mob had been, to the ground that had been churned up by hundreds of feet. Ann caught his anxious expression and rested a hand on the side of his face.

'Listen, pet,' she said, 'don't let that scare you.' She nodded at the aftermath of the riot. 'People are starving and they're desperate to get what little food there is. But most of us share. All we have is each other.'

'Thanks.'

The nurse peered at the darkening sky above.

'Looks like it's going to rain today.' She turned back to Arthur. 'Take care of yourself and, like I said before, pet, if you need anything I'm usually in our little makeshift hospital.' And with that, she was gone.

Nurse Ann was right. It did rain later that day. It began suddenly; there was a roll of thunder directly overhead, followed straight away by the torrent.

It wasn't just any drizzle or any shower; it was a supernatural rain that Arthur had only seen once before.

Arthur was surprised that, as soon as it began, the wolves actually permitted the prisoners to stand among the tiered seating. This was one dispensation he supposed the Wolfsguard had to give them. Drops the size of basketballs fell from the emerald clouds, which shot out bolts of lightning with them. Within minutes, the pitch was flooded and the water was seeping halfway up the tier towards the huddled crowds.

Now would be a good time to escape, Arthur thought, looking around him. Except that there were at least two guards at every exit.

The shower only lasted twenty minutes or so and, though the clouds didn't disperse as normal, they were certainly a shade lighter than they'd been during the storm. What happens now, Arthur wondered, staring at the flooded sports pitch. He got his answer almost immediately as members of the Wolfsguard marched through the prisoners, handing out buckets and waterproof sacks. One of them thrust a rusty coffee tin into Arthur's hands.

'You know what to do,' he barked before moving on. Arthur opened his mouth to say that actually he didn't have a clue what he was supposed to do since he'd only been here a day, but then wisely shut up when he noticed that the other prisoners were already following orders. He watched as they dipped their buckets or water-carriers into the edge of the flood, filling them up. Then they carried them back up to the top of the tier and poured the water down drainage holes he hadn't noticed previously, before going back for more. By the sound the water made drizzling down the pipes, Arthur could tell they went very deep, probably leading outside the stadium.

'We can't possibly drain this whole pitch,' he murmured to himself, looking at the flood. It easily reached halfway up the bottom tier, which made it about ten feet deep. And yet people kept filling their buckets and pouring them out.

'Of course we can,' muttered an elderly woman who was passing to refill her own sack. 'We've done it before, we'll do it again.'

Arthur stood there for a moment, watching the work. So that was why the pitch wasn't flooded like outside. The prisoners had to drain it every time it rained. He let the realisation sink in for a moment before walking down to the edge of the flood and joining in with the other detainees.

They worked right through the day and through most of

the night without a break. If any of the prisoners did risk sitting down to rest, the guards would shout a warning to get back to work. If that didn't encourage them enough, they'd take out their batons. One swift clout around the ear was usually enough to remind the prisoner of their work ethic.

As exhausted as Arthur's legs had been the day before while swimming down Henry Street, his upper arms and shoulders were twice as fatigued now. Yet his coffee can was tiny compared to some of the water carriers others had been left to deal with, so he couldn't imagine how worn out those poor souls were. As the day grew darker, he was tempted to take the pizza crust out of his pocket and devour it whole. Two things stopped him. First, he knew he'd be gladder to have it when the work was finished and, second, he was worried that if he did take it out the guards would simply confiscate it.

He didn't think they were making much progress on the flood, but after the first few hours of work he started to see a notable difference. Three rows of seats had been reclaimed. One thought circled through his mind as he worked. One single, solid thought. Ellie was right. The Norns were right. Loki's third child did, indeed, unleash Hell on Earth.

He didn't know what time it was when they finally finished. His watch had stopped when he had been in the water. But, judging by the level of the moon and the faint glow of a new day's light in the east, he guessed it was some time between six and seven in the morning. Close to dawn, anyway.

Everyone went back to their spot on the pitch, which was now muddier and slicker than ever. He lay down by the advertisement board and munched on the pizza crust. It was, as he'd expected, very stale and tough. But it was delicious nonetheless. He ate half of it and put the remainder back in his pocket for safekeeping.

Despite his exhaustion, he swore to himself he wouldn't go to sleep. He couldn't spend much longer in this hell-hole. It was time to escape and he needed a plan.

CHAPTER ELEVEN

Morning came. But before the breakfast rush could start, Arthur rose and hurried in the direction of the first-aid area. He found Nurse Ann without much trouble; she was already up and tending to an elderly man who was in the middle of a violent fit of coughing. When he could breathe again, Ann turned to Arthur with a quizzical expression.

'Morning, pet. Is everything OK? Do you need help with something?'

'Yeah.' Arthur led her out of the patient's earshot. 'I need help to get out.'

She shook her head dejectedly. 'It's impossible, pet, so don't–'

'It's not. You said it yourself. A few hundred people could never hope to escape, especially in this weakened state. But one person, on their own …'

'People have tried it before, pet. People on their own or in groups. Some of them made it through the stand but they were all caught. Caught and punished. You can't be serious.'

'I am serious. I have a certain experience in things like this so trust me. I've been thinking about it for hours. Listen ...'

Arthur had, indeed, mulled over his options thoroughly. There were exits at pitch level but he couldn't escape through those because they'd been sealed up against the flood with thick steel doors. And even if he did somehow manage to open one of the doors as much as an inch, the water would rush in before he'd have a chance to rush out. It was impossible to get through.

The only option would be to go back the way he'd come: up through the seating and back down the outer stairwell. This was fraught with its own problems. First, lots of guards were always milling around the stands, keeping watch or relaxing on their breaks. Second, if he did somehow manage to get to the top of the tier, the outside stairs were even busier, with guards coming to and from the jet-ski landing area. But it was his only chance. He explained his plan to Ann.

'You need some sort of distraction,' she noted. 'So that you can reach the stairwell without being seen, I mean. Something to take the guards' attention away from the stands for a few minutes.'

'The morning feeding should serve that purpose. But I will need your help – to keep a watch for me in case the breakfast isn't distracting enough and let me know if a guard is coming my way. Please, Ann!'

'What happens if you do manage to reach the stairwell?' asked the nurse.

'I have something that will help me get out,' said Arthur, thinking of the hammer. 'And I saw where they put it. Anyway,' he added with a wry smile, 'I've been in worse jams than this.'

'Something about you makes me think that's true, pet.'

The nurse looked doubtfully into the stands around them, at the dozens of guards stalking over and back. Her eyes fell to the patients around her – all the people who were dying purely as a result of being put in this horrific situation. Finally she looked at the boy with the eye-patch.

'All right,' she said in a low voice. 'I'll help you. But first tell me your name.'

'Arthur. Arthur Quinn.'

Arthur and Nurse Ann waited at the edge of the pitch and watched the doors to the stadium back-rooms in silence. Finally the chef and his two assistants stepped out onto the stands and walked around to the serving trough. Throngs of people were already swarming forward and a few stragglers were chasing after them, hoping they weren't already too late to get a good spot. The only people left on the pitch were the sick, weak, very young and very old, as had been the case the previous day. Many of those nearest Arthur watched him, no doubt wondering why such a fit young man wouldn't take his place in the mob. However, he doubted they'd rat him out to the Wolfsguard. They might not help him but at least they wouldn't hinder him.

He watched as the chef chucked more of the un-appetising goop into the trough while his deputies tossed scraps out among the crowd. From Arthur's position today, the mob seemed even more fevered, more frantic to get the food. They were probably extra aggressive after the previous day's hard labour. When more of the Wolfsguard left their sentry positions to join in the fun, Arthur knew his moment was coming. He kept a close eye on them as they hurled the dregs of the breakfast over the heads of the prisoners. One guard on the tier nearest Arthur still hadn't joined in, but he was on his tip-toes, narrowing his eyes to get a better look. Eventually, he decided that he was missing out on too much amusement and went to join the others.

'Are you sure you want to do this?' Ann murmured under her breath, keeping her own eyes on the breakfast riot.

Instead of answering – and before either of them could change their minds – Arthur crept onto the first step of the tier, taking care that no other guard was nearby or watching. Then, keeping low, he quickly took cover between the first two rows of seats. He peered between two plastic chairs at Ann's anxious expression. She smiled helplessly and gave him a thumbs-up. As soon as he got the sign, he grabbed on to the back of the seat above him and vaulted over to the next row. He looked back at the nurse again, who turned her head from left to right, surveying the whole arena and especially the hungry throng. Seeing that the coast was clear, she gave him another nod and Arthur leapt up to the next row.

They continued like this for the next few minutes. Arthur would vault or climb over a row, then the nurse back on the pitch would give him the OK to move to the next row and so on. But then, just past the half-way mark, she was about to give the thumbs-up when she stopped suddenly and shook her head almost imperceptibly. Arthur followed her gaze and saw that one of the guards who'd been watching the mob had had enough and was moving back to his post. He was swinging a baton and humming tunelessly to himself.

Arthur had few options. He could retreat to the pitch and try another time or he could stay here and hope the guard wouldn't see him. But judging by the route the wolf-man was taking, he'd end up passing right by Arthur. He'd never be able to stay hidden. There was, however, one other possibility and, before sense could overrule his nerve, Arthur took it.

He ran down the row of seating away from the approaching guard, keeping hunched over and his footsteps light so he wouldn't be heard. When he reached the end of the row, he found himself on the staircase leading to the door he'd come through originally. The steps were wide and the incline was low, so running up while staying hidden was exceedingly difficult.

His heart was pounding by the time he reached the top. He threw all caution to the wind, swung it open and leapt through to the stairwell. He leaned back against the door and took a second to catch his breath. There wasn't as much sound from the landing area below as there had been the day he'd arrived. Arthur assumed many of the on-duty wolves were still watching the feeding frenzy.

He looked at the door to his left. It led to the room

where he'd seen the guard go with his backpack. He didn't care about the bag: it had been a cheap and flimsy freebie he'd gotten at a summer camp a couple of years ago. All he really wanted was the hammer inside.

Arthur pushed the door open and went through. It was nearly pitch black in the room, aside from a pale-blue emergency light directly over the door. This illuminated the space enough for him to take in his surroundings. It was more of a warehouse than a room and piles of confiscated belongings were stacked along the four concrete walls. He walked through the aisles, passing a heap of children's toys – dolls and teddy bears gazing up at him with glassy eyes – and another with nothing but electronics – mobile phones, laptops, cameras and so on. He noticed a box on the floor full of car keys and wondered why the wolves had bothered taking those. Surely no car could be useful after the flood. There were books and photographs and flashlights and medical supplies and clothes. Finally he found a mound built of every type of bag, from purses to sports bags. His own backpack had been thrown onto the top. He pulled it down and, holding his breath, ripped it open. He gave a gasp of relief when he saw that the hammer was still inside, lying next to the food he had stolen from the toy store. Smiling, he slung the bag over his shoulder then headed back towards the exit.

As he neared the door, he heard voices beyond it. He pressed his ear to the small gap between the door and the frame, keeping his breathing calm so he could hear clearly. There were guards outside, rushing down the stairs.

'Tell me again what he looked like,' one of the guards was saying.

'About yay high, brown hair, wearing a T-shirt and jeans,' said another one. 'He had an eye-patch, for Loki's sake! Shouldn't be that hard to find.'

Arthur put his back to the wall. They were talking about him! The guard must have seen him burst through the stairwell door.

'OK, OK,' the first Wolfsguard was saying. 'You check downstairs with the others. I'll have a look in here.' As the door to the room started to open, Arthur ducked behind a stack of unmarked boxes. He held his breath and peeked through a gap as the guard entered the room, shining a flashlight around the mounds of loot. The guard walked forward, his heavy black boots clicking on the concrete floor as he moved the beam of light ahead of him. Any minute now, he'd turn around and start searching in Arthur's direction and then there'd be no hiding. Arthur would be sent back to the stadium or worse. He couldn't even imagine what would happen if the wolf discovered the hammer.

While the guard's back was turned, Arthur took his

chance. He crept around the stack of boxes and edged towards the open doorway. He could hear the sound of running footsteps and barked orders coming from the lower floors as other guards searched for him. He glanced over his shoulder: the guard in the room still had his back to him, scanning the mounds. Arthur took a long stride forward and as he did–

Splech!

Arthur looked at his sock as it squelched loudly.

What a traitor, he thought.

'Oy!' roared a voice from behind him as the guard swivelled on the spot. 'Stop right where you are!'

Arthur did the exact opposite, running out of the storeroom, slamming the door behind him and turning the lock on the outside. Behind him the guard pounded on the door, alerting those further down the staircase. As soon as they spotted him, they bounded up the steps. The guard in the storeroom then started to throw his weight against the door in an attempt to break it open. Arthur looked around frantically, trying to find an escape route. To his right was the door leading back to the camp itself, and pounding up the stairs to his left were a dozen of the Wolfsguard, armed with batons and crossbows. In front of him was the edge of the staircase and beyond it a narrow gap with a sheer drop to the ground floor, four storeys down. There was a low safety wall around the edge. He glanced over and could see even more guards sprinting up the stairs.

There was nothing else for it. Arthur jumped onto the wall, took a deep breath and looked down at the flood below. What he saw made him pause. This is insane, he told himself. If I jump and miss the water I'll end up as a puddle of blood, gore and shattered bones on the concrete. But if I don't jump the guards will catch me and probably submit me to a fate worse than death.

His thoughts were cut short as the guard burst out of the storeroom behind him. Barely realising what he was doing, Arthur leapt feet first off the edge. He held his breath as he plummeted, keeping his body as straight and rigid as possible, ready for the impact. The bag slid awkwardly around on his back, threatening to unbalance him. Regardless, he kept his mind fixed on his intended destination: the flood below.

He soared past a row of jet skis idling at the landing bay and smashed into the water. The wave from his impact sent one guard – who'd just arrived on his jet ski – flying from the vessel, and the force of it knocked the air from Arthur's lungs. Seconds later, his feet hit the submerged ground and he pushed himself back up towards the surface. He gulped in air greedily then saw that the jet ski the guard had fallen from was just beside him. The engine was still running. He swam to it, gripped one of the handles and pulled himself up. The original driver was swimming towards it now too, roaring every expletive under the sun at him.

Arthur looked at the controls. He had never operated anything like this; he'd never even driven his dad's car around the driveway at home. He twirled one of the handles and the jet ski revved; the front end of it soared straight into the air, almost throwing him off and sending the guard somersaulting backwards in the water. But he managed to hold on and eased his grip on the control. The jet ski settled down and, with a tweak of the second handle, started moving towards the exit.

The guards who'd been running up the stairs had turned and were now racing back down. When Arthur saw them coming he revved the engine once more. The jet ski knocked off one of the side walls but he managed to get it under control and steer it out through the door to freedom.

He didn't know which way to go but remembered coming from the left-hand side the night he was captured. He figured that the guards probably travelled all over the city but he just didn't feel safe retracing their exact steps, so he chose to go right. As he started to turn, he heard more engines behind him. He looked over his shoulder to see that a handful of guards had reached their jet skis and were revving them up.

Arthur twisted his own throttle and the jet ski flew away from Croke Park, slicing through the water with ease and sending waves over the rooftops of the buildings on both sides. Without looking, he knew that the guards were on his tail; he could hear the engines roaring aggressively behind him. He hunched over the controls, willing the engine to work harder, to go faster.

Just then, something appeared in the corner of his vision. Movement. He glanced back to see a person on one of the rooftops. Arthur was going so fast he couldn't work out if it was a man, woman or child, but he managed to see what happened next.

The person pulled something out of the water in Arthur's wake. If he hadn't been looking for it, he'd never have spotted it. It was a metal cable and, as the person held it, it ran taut across the water. The pursuing guards crashed straight into the cable and were thrown backwards and off their jet skis. Arthur slowed and turned to get a proper look.

Before the guards could resurface and get back on their slowing skis, more people leapt and slid from where they'd been hiding on the rooftops. They swam to the skis and boarded them. Arthur hadn't a clue who his saviours were, but he was thankful they'd been there just at the right time to save him.

CHAPTER TWELVE

In total, there were five people in the group that rescued Arthur from the pursuing Wolfsguard: one either side of the cable, holding it taut, and three more who commandeered the driverless jet skis. As Arthur watched, one of the cable holders dropped their end while the other one coiled it in; then they both slid down the roofs and mounted their own jet skis which had been hidden behind the roofs of the houses they were on.

The guards had just broken through the surface of the water and were floundering about angrily as Arthur's saviours sped off. Arthur wondered who they were. After all, they hadn't looked much older than him. But, he decided, any enemies of the Wolfsguard were friends of his. So, hoping that, whoever they were, they were trustworthy, Arthur followed them. It was difficult at first to keep pace. His rescuers clearly had a lot more experience on jet skis than he did. He'd just gotten used to the quick turns they were making when they took a particularly sharp twist down a narrow alleyway between two tall office buildings.

The alleyway was just wide enough for the jet skis to go down in a single line and Arthur really had to concentrate to make sure he didn't bounce off the side of the tall, plain walls. They emerged from the alley into a wide open space with half-submerged fences around the perimeter. Arthur peered under the water to see a few cars parked there and a white grid painted on the ground. It had been a car park before the flood had taken over, he realised.

The other jet-ski riders hid around the corner from the alley opening. Arthur did likewise. As they waited in silence, he took the chance to study his saviours properly for the first time. They were all in their teens or pre-teens and most of them looked exceptionally fit. They each wore a swimming suit of some sort – either full-body neoprene wetsuits or a simple pair of surf shorts. The sole girl among the group was wearing a one-piece swimsuit: it was pink with little yellow palm trees on it that seemed out of place in the post-apocalyptic urban landscape. She was in her mid-teens, had dreadlocks down to her waist and several beaded bangles around both wrists.

Next to her was a boy who looked a little younger than Arthur. He had a crooked nose, as if it had been broken on several occasions, and was pudgy around his middle, his gut hanging over the waistband of the neon-green beach shorts he was wearing. He had a backpack slung over his shoulders into which Arthur had seen him put the wound-up cable. By the way the bag sagged against his bare back, Arthur supposed it must be very heavy, but the boy didn't seem to mind. Despite his young age, with his nose and girth he gave off the air of someone you wouldn't want to trifle with. The other cable-holder was a boy who looked to be around Stace's age. His face resembled a map marked out by lines of acne and he was also in surf shorts, covered in a Hawaiian pattern. He was wearing a sleeveless blue hoodie, swinging open to reveal his skinny bare chest.

The other two were in full wetsuits. They each had diving gear pushed up to their foreheads – goggles and snorkels – and a pair of flippers sitting in their laps. Arthur could tell from their broad-shouldered frames that they were clearly the strongest swimmers of the motley crew. As the group waited in hushed silence, they took off their snorkelling gear. The first was a boy of about fifteen with a totally shaved head and bulky upper frame. The second was a slim young man with a mop of wavy black hair, who looked to be at the older end of his teens. He clearly hadn't shaved in a while and was sporting an impressive amount of dark facial hair all over his jaw. Arthur guessed that he was leading this gang.

'Who are you all?' he asked, somewhat excitedly.

'Shh!' said the girl with the dreads, who was next to him, clapping a hand over his mouth. It was a little too tight and he had to struggle to breathe through his nose. She put a finger over her own lips then pointed her thumb over her shoulder. He nodded to say he'd understood and she withdrew her hand. Arthur smiled at her gratefully, but she didn't return the expression. She merely stared forward, listening intently.

Then he heard it himself: the sound of approaching engines, roaring as they slashed through the water. More guards had obviously left Croke Park in pursuit of him. Except that now, after the humiliation of losing the jet skis, they'd be even more vicious, even more unforgiving. His heart pumped faster and louder in his chest and he tightened his grip on the handle of his own jet ski, readying himself in case they had to make a quick escape.

The noise became deafening as it got nearer, bouncing off the vacated buildings and sending Arthur's senses into overdrive. He could picture the guards in his mind's eye, thrusting forward on their jet skis, hunched over the controls, their faces sneering and red with rage behind the black masks.

The Wolfsguard passed right by their alleyway, sending waves careening down the lane and into the parking lot. They all looked at each other with wide-eyed apprehension, waiting in silence for more engines to approach. But none did. As suddenly as the racket had begun, it dwindled into the distance.

'All right,' said the tubby, tough-looking boy who was holding the cable, when the noise had faded. 'Let's go.'

'Wait!' Arthur moved his jet ski closer to the stubbly-faced leader. After his time in Croke Park, he wanted some answers, *needed* some answers. 'Please tell me,' he said. 'Who are you all? What's been going on?'

The leader eyed him suspiciously and Arthur stared stubbornly back.

'Who are you?' he demanded again.

The leading boy looked from one of his companions to the next then turned back to Arthur, smiling.

'Why would we tell our prisoner that?'

'*Prisoner?*'

'That's right. Now you can come with us or we can leave you here for the wolves.'

'But—'

'What's it going to be?' urged the fat one.

'Where are you taking me?'

Miss Dreadlocks pumped her engine and said gleefully, 'To see our gracious leader!'

Rather than heading back up the alleyway and risking running into more of the Wolfsguard search party, the guy with the tightly shaved head cut a gap in the fencing around the car park and led them through it, heading back towards the city centre. He seemed to know his way around the sunken city best – a skill that Arthur assumed would be hard to come by – and he led the way. During the day that Arthur had had his little sandpit-boat, he'd only been able to find his bearings because he knew the route home so well. But Mr Egg-head confidently navigated along streets where the only visible landmarks were the top storeys of Georgian houses that all looked the same to Arthur.

Before they had set off, Fat Boy had tied one end of the cable around a hitch on the front of Arthur's jet ski and secured the other end to a similar hook on the rear of his own. Arthur guessed that they couldn't care less about him, but weren't very keen on losing his jet ski. As Fat Boy sped off in front of him, Arthur had to be sure to keep up the pace otherwise he'd be thrown off the ski. He wasn't particularly happy about being their prisoner, but figured it couldn't be any worse than what he'd just come from.

The leader, Stubble-face, was right behind Egg-head. They were followed closely by Miss Dreadlocks and Spotty Teen, both side by side. Fat Boy and Arthur trailed at the rear of the convoy and Arthur couldn't help but feel unprotected in this position. Every second he expected to be ambushed by some of the Wolfsguard, and he wondered pessimistically if the others would bother saving him twice in the same hour.

He wanted to ask where they were going but knew he'd get no response. He could see their eyes flitting from side to side, constantly on the lookout for more guards. Egg-head took them down any side streets and narrow laneways he could, avoiding the main roads or avenues at all costs. Then he led them into a cul-de-sac. For a split second, when he saw the dead end, Arthur was sure that they'd wandered into a trap. But Egg-head disappeared through the tiniest gap in the wall, which Arthur hadn't even noticed. They followed through one by one, bouncing against the wall on either side, and into another street beyond.

Eventually they arrived in the shadow of a large

building. They took the jet skis through an open square space – Arthur looked down through the flood to see a couple of delivery lorries parked there – and into a hidden nook between two buildings. A speedboat was already moored there and it was a tight squeeze to fit the skis but they managed it. Once the vessels were all out of sight of the main thoroughfare, they shut off the engines and clambered through a window in the taller building. They went one by one, either climbing over the jet skis or swimming across to it.

The space inside was dim – lit only by the weak green light coming through a row of windows. Cardboard boxes, shelving units and various pieces of dusty junk filled the narrow, anonymous corridor that led off into further darkness

'Hurry up,' Stubble-face said once they were all in. 'She'll be waiting for us.'

Arthur followed as quickly as he could and, if not for Fat Boy guiding him through the gloom with one hand on his shoulder, he was sure he'd have stumbled. Suddenly, a rectangle of light cut through the blackness as Stubble-face swung a door open. He went through and the rest stepped in after him.

Arthur couldn't help but gawp at the sight that awaited him beyond the doorway. They were in a shopping centre.

All the shops were shut and in darkness but the wide and open central area was ablaze with electric lights buzzing overhead. Somewhere in the distance he could hear the low rumble of a generator. The whole place was impossibly bright – especially after he had become used to the green, murky daylight – and Arthur had to squint until his eye adjusted to the glare. Sleek lines and chrome were the order of the day and generic muzak played from the overhead speakers. They were on the upper floor and, as he looked down, he could see that the ground floor was flooded as expected. Unsold products of every sort – clothes, electronics, food – all floated on the still water. But up here, the centre was vibrant with bustle and life.

People charged from one shop to another, loading bags with whatever took their fancy. There weren't many – fifteen, twenty tops – but the way in which they ran about, elatedly taking what they wanted, made the scene seem so much livelier. The people were mostly under the age of eighteen – although there were a couple of adults here and there. Most were wearing a patchwork selection of clothing. Clearly they'd had to make do with whatever clothes they could find for a few weeks now. That wouldn't be the case any longer, Arthur thought, watching one girl pile several pairs of jeans, hoodies and T-shirts into the bag she was carrying. With the stores themselves still in darkness, and by the way the shoppers were haphazardly grabbing stock, Arthur realised something.

'They're stealing,' he uttered, before he could stop himself.

'It's not stealing if no one owns it any more,' protested Spotty Teen.

'Sorry. I do understand, you know. You're taking what you need to survive. We've all had to do that.' He thought of the supplies he'd taken from the toy shop.

'Come on,' said Stubble-face. 'You have to meet someone. She'll know what to do with you.'

He strode quickly away as the others joined in with the salvagers, dressing themselves with brand-new clothes. Stubble-face had a long gait and Arthur had to half-jog to keep up.

'Where is she?' The teenager asked a passing boy whose arms were overflowing with tinned food.

'She's in the café there, going over the checklist.' He nodded past them and they walked in the direction he'd indicated.

The open-fronted café was in darkness but enough light spilled in from the centre for them to make out the figure of a girl sitting at one of the tables. Arthur could hear a boy opposite her detailing everything they'd taken as she marked the items off a list in front of her. She was wearing a heavy-looking jacket, full of pockets, and had a long stick strapped to her back. Her hair was a dusky shade of auburn, tied back in a tight ponytail. Arthur knew who it was even before Stubble-face said her name.

'Ash, we found someone.'

The girl turned around to look at him and Arthur rushed straight forward. He embraced her in a relieved hug for a second before Stubble-face yanked him off her, sending him flying to the floor.

'Ash, I can't believe I found you!' he cried, back on his feet before the older teen could react a second time. He beamed at the girl, but then his heart sank when he saw that she was looking back at him with a puzzled expression.

'It's me, Ash,' he said.

'Yes,' she said eventually. 'It's you.'

'No, you don't get it. It's *me*. It's Arthur!'

'Is that so?' Ash looked from Stubble-face to the boy with a bemused expression, as she tried to figure out if she should remember him. Eventually she said, 'I'm sorry, Arthur, but I don't know you.'

'Yes, you do! At least, I know you. I'm Arthur. I moved into your estate last October and ... and ... I'm your best friend ...' He trailed off as her face remained blank.

'I think I'd remember that,' said Ash, sceptically. She

turned to the other boy. 'Where did you find him, Donal?'

'He escaped from the Croke Park camp,' answered the boy Arthur had been calling Stubble-face in his head.

She looked surprised now, sort of interested. 'Really? Well, that's a turn-up for the books.'

'Why's that?' asked Arthur.

'Because in all the time that camp has been open, not one person has managed to break out that we know of. Except you.' She looked away thoughtfully, then turned back to Donal. 'We'll bring him to headquarters and lock him up, as a precaution.'

'What! Why?' Arthur looked at Ash.

'Because we don't know if we can trust you. You could be a spy for Loki for all we know.' She considered him thoughtfully. 'Although I doubt you're any real threat to us.' She turned back to Donal. 'Keep an eye on him until we get back to base.'

The teenager nodded and grabbed Arthur in the crook of his arm, starting to pull him out of the café.

'Wait! Please!' Arthur begged as Ash turned back to her checklist. 'You have to listen to me!' His socks slid over the floor, refusing to give him any traction. He searched his memory for anything that would change Ash's mind. Every moment he'd ever spent with her rushed through his brain, images flickering like a movie screen. Every moment. Every laugh. Every smile. Every story. And then–

'Remember Clare Pond!' he exclaimed finally, just as Donal had him at the door.

'Wait!' Ash ordered, looking up. 'What did you say?'

Arthur shrugged out of Donal's strong grip and walked back to her.

'Clare Pond,' he repeated breathlessly. 'She was your friend before you started school. But she went to a different school and after that she didn't want anything to do with you. You were hurt, very hurt. But then you saw her briefly last summer and she'd changed. She was nice to you. She even apologised.'

As Arthur blurted out this story Ash's mouth opened in shock, her eyes fixed on him.

'I … I never told that to anyone,' she said.

'No one but me.'

She looked him straight in the eye. 'Who are you really?'

Pulling a chair out from under the table, Arthur sat down. 'I've proven that I know you, that I'm your friend,' he said.

'No, you've proven that you know Clare Pond, not me,' she said warily.

'Ash, I know you don't believe me, but you have to. If you just give me a chance, I think I can convince you. But

'I'll need your help. I need you to answer my questions first.'

'Convince me? Huh. We'll see,' she said somewhat reluctantly, keeping an eye on Donal to make sure he was close in case Arthur turned out to be some sort of nut. 'Go ahead then. Ask.'

'What happened, Ash? How did you get to be here? What happened with Loki?'

'What do you mean?' She shot a confused look at Donal, then back to him. 'Everyone knows that. You'd have to have been living under a rock not to know about the Great Flood. Anyway, I don't like to talk about it. I don't even like to think about it.' She looked down at her hands; her knuckles were white, she was gripping the table so tightly.

'You have to tell me. Just humour me. Imagine that I actually have been living under a rock. Please, Ash, please!' He laid his hand over one of hers. 'Ash …'

She jerked her hand away uncomfortably. 'All right. Where do you want me to start?'

'With the flood.'

'OK.' Ash gathered her thoughts for a moment before beginning. 'It was late October last year when Loki first appeared to the world. He came out of nowhere and no one has any explanation for where he was before then. He … uh … he …'

She looked away, her eyes turning glassy as she bit her bottom lip in guilt.

'What happened, Ash? What did he do?'

She stared at a spot on the floor, not saying anything.

'I'm to blame,' she told him eventually. 'I'm to blame for everything. For all of this, for the way the world is. I was walking home from school that day. I don't know why. I usually get the bus. But I wanted to walk. Something felt like it was missing so I decided to walk so I could have time to think. Anyway, that was when Loki abducted me. I didn't know what was going on but I was so scared. He took me to a tunnel under the new metro site and forced me to open this underground cavern that the World Serpent was in. I don't know why he chose me, but he needed someone and I guess I was an easy target. You see, he wasn't able to touch the key that opened the cavern. It was some kind of pendant.'

'Like this?' Arthur pulled the pendant out of his T-shirt.

'Exactly like that,' she said, her eyes bulging at the sight of it. 'How did you–'

'I'll tell you after. Go on.'

'OK. Loki blew a hole in the wall of the cavern to release the Serpent into Dublin. While he was doing this I managed to sneak away and escape back up the tunnel.

But at that moment I don't think he really cared. I'd done what he needed. The monster was free. Loki and the World Serpent started their conquest of humanity that day. By the time I got back to the surface, they'd already brought the Great Rain and within a few hours the whole country was flooded. I rushed home but I was too late. I discovered that he'd destroyed my house and taken my family.'

Arthur felt himself breathe a sigh of relief; the rest of the Barrys weren't dead at least.

'No one knew what to do. The rain clouds spread every-where – all over the world – and they flooded everywhere. The army tried to take him and the Serpent down, but they failed. Even the UN sent in troops, but Loki changed them and now they're part of the Wolfsguard. It's like this the world over.

'Now the Wolfsguard act as Loki's police force and they're not afraid to use violence to keep the people in line. The day after the flood they started rounding up everyone who'd survived. They took people in boats to camps like the one you were in. Large, open spaces with high enough walls to keep the water out.'

'And when it rains, the prisoners are forced to drain the place,' murmured Arthur, 'one bucketful at a time … How many camps are there?'

'Who knows. We think there may be as many as ten in the city but beyond that it's anyone's guess. Some prisoners don't go to the camps. If they've got a useful skill, the wolves use them. Doctors or vets, I guess. Or mechanics who can build and mend jet skis and weapons. Some of them – the stronger ones – get turned into wolves. At least that's what we believe. Anyway, I managed to avoid capture, keeping to side streets in a raft I made, hiding in vacated buildings that rose above the waterline. As I moved through the city I found other survivors hiding. Mostly kids. It was easier for them to hide. We banded together for safety and they kind of adopted me as their leader. I don't really know why, especially after what I did.'

'You're clever, Ash,' Arthur said. 'Clever and strong and brave and full of ideas. Everyone knows it the moment they meet you. And all these people,' he waved a hand at the centre, 'they know it too. They know you would never have helped Loki if he hadn't forced you. If you weren't the person you are, we could never have stopped Loki before.'

'I don't understand what you mean. No one stopped Loki. That's why we're in this mess.'

'Yes, you did. We both did. And we will again.'

'We can't. No one can defeat him. We're just trying to survive and not get caught.' She pointed out of the café to where people were still loading up trolleys with essentials. 'Do you think we like this? Having to hide and scavenge and steal? It's the only choice we have if we want to go on living!'

'Ash, we can stop him, trust me. Think of your family.'

'And the others,' added Donal behind him.

'Others?' Arthur asked. 'What others?'

'A while ago, we managed to hack into the Wolfs-guard's computer system,' Ash explained. Even in this terrible situation, she was still an electronics wiz, thought Arthur proudly. 'And we found out that Loki has eight people held in his inner sanctum.'

'Who are they?'

'My parents,' Ash began, counting them off on her fingers. 'My sister Stace and my brother Max. Then there's someone called Joe Quinn and someone else known simply as Fenrir. The last two are kids about our age called Ellie and Xander Lavender. I don't know anything about any of these people apart from my family and I certainly don't know why Loki would want any of them. But they're obviously important in some way. I just hope they're important enough to keep alive.'

Arthur felt like jumping for joy. They were all alive! Held captive by Loki but alive nonetheless!

'Ash,' he said urgently, leaning forward, 'Joe is my dad.

187

Ellie and Xander – Ex, as he likes to be called – are our …
well, *my* friends. And Fenrir helped us defeat Loki before.
They're all his enemies or family of his enemies.'

'OK, Arthur. You seem to know an awful lot about
Loki. I think it's time you told me your side of the story.'

'This will take a while,' he warned her. And he was
right; it did.

CHAPTER THIRTEEN

While Arthur told her his story, Ash's rebels (as he'd come to think of them) had been busy accumulating all they'd salvaged from the deserted stores and then loading it into the waiting speedboat, which was now packed to the brim. As Ash, Donal and Arthur arrived at the window through which they'd entered, Arthur could see that the rebels had done a sterling job of fitting most, if not all, of their findings into the little vessel. It was painted white, though the sludge that covered it from years of use made it closer to a charcoal grey. Despite its apparent age, it seemed to be in reasonably good condition and the engine was ticking over smoothly as the rebels got ready to leave. A few of the kids had squeezed themselves into the boat along with the loot; a couple of them were even perched on top of the sacks full of clothes, batteries, torches and food.

The rest of the rebels – including Arthur's rescuers – were seated on jet skis, two or three per model. The ski nearest the window had been left for Arthur, Ash and Donal, so they climbed out onto it. Donal got on in the steering position with Ash behind him and Arthur behind her. They clamped their arms around each other tightly then Ash gave a thumbs-up to Donal.

'Ready!' Donal called to Egg-head, who was already turned in the direction of the exit. He nodded, revved up his own ski, which had two young women as passengers, and sped off. The rest followed straight away and, as soon as they could, arranged themselves in a tactical formation with the speedboat in the centre, guarded on all sides by the jet skis. As on the journey to the shopping centre, Egg-head led them, swooping down narrow streets with grace and ease, always two steps of the route ahead of the rest.

Arthur gripped Ash tighter. She glanced over her shoulder and flashed him a reassuring smile. He smiled back, still not quite believing that he had found her. He had actually found her. In a city that was submerged and with its survivors captured or scattered he had managed to find the one person he really needed to. It was only sinking in now what a great and miraculous thing this had been. It was almost as if someone had guided him to her.

But after a devastating and depressing couple of days, he really didn't care how it had happened. Discovering that Ash was not only still alive but also free, and had a group of rebels following her, was just the boost Arthur needed. With her to help him, he suddenly felt that maybe, just maybe, they might have a chance against Loki. Although he still had to convince her that she could help.

He thought back to what he'd told her in the shopping centre. After he'd filled Ash and Donal in on everything she'd forgotten, his best friend hadn't said anything for a few minutes. He had given her the hammer as evidence when it came up. She held it in her lap, feeling the heft of it, then she put it back on the table with a thunk. When he'd finished, Ash had pushed her chair back, the legs scratching against the tiled floor, and started pacing the empty café. She walked to the far wall and Arthur watched as she studied the menu blackboard hanging there. The lunch deals were still written on it in multi-coloured chalk, with little doodles of flowers and butterflies decorating the list. She rubbed a thumb across one butterfly, slicing it in two. Now it was just two C-shaped wings with no body to bind them together. Without warning, she rolled her hand into a fist, scrubbed a thick, straight line through the entire menu and turned back to Arthur and Donal. She brushed her hands clean as she strolled back towards them.

'That's a lot to take in,' she said.

'It is,' Arthur nodded, observing her closely.

'How do you expect me to react to all that?'

He shrugged his shoulders emphatically. 'I dunno. I was hoping that you'd believe me.'

'What do you think, Donal?'

He grimaced. 'It's a difficult one to buy,' he said. 'A bunch of kids defeating a Viking god of mischief and his all-powerful XXL snake? But then again, only a year ago no one would have believed in Loki or that all this,' he waved an arm about the deserted centre, 'could happen at all. We live in a different world now.'

'True,' Ash said, mulling over the prospect. 'That's very true.' She reached the table again and looked Arthur square in the face.

'OK, Arthur,' said Ash. 'My instinct says that I should trust you. And I think I do. But that doesn't mean I believe your story.'

'But the hammer–'

'Is a nice find and we might have use for it–'

'But–'

'Let me finish. For days after the flooding, I was sure I was dreaming. I had completely convinced myself that I would wake up at any second to the smell of sizzling bacon. It took me a while to realise that it wasn't a dream, that this was all really happening. What I'm trying to say is we all have different ways to deal with what the world is today. You can believe your fantasy but don't expect me to do likewise. The time for daydreaming is over.'

Arthur opened his mouth to protest, but Ash shot him down.

'That's the best you're going to get out of me at the moment,' she said. 'It'll take a lot more than a nice little kid's story to convince me. But right now, we should go back to HQ.'

Despite the weight of the extra riders, the jet skis seemed to be as fast as ever as they glided through the waters that covered Dublin. Arthur supposed that the Wolfsguard made sure that their main mode of transport would be kept in good condition. The speedboat was also flying along and the couple of rebels perched on top of the salvage kept watch for any approaching enemies through pairs of binoculars. Even with that precaution, Arthur was worried that some guards would spot them. The sound of jet skis racing through the city was loud enough, but adding the angry roar of the speedboat to the mix seemed to be a recipe for disaster. Yet as they skimmed along the water, luck seemed to be with them. For the moment, at least.

Arthur had completely lost track of where he was shortly after leaving the shopping centre, but at one stage they were forced to pass through a wide open space, where there was no trace of any building or tree poking above the surface of the water. It was as if they were cutting across an open lake and he could see the flood receding over the horizon. When he looked down, all he could see was the darkness of deep water and his eyes couldn't even pick out the bottom. Suddenly he realised where he must be.

'Are we over the River Liffey?' he shouted at Ash, raising his voice so she could hear him over the engines.

She nodded and he gazed with wonder at the water again just before they ducked back down some more side streets. The Liffey had overflowed into an even greater river than usual, flooding the streets and laneways around it, covering even the bridges. He realised that crossing it meant they were heading for the south side of the city.

Moments after that, one of the watchmen on top of the loot started waving frantically to slow down. The drivers obeyed and instantly they all heard the sound of engines behind them. Arthur realised that if they could hear the Wolfsguard then the Wolfsguard could probably hear the rebels' engines in turn. With the expanse of water making any sound echo more than usual, it was nearly impossible to tell how far off the noise was, but he waited for the inevitable sound of them drawing closer. However, seconds later it faded away. Clearly the Wolfsguard hadn't realised that the engines in the distance weren't those of their colleagues and were heading off in a different direction, or they had already reached their location. Arthur breathed a sigh of relief as they moved off once more.

Soon after, the convoy started to slow down. They passed a few tree tops just above the surface of the flood; strands of moss and weeds clung to the gnarled branches. Arthur peeked past Ash's shoulder at the construction looming out of the water ahead of them. Grey stone walls stretched off in both directions at right angles to each other. Beyond the walls, he could just about see the building itself. Like the perimeter walls, it was a stone structure, with an unusual rounded end and two storeys rising above the water. Tiny square windows punctuated every few feet along the surface of the building, with blackened iron bars criss-crossing them. The other end of the structure was attached to an equally tall square building, more traditional in design, with large Edwardian windows blocked up with bricks and a flagpole thrusting up out of the flood. Half an Irish tricolour hung there, shredded and hanging limp and soaked along the pole.

They idled down the width of the outer wall, past the lifeless flag and towards a clump of trees that matched the structure itself for height. There wasn't much space between the trees and the wall and Arthur was sure that the speedboat wouldn't fit. Yet somehow the driver manoeuvred it through the gap. It pulled at branches as it went past and they flicked back into place with a twanging sound. The trees were packed so tightly together here that they formed the perfect cover and hid the boat and the skis which followed it in from any prying eyes. As they approached a corner of the wall, Arthur noticed a pair of teenagers in swimsuits perched on top of the barricade. They threw lengths of rope to the riders when they were close enough. The riders looped one end around the steering panel while the other was securely knotted to a hook on the wall. Once all the vessels were moored – they bobbed softly between the walls and the cover of the trees – the passengers started disembarking.

Those on the speedboat went first: up a rope ladder slung over the edge of the perimeter wall and then along the top of some other wall leading to the main building. They were lithe and moved with confidence, as if they had done this many times. Every one of them went with sacks full of their takings slung over their shoulders. When all those on the boat had left, those on the nearest jet ski bounded across to it, picked up more of the loot and then followed up the ladder. This was repeated a few more times until the boat was unloaded. Finally, it was Arthur's turn to alight. Donal pulled the jet ski as close as he could to the boat and nodded. Arthur scrambled across the gap and the boat tilted as he landed in it. He took a moment to regain his balance, then crossed to the ladder and scaled the wall. The pair who had tied off the vessels gave him a hand up. Meanwhile, Ash and Donal were making their own way up the ladder behind him.

When he reached the top of the ladder Arthur could see a wall running perpendicular to the one he was on. The last few riders in front of him had made their way across it to the rooftop of the building opposite. They disappeared one by one through a hole in the roof. Below Arthur was a courtyard, as full of water as the area around it. The walls enclosing the courtyard were incredibly thick: three feet at least. The construction of the place should keep any would-be invaders at bay, he thought, or at least keep them out long enough to give the rebels time to escape.

Arthur moved over the perpendicular wall, taking care

as this one was narrower than the outer fortification. He reached the roof – it was sloped slightly but luckily the slates weren't too slippery. Waiting for Ash and Donal to join him, he savoured the chance to take in the view from this height. The city was submerged in every direction, although a few of the taller buildings towered over the still water. The silence hanging over the place was so thick that he could almost touch it. Tendrils of smoke rose from buildings here and there. The one thing that caught his attention was a break in the clouds to the west. He could just make out a patch of the blue evening sky through the hole.

'Look at that,' he said to Ash as she and Donal joined him on the rooftop.

'So what?' Ash replied, as she glanced at the sky, uninterested. They strode straight past him over the slates. 'This way.'

Ash led them to the hole in the roof. It had a domed perspex trapdoor raised beside it and it was so dim inside the building that Arthur couldn't make out anything in there. Without warning, Ash leapt straight into the hole. Donal indicated to Arthur that he should follow. Arthur looked down into the hole and couldn't see anything but darkness. Donal nodded at him reassuringly and finally Arthur stepped off the edge.

He was surprised when he fell less than four feet and landed on something soft and bouncy. He felt around him to discover that it was an old, musty mattress. Actually, not just one, but a pile of old, musty mattresses stacked six feet high. Ash was already standing on the floor, looking up at him. Arthur slid off the mattresses to stand by her. As he did, Donal made his entrance in a similar manner, then reached up and closed the perspex trapdoor with a resounding thud.

As his eyes adjusted to the gloom, Arthur could see that they were in a dank and stuffy attic, full of basic-looking beds, tables and more mattresses than he could count. Footsteps had shuffled through the dust on the floor, leading away from the stack he'd landed on and out through a door at the far end of the room. Without another word, Ash and Donal followed the trail and Arthur hurried after them.

Beyond the door was a narrow stone staircase leading downwards. Some of the small square windows he'd seen outside allowed a small amount of the gloomy daylight into the interior, but aside from that it was almost as shadowy as the attic had been. They continued straight down the steps, taking care not to slip on the slick treads. The corridor at the bottom of the stairwell was in near full darkness so Ash took Arthur's hand and dragged him along. Her skin was warm and soft. Their footsteps resounded in the gloom and he could sense that the walls on either side were close by. Finally, they came to a wooden door, which Ash pushed open onto an even narrower corridor. A couple of candles burned in this passageway – and they were badly needed. The stone floor here was uneven, with plenty of fissures to trip one up. On the right-hand wall was a line of thick timber doors. Arthur didn't have time to investigate as Ash stalked along at a brisk pace. They came to the last door and Ash turned to Arthur.

She had a wry, knowing smile.

'Welcome,' she said, 'to our current headquarters.' She swung the door open to reveal the room beyond.

It was just like those old prison movies Arthur's grandfather had liked to watch; in fact it really reminded him of the one where the guys drove all those Mini Coopers. The room was vast and four storeys high. The brick walls were painted a dull shade of cream and the floor was covered with massive flagstones. The first and second floors had balconies running all the way around the edge of the expansive room, which were completely fenced in with iron railings. A steel staircase led from the centre of the ground floor up to the level of the second storey. A bridge cut across the steps at the first and second floors; these were also covered in iron caging and led to the respective balconies. The centre of the ceiling was a clear-glass skylight and, although parts of it were covered in some sort of mossy growth, presumably because of the damp, Arthur could see the filthy green clouds beyond. Arched iron girders held the glass in place, completing the menacing feel of the room. All along the walls on each level was a series of wooden doors, just like the ones he'd seen in the corridor, with little square hatches set at an adult's eye-level. Small, boxy cells lay behind these doors. When Ash had opened the main door, a wave of heat whooshed out to meet him and he could feel the still, clammy hotness in the room. But most astonishing to Arthur were the inhabitants of the prison.

Close to a hundred people were milling around, moving from one cell to another, chatting or catching up with the returned rebels and cooing over the haul from the shopping centre. Most hadn't reached adulthood yet, although a handful of men and women were scattered about. A group of teenage boys and girls in one cell raced out and appeared to take all the food. He could smell the homely scent of cooking emanating from that cell. A few preschool kids – most no taller than his hip – clattered along the steel-gridded second floor, across the bridge and down the steps. The noise of their running rang throughout the room, bouncing off the ancient stone walls. A small cluster of kids Arthur's age were huddled in one corner, leaning back on fusty mattresses, reading. They barely looked up to acknowledge the others' return. There were groups cleaning, napping, eating, laughing and living. And all of them, Arthur was pleasantly surprised to see, seemed happy and healthy.

'What is this place?' Arthur murmured, following Ash as she headed further into the room.

'Kilmainham Gaol,' she said. 'Don't tell me they don't have this in the world you remember?'

They had and, though he'd never visited it, he'd read all about the building in history class. It had been a working prison for centuries and then, during the War of Independence, it had been used to house the Irish rebels. Now it was a museum recounting the history of the war and its famous prisoners. Quite a suitable place for these new rebels to hide, Arthur thought, and he told Ash as much.

'I guess it is,' she agreed. 'We've been moving about a lot since this all started, collecting more refugees as we go. We stay somewhere until the Wolfsguard find us and then we move on. This place has lasted the longest. The thick walls have kept the water out. There's no electricity but we have gas cookers and the skylights provide us with enough light during the day. We don't use flashlights at night in here unless it's really important. It's the perfect hiding place, really.'

'Why are there so few adults? I only see – what – six or seven grown-ups.'

'I guess kids were better at hiding from the Wolfsguard. Or maybe easier to hide.'

'But how did you get away from the Wolfsguard any time they found you before?'

She headed up the stairs at a brisk pace and Arthur followed quickly.

'I told you: we're able to hack into their computer system and radios, so we knew they were coming,' she explained. 'But I can tell you more about that tomorrow. I thought I'd show you your room and let you get some rest now.'

She led him up the stairs to the second floor and started crossing the bridge. Arthur stopped for a moment and looked out over the entire scene. When Ash saw him waiting, she went back to him.

'It's amazing,' he uttered, full of awe.

'What is?' She followed his gaze, studying the happy faces sorting through the salvaged goods.

'This. All of it. What you've done here.' He looked her in the eye. 'You saved all these people.'

She shook her head, her cheeks turning a deep red. 'No,' she said modestly. 'It wasn't just me.'

'It was, Ash. You led them. You saved them.'

'I didn't save the ones that count, though.' She grimaced as she said it, feeling instantly guilty. 'That's not what I mean. They all count. It's just–'

'I know.' He laid a comforting hand on her shoulder. 'Your family.'

'And yours.' She kept staring at the people below them, not saying a thing, before finally getting the courage to turn back to him.

'We'll save them, Ash.'

'You really believe that, don't you?'

'I have to. Don't you?'

Without another word, she walked off towards his cell.

Loki's throne was a thing of wonder. It was forged from solid gold. A life-sized wolf sculpture was carved out of the left-hand side. The narrowed eyes, lips drawn back in a snarl and sharp little lines incised along the back of its neck indicating its bristling hair gave the carving a sense of menace. A golden sea serpent was coiled on the other side, two fangs bared with a pear-shaped piece of emerald dripping off one point, like venom. Both beasts' heads were at just the right height for armrests. The back was shaped like a tree, rotting and crumbling, with a woman standing next to it, draped in robes of gold. Her lips were turned up in a half-smile but the empty metal of her eyes gave her a cold and forbidding expression.

The softest cushions imaginable adorned the seat, with covers crafted from tightly woven silk and stuffed with down from the long-extinct dodo. The throne was tall, so a footrest was necessary to ensure that Loki's legs didn't dangle as he lounged back in the chair. Tonight's ottoman consisted of a single cushion balanced on the back of a young boy on all fours.

The boy was squirming so Loki gave him a swift and vicious kick in his already tender ribs.

Max tumbled aside, tears in his eyes.

Loki surged to his feet and glared down at him.

'What are you crying for? It's an honour to serve me, isn't it?'

Max whimpered that it was, nodding frantically to emphasise his agreement.

'You have a choice. Be a good – and unmoving – little footstool. Or you go back to the cage. And I don't think you like the cage very much, do you?'

Max shook his head and clambered back in position,

holding the cushion in place until Loki was comfortable once more.

'Much better,' said the Father of Lies, returning to his thoughts.

He had been pondering the disturbance before Max had moved. He had first felt it a couple of days ago: the faintest of vibrations in the fabric of reality, rippling like a pebble dropped in a pond. Something wasn't right. Someone was interfering.

Loki drummed his fingers on the golden wolf's head and looked in the direction of Hel.

It couldn't be, he thought. No. Not Arthur. Impossible. He had watched the boy disappear, watched reality change around him.

Yet a nagging doubt remained. The boy had proved exceptionally lucky in the past. Perhaps he'd been getting help all along. And if this was true, then there was the slimmest of chances that it *was* his presence Loki had sensed.

He shrugged mentally. Even if the boy was back, Loki wasn't concerned. He had a back-up plan. He hadn't come this far just to let that brat ruin everything once more.

He grinned.

But despite the smile, his throne had never felt so uncomfortable, as if it wasn't meant for him.

He looked down at Max on hands and knees, making the perfect footrest.

Then, just for fun, Loki kicked him in the ribs once more.

Hard.

Chapter Fourteen

Somebody was in Arthur's room with him. He could hear them moving about even before his good eye fluttered open.

The evening before, Ash had brought Arthur straight to his cell without saying another word. He had peered into it from the doorway as Ash stood at the small rectangular window, the green of the darkening clouds illuminating her face with an eerie glow. The room was a perfectly square box: nine feet long by nine feet wide by nine feet high. The stone walls were finished with whitewash, which was slowly peeling away. There was a white ceramic basin in one corner, half-filled with water. Next to it was a clean yet ragged piece of cloth and next to that was a bar of soap, the brand name long worn off by use. In the other corner was a bare mattress; it looked lumpy and a particularly sharp spring had ripped through the outer material at one end, but Arthur was nonetheless thrilled at the sight of it. He could see nothing else in the room, save for a spider creeping across the ceiling and into a crack.

'It's probably not what you're used to,' Ash said, still looking through the barred-up window.

'Ash, it's great.'

She looked at him. 'Hope you don't mind there's no blanket. It gets pretty hot in here, as you can imagine. The water outside probably insulates us.'

'It's fine, honest.'

'And, sorry, but you should leave the door open. We closed them when we first got here but the hinges and locks are so rusty that a couple of us nearly got stuck inside. It took half the day to pry those doors off.'

'It's perfect, Ash.'

She walked to the door, then paused and turned.

'You should rest up,' she advised him. 'Supper is in a couple of hours so come and join us then.'

Before he could even thank her, she was gone, marching swiftly back across the steel gangway, her boots clanging on the metal as she went. He turned around, let the heavy backpack slide off his shoulders and flopped onto the bed, thankfully. He shut his eyes – even the damaged one behind the leather patch – and sighed with exhaustion. As he lay there, his clothes suddenly felt heavy and constricting. He pulled off the socks. They were now so crusty with mud that they were almost moulded to the shape of his feet. He wiggled his toes, glad to let them breathe for the first time in days. Then he unbuckled his belt and slid off his jeans. Like the socks, they'd become mud-encrusted at the cuffs. Finally, he pulled his T-shirt over his head and threw the whole lot in a pile on the opposite side of the little cell. He turned onto his side, facing the blank wall, and before he could stop himself he was sound asleep.

He had no dreams and didn't even stir once in the night, such was his exhaustion.

He woke to the rustling sound of someone in his cell. The sharper light of the morning was streaming in the tiny window. Arthur could feel a crick in his neck and pins and needles all along his left-hand side. I should have used my clothes as a pillow, he admonished himself, before turning to the source of the noise. The girl with the dreadlocks who had rescued him the day before was there, with a clothes basket under one arm. Feeling suddenly exposed (especially since he was only in his underwear) Arthur wished he could cover himself up, but he saw that the girl was lifting his grubby garments and dropping them into the basket.

'Uh …' he started, unsure how to go on.

'Oh,' she said. 'You're awake.'

'Yeah …'

'You slept right through the night,' she told him. 'Missed supper and all. You must be starving!'

Now that she mentioned it, he could feel hunger pangs in his stomach. He nodded.

'It's OK. We're still in the middle of breakfast.' She held up the basket for him to see better. 'I was just going to drop your clothes into the laundry room. I left some clean ones for you there.' Arthur saw a stack of brand-new clothes on the ground by the basin: T-shirt, jeans, underwear, socks and even – his heart leapt with joy – a pair of new trainers.

'I hope they fit OK – I had to guess your size,' the girl continued.

'Thanks,' he said, genuinely grateful.

'Anything in the pockets?' She held up his jeans from the basket.

'Just my keys, I think.' He reached out for the trousers and she threw them to him. 'And my phone, maybe, but it's probably damaged beyond all repair now. It's had one too many dunkings.' He pulled the items out of the pockets but was surprised to find a third object in his palm as he handed Miss Dreadlocks back the jeans.

'What's that?' she said inquisitively.

'Nothing much,' he said, staring at the pizza crust. His fingers wrapped around it tightly.

Looking up, he saw the girl watching him curiously. 'I just realised I don't know your name,' he said, offering her his free hand. 'I'm Arthur, Arthur Quinn.'

'Orla, Orla Doyle,' she said, smiling. 'Nice to meet you Arthur Arthur Quinn.'

'And you, Orla Orla.'

She took the filthy jeans back and left with a grin. As soon as she was gone, Arthur unclasped his hand and looked down at the crust. He turned it slowly around in his fingers. At the memory of the people locked up in the camp, a wave of sadness surged through him. He thought of Nurse Ann, who'd offered him the leftover and who had helped him escape, and remembered the kindness in her eyes despite the situation they had found themselves in.

With a sudden and urgent sense of resolution, Arthur put the crust on top of the stack of clothes. He dipped the soap into the water in the basin and scrubbed his face, hands, torso and legs. Then he patted himself as dry as he could with the small rag, before pulling on the fresh clothing. He slid his feet into the shoes and laced them up. Finally, he stuffed the crust into his jeans pocket and strode out of the cell. The new jeans were stiff and he could feel the crust pressing into his right thigh. It was as if it was pushing him forward, urging him to make a difference, convincing him to save everyone.

As he walked along the upper gangway, he looked over the edge, taking in the whole impressive room. The gaol was even livelier than it had been the previous evening. People were hustling to and fro. Some were carrying baskets or bags of dirty laundry and taking them into the outer corridor. Others were eating breakfast huddled on the dusty floor or crouched on steps or lying across mattresses or even sitting on a couple of long benches that he hadn't noticed the night before. There was a short queue leading into one of the cells. It was the same cell he'd smelt the aroma of cooking from when he'd first arrived. And, though he couldn't see into the cell now thanks to the line of waiting people, he could still catch the scent of toast, which made his stomach rumble loudly.

Arthur made his way straight down the stairwell and joined the end of the breakfast queue. As the line moved forward – more quickly than he expected – he kept an eye out for Ash or Orla or even Donal. But he didn't spot them anywhere among all the unfamiliar faces. Some of the faces looked back at him suspiciously, wary of the newbie. They glanced away when he caught them staring.

After a few minutes, he reached the front of the line. This cell was about twice the size of the others and a long counter had been set up in it, splitting it in two. Tins of fruit, vegetables and lots of beans and peas were piled high on the counter. Next to them was a large pot filled with steaming porridge. A boy wearing an apron, who looked about ten, was behind the counter, busy ladling the sticky gloop into plastic bowls and then handing them to the queue. Arthur took one.

'There's honey and jam and sugar over there,' the boy told him, pointing next to the stacks of tins. 'And water and orange juice behind you. If you want toast or bread, Katie will have some ready in a bit.'

Arthur helped himself to a glass of juice and heaped two spoonfuls of sugar onto the porridge, then looked behind the counter. In the far corner of the cell there was a toaster, a little gas-powered hob with the flame glowing blue and even something called the Breadmaster Supreme. Arthur guessed that these all came from looting raids and he was starting to wonder how the electrical ones were powered when he noticed the cables running from an extension lead to an exercise bike in the next cell. A boy who looked a couple of years younger than him was pedalling furiously, generating electricity. It looked like one of Ash's inventions, Arthur thought. He turned back to the girl,

Katie, who was busy slicing freshly baked bread and popping the slices into the toaster. When they were browned enough, she dropped two slices onto a plastic plate and handed them to Arthur. He slathered them in butter and had swallowed half a slice before he had even left the cell.

He sat by himself, leaning his back against the wall, and wolfed down the food so quickly that his stomach growled angrily afterwards. But that didn't stop him going back for seconds and even thirds. He felt so bloated when he was done that for a moment he couldn't move. As the feeling finally wore off, he brought the used dishes back into the kitchen cell. Breakfast serving had finished and Katie and the porridge-boy were now busying themselves preparing the ingredients for more bread. When the boy saw him coming with the dishes, he nodded to a basin of sudsy water on the floor. All the cleaned plates and bowls were stacked next to it on a tray, dripping dry. He washed his own dishes and left them with the rest.

'Excuse me,' he said, getting up to go. 'But have you seen Ash anywhere this morning?'

'She and the others have gone for more supplies,' Katie told him, squinting at a measuring scale as she tipped flour into it.

'Any idea when they'll be back?'

'Not till this evening some time, I reckon.'

He left the cell and looked around. Most people were working: cleaning up after breakfast or sweeping the floor or carting more mattresses from the corridor. One girl was even in the process of hanging an old landscape painting that she'd found somewhere. He watched with quiet fascination as she hammered a nail into a wooden lath attached to the wall. She stood back proudly and admired her work. A couple of passers-by patted her on the back, telling her what a good job it was. And though the painting did little to counteract the harsh, stony surroundings, Arthur had to admit that it did make the place seem more homely somehow. And of course, that's what they were doing, he realised as he looked on: they were making this place their home.

He felt like he should help them, especially after the hospitality and food they'd shared with him. So, when he noticed a tired-looking broom leaning against one wall, he took it and proceeded to sweep the floor. The dust rose about his shins in little clouds, smudging his new jeans, but he didn't mind. He just concentrated on the work, moving around the floor, in and out of each cell, and after a couple of hours he had several little hillocks of dust piled on each storey. He found a scrap of a cereal box in one bin and used it as a little shovel to scoop up the dirt. When he was done with that, noticing that Ash still hadn't come back, he looked for something else to do.

A young boy came speeding out of one of the cells and bumped right into Arthur's leg. He fell backwards onto the floor and looked up at Arthur with fear in his eyes.

'What's the matter?' Arthur said, giving him a hand up.

'Th-there's a *huge* spider in there.' He pointed an accusing thumb over his shoulder in the direction of the cell he'd bolted from.

'You don't like spiders?'

The boy simply shook his head, turning red.

'It's OK, it's nothing to be embarrassed about,' said Arthur, thrusting the broom forward dynamically. 'Lots of people are afraid of spiders. Luckily I'm not one of them. I'll take care of it with my trusty broom!'

The boy waited by the door as Arthur went in. A flimsy web had been strung across one corner of the cell and a tiny grey spider was scuttling up a thread towards it. In one swift arc, Arthur swept the broom across the wall, taking the web and the spider with it, and flicked them out the door.

'All gone,' he exclaimed, turning back to the boy, whose face was beaming with an appreciative smile.

'Thanks!' the boy said as he ventured back in again. 'There's loads of spiders everywhere.'

'Well maybe I'll just clean them all up,' Arthur said, heading out.

'You're him who was at the camp, aren't you?'

Arthur stopped in his tracks, looked back at the boy and nodded. The boy dug around in his pocket and eventually took out a crumpled passport photo. He handed it to Arthur. It showed a man in his early twenties who had the same hazel eyes as the boy.

'That's my brother. He took care of me. But then we got separated during the flood.'

'Oh.' Arthur didn't know what else to say as he looked at the photo, holding the wrinkled paper carefully between his fingers.

'Did you see him there? At the camp?'

'Oh,' Arthur said again. He looked directly at the young boy. 'No. No, I'm sorry.'

'That's OK,' the boy said dejectedly. He put out his hand for the photo and Arthur gave it to him. 'I just thought you might have.'

The boy turned away, putting the photo back in his pocket for safekeeping. Arthur wanted to tell him that it'd be all right, that they'd get his brother back, that they'd get them all back. But that might not be true; it could all be a lie. He would definitely try to get them back. And he knew there might be comfort in telling the boy that, but he couldn't lie to him. At the end of the day, there would be no comfort in lies.

Arthur spent the next while rounding up all the spiders in the main area and taking them out to the candlelit corridor. It was the one promise he could keep to the boy.

'Sleep well?'

Ash was standing in the doorway to his cell, leaning against the jamb. She was still wearing the many-pocketed coat that she'd had on the day before. Her hair was tied back but tendrils of it had escaped and she looked a tired mess.

After spending a couple of hours spider-hunting, Arthur had found a box with paperback books in one storage cell. He borrowed one and returned to his mattress. It was a fairly straightforward murder mystery and he'd read half of it already, although he hadn't been concentrating on the words. He wouldn't have been able to concentrate on much besides the most menial tasks, but at least the very act of reading seemed to make the time move quicker. He hadn't even heard any kerfuffle down below to let him know that Ash and the others had returned.

'I slept great, thanks.' He shut the book and left it on the ground next to him, then nodded to her dishevelled appearance. 'You guys have trouble out there?'

'Not much,' she said, coming into the room to sit on the end of the mattress. She twanged the loose spring with a finger. 'We just had to make a quick get-away and then came the long way home so no Wolfsguard would follow us. But we got a good haul.'

'Great.' He sat up and tucked his feet underneath him. He knew he needed to talk to Ash. He hadn't been here long, but every hour he stayed quiet was another hour that his dad and his friends could be tortured by Loki. He'd been planning what he would say, while his eyes had read about a private detective and the dame that walked into his life. But now that Ash was here, giving him her time, the words got stuck in his throat.

'Listen, Ash,' he started finally. 'I've been thinking.'

'Oh yeah?'

'Yeah.'

'And what have you been thinking about?'

'It's just that …' He took a breath. 'How long can life go on like this?'

She raised her eyebrows but Arthur continued before she could say anything.

'Taking what you need and moving from place to

place when the wolves come … I mean, eventually you're going to run out of places to go and stashes of food.'

'So what do you suggest, Arthur?' She crossed her arms, almost petulantly. 'That we stop moving? That we give up?'

'No! Of course not.'

'What then?'

'Well …' Here goes. 'Attack.'

'Attack?'

'Attack Loki.'

'Are you serious, Arthur?'

'Of course.'

She stood up, looking at him as if he was nuts. 'We can't attack him! We can't attack any of them!'

'But we have to!' Arthur got to his feet. 'We can't just sit here, barely getting by, living from day to day. The only thing that will ever change is that our luck will run out. It's inevitable. But there's one way to make things better. And that's to stop Loki.'

'Arthur, we're just a bunch of kids. We're not an army. Any attempt to take on Loki will get us all killed.'

'We stopped him before.'

'You keep saying that, but it's not true, Arthur. It's not true! And the sooner you realise that, the better. He's a god, an all-powerful magical being. If he couldn't be stopped by the army, what chance do we have? I don't even think a god *can* be stopped by mere mortals.' She spat the last two words out in disgust. 'If you think I'm going to help you in some hare-brained scheme that could lead him here and bring his anger down on all of us, on all of *them*,' she gestured violently out the door, 'then maybe you'd better leave.' She turned and stormed out of his cell, almost running along the gangway. Arthur followed. He grabbed her shoulder and swivelled her around to face him.

'What happened to you, Ash? When I knew you before you were so brave, so full of courage–'

Angrily she brushed his hand from her shoulder, cutting him off mid-sentence. 'There's a difference between courage and stupidity, Arthur, and what you're talking about is stupidity.'

'Ash, you have no idea–'

'No! *You* have no idea. You have no idea what it feels like to be me,' she said in a low, breaking voice. 'To be the one who started all of this. To be the one left behind. To know that your family are locked up somewhere because of you. To know that all these people – *all the people down there* – rely on me. To know that I have to make it better for them. I can't fail in that, Arthur, and I won't.'

'You're right,' he said softly. 'I don't know what it's like. I can guess, though. I can guess because, in another world,

I was the one who freed the serpent. And it all fell on my shoulders. But that time, we got through it together: you and me. And we can do it again. We just have to–'

'We're *safe* here, Arthur.' She waved her arm over the people below. They'd already started queuing for supper. 'We're alive here. That's all that matters.'

'But for how long?'

Ash gave a loud, exasperated sigh and strode off.

'The girl I knew wouldn't be afraid!' Arthur called after her. 'The girl I knew wouldn't give up. The girl I knew would do whatever it takes to save those people in the camps.' He knew what he was about to say and he knew how it would push Ash's buttons, how it would hurt her to hear the words. But he had to say it; it was the only way he might get through to her. 'The girl I knew and loved wouldn't *abandon* her family to who-knows-what *cruelty*! To the *agony* that a god can inflict!'

She stopped suddenly, caught by his callous words. Red-hot guilt surged through Arthur and he instantly regretted what he'd said. The words had carried more of a sting than he'd imagined.

Ash turned on him, her face red with rage and tears pouring down her cheeks. She stomped back to him and, before he could react, slapped him across the face, hard. The smack echoed throughout the cavernous room and a sudden silence fell. They looked at each other, both equally shocked. Arthur found he couldn't move, not even to rub the red welt he felt rising on his cheek; and neither, it seemed, could Ash.

As Arthur opened his mouth to apologise, the earth suddenly started to shake. The whole building shuddered: metal grinding against metal, stone crunching against stone. Screams rose from the ground floor as the children below clung on to anything they could find. When they realised that nothing was stable, they just held on to each other. One teenage girl toppled down the stairs, tumbling head over heels down the narrow steps.

All over the city, buildings quaked. The waters of the flood churned and boiled, smashing against the sides of the structures, then receding like an angry sea, revealing cars and vehicles underneath. And beyond the city, beyond even the country, the world shook, quaking to its very core. In every corner of the Earth, frightened people huddled, clinging on to each other, certain that the end had finally come, that Loki had decided to destroy the world completely.

The gangway Arthur and Ash were standing on had been constructed in sections. When the quake had started, Ash had been thrown backwards onto a different section and, as Arthur hugged the railing for dear life, he realised with horror that the bolts holding Ash's section to the ceiling were coming loose. As the earthquake continued, a single end of her section came away from the ceiling completely. It swivelled outwards and one side was now hanging over the terrible drop to the ground floor. Arthur watched with dread as she lost her footing and slid towards the precipice. Quick as he could, he reached out to her, about to yell her name when–

The tree Yggdrasill is dying. The rot has spread over its bark, from the root to the tip. The wind lashes its side, tearing weaker branches as if they are as insubstantial as the wing of a moth. With a groan heard in all the worlds, the tree splits in two, straight down the middle, exposing–

'Ash!' Arthur shook his head to clear it, blinking the vision out of his eye and concentrating on his friend. Sliding rapidly towards the edge she looked up at him, saw his outstretched hand and grabbed it just as–

–sick timber within. It is not the healthy, creamy colour that a tree should be, but rather a noxious blue. The timber is soft and crumbling, not strong and unyielding as it should be. The left half of Yggdrasill falls away, over the cliff edge, while the other half, miraculously, stays standing. But it cannot last much longer–

The section Ash was on fell away completely, crashing to the ground, narrowly missing a huddled and terrified group of girls. As Ash swung below him, Arthur tightened his grip on her hand, almost cutting off the circulation to her fingertips. He leaned over, wrapped his second hand around her arm and heaved upwards with all his might, hooking his feet into the railings to get some extra purchase. As he pulled her up, Ash grabbed the edge of his section with her other hand and helped heave herself onto it. With one last lurch, Arthur dragged her up over the edge of the section and the two of them collapsed backwards, gasping for breath.

'It's stopped,' Arthur murmured, noticing that the world wasn't shaking any more. He could hear the water outside, still crashing against the walls, and the sounds of frightened sobbing from the ground floor.

'What *was* that?' said Ash. She'd been lying half on top of him and now rolled to the side and sat up straight.

'Some kind of earthquake, I think.'

'No. I meant what was that tree?'

Arthur looked at her through his widened eye. 'You saw it too?'

'When I touched you I saw it. This gnarled old tree splitting in two. What was it?'

'It's called Yggdrasill, the tree of life. As it rots, so does our world. So do all worlds. If it falls then that's the end of all existence. For good. That's what's at stake, Ash. That's why we have to do something. It doesn't matter whether we survive or not. If we don't stop Loki, then nothing will survive. The end of all creation.'

She looked at him with a glimmer of that determination he had seen on her face many times before and said, 'Then we don't have a choice. Let's do it.'

'Let's do what?'

'Attack.'

CHAPTER FIFTEEN

'I have an announcement to make,' Ash said in a loud voice that rang through the gaol.

After making her decision, Ash hadn't wasted any time. The gangway section that had fallen had left a four-foot-wide gap between the two of them and the stairs; it was just short enough to take a running jump across. When they had both gotten safely over, they rushed downstairs to see the damage for themselves. The kitchen cell was a mess: there was sugar all over the floor and unopened tins of food still rolling around from the after-shocks. Tight knots of people had gathered in groups, examining each other's injuries. They were relieved to find that no one had sustained much more than a few bruises and some nasty grazes. The painting Arthur had watched the girl hang earlier had fallen from its hook. Upon collision with the concrete floor, the frame had snapped in two and the canvas itself had torn slightly. As Ash was tending to the wounded and handing out first-aid kits, he went to re-hang it, but when he picked it up the whole thing fell apart in his hands. He let the remaining pieces of frame clatter to the ground. He didn't understand it, but seeing the ruined painting like that made him even angrier about what Loki was doing to the world.

When everyone had been accounted for and attended to, Ash called them all together in the middle of the floor. She then walked back up a few steps of the staircase and turned to face them, clapping her hands to get everyone's attention. When the low murmur of chatter finally stopped, she met Arthur's eyes for a moment, then turned her attention to the crowd and started to speak.

'What happened here, right now, is a sign,' she said, her voice booming. 'It's a sign that we can't afford to hide any more. We have to come out of the shadows and fight back.'

'Fight who?' called a boy's voice from behind Arthur.

'Loki. Who else?'

A clamour of agitated voices rose straight away, all talking over each other, all shouting their own opinions. Ash tried to calm them down again, but her voice wouldn't carry over the chattering mob. Arthur watched as she hastily pulled off a boot and clanged the heel against the iron rail of the staircase. The sound rang sharply off the walls, and it was enough to force the crowd to focus back on her. Silence fell once more, but Ash held on to the boot, just in case of more interruptions.

'Listen! You have to listen to me!' she exclaimed. 'Our families are out there, held prisoner by Loki—'

'Yours maybe,' a girl's voice cut in loudly enough for everyone to hear. 'We don't know about our families. They could be safe somewhere else, or they could be …' Her voice trailed off.

'Yes,' Ash said, looking in the direction of the voice. 'I know Loki has my family. I don't deny that I want to save them. But I want to save all the others too. I want to save everyone in the camps.' She sighed. 'I want to save us.'

'But we're safe here, we're happy here,' called up another voice.

'I know. And I was happy here until a few minutes ago so, believe me, I understand how you feel. Which is why I won't force anyone to fight. But I understand now why we need to fight. Things are not going to stay like this. Things are going to get worse and quickly. If we don't do something now, Loki will destroy everything.'

'This has something to do with him, doesn't it?' said Donal, turning and pointing to Arthur. Dozens of heads swivelled to look at him, and he stared back defiantly. 'Are you saying you believe that crazy story he told you yesterday?'

'You're right, Donal. It does have to do with him. I'm still not sure that I believe his story, but I do believe one thing: that Loki has to be stopped and that we have to try. No matter what happens, we have to try.' She stopped and looked at the crowd before her. 'Whoever wants to join me, whoever wants to take up arms against Loki, whoever wants to stop him and save the world, whoever wants to fight, meet me here in an hour, before it gets dark. But anyone who doesn't, all I ask is that you stay in your cells until the meeting is over and don't get in our way.'

Murmurs of protest rose from the crowd.

'I hope to see some of you in an hour,' Ash finished, before descending the steps to rejoin Arthur. As she walked over to him the crowd dispersed into different corners. Dozens of whispered discussions were in progress – many of them heated.

'Will it work, do you think?' he muttered to her.

'I hope so,' she answered, keeping her eyes fixed on the assembled crowd. 'I really hope so, because if we are going up against Loki we'll need all the help we can get.'

231

That hour felt like the longest of Arthur's life. He and Ash busied themselves by tidying up the kitchen cell. Every few minutes they would look out into the main room and see that more people had left the space, retiring to their cells. When the kitchen was as tidy as it could be, they went back out and sat on the central stairway. The main area was now empty and still, save for the quiet mumbling from the cells all around. Arthur was sitting behind Ash and stared at her hunched-over back. If no one came, it would be up to the two of them. The two of them against Loki, his children and an army. He didn't like their chances. They had had the dead army's help against the World Serpent and then the help of Fenrir, Ellie and Ex against Loki for round two. More importantly, Loki hadn't had a stranglehold on the world either time, nor did he have their parents as hostages.

'The hour's nearly up,' Ash said, looking at the water-resistant sports watch on her wrist. 'I just have to get some stuff from my cell. Will you give me a hand?'

'Sure,' he said and followed her up to the first floor. Her cell was almost identical to his, with the plain white basin on the left and the lumpy mattress on the right. A cardboard box sat against one wall, which Ash knelt down by. She picked out a large felt play-mat and handed it to Arthur; he remembered that he had had something similar when he was younger for driving toy cars around on. Then she grabbed a plastic carrier bag and put it on top of the mat. He peeped inside to see that it was full of toy animals, building bricks, crayons and markers. Finally, from the bottom of the box, she took out a black laptop case.

Ash nodded at Arthur. 'Let's see if we're on our own then.' They left the cell and looked over the edge of the gangway. A small gathering of people waited below.

Arthur recognised most of them as they walked down the steps. All the people who'd rescued him from the Wolfsguard were there: Donal, Orla, Egg-head, Fat Boy and Spotty Teen. The boy who'd been terrified of spiders was there, too. There were also a couple of others he didn't know. They peered up apprehensively at Ash.

'Glad to see some people showed up,' she said, putting the laptop case on one of the long benches.

Ash took the laptop out and it was unlike any computer Arthur had ever seen. It had the usual keypad and slim monitor but it was all connected to a chunky contraption consisting of gears, wires and one thick handle. She pulled out the handle and started winding it. After a few seconds, the laptop blinked into life and the handle cranked itself around.

'A wind-up computer!' he said with awe. 'That's just amazing, Ash.'

Ash blushed. 'Well, I've always been good with–'

'Electronics. I know.' Arthur grinned at her.

She stared at the screen as the laptop booted up. Arthur watched her fingers glide effortlessly over the keys as she typed in the password. It was so familiar seeing Ash like this. His heart soared in a way he had never felt before.

As the computer started humming, she nodded to Donal. He took the play-mat and bag of toys from Arthur, then unfurled the mat over the bench.

'Do we have any weapons?' asked Arthur hopefully as the computer booted.

'Just this,' said Orla, reaching into a backpack at her feet. She pulled out something that looked like a slimmer and lighter version of a shotgun. The handle and barrel were black while the rest of the body was green. A sight sat on top.

'Tranquilliser gun,' Orla explained, noting Arthur's expression. 'We found it in a big house a couple of weeks ago. I'm pretty sure it belonged to a vet.'

'Do you know how to use it?'

'It's straightforward enough,' said Donal. 'Put the darts in, aim, pull the trigger.'

'How many darts do we have?'

Orla kicked the bag.

'Half a dozen,' she said. 'We had more, but we wasted some of them on the Wolfsguard, only to quickly discover that the needles couldn't pierce their armour.'

As she put it back in the bag, Ash turned to Arthur.

'There are a few things you should know,' she said. 'When we all banded together months ago, for a while we actually considered attacking Loki then. But we couldn't get a proper plan sorted and, to be honest, we got too comfortable in our safe little community. However, we did learn some things that might be useful now.'

'Tell me.'

'As I told you, we were able to hack into the Wolfsguard database.'

'Yeah. That's how you found out who Loki was holding prisoner.'

'Right. But we also found out where Loki's base is and a little bit about the layout.'

'Great! Where is he? How fast can we get there?'

'You saw it yourself when you first got here. Remember you pointed out the gap in the green clouds?'

Arthur thought back to his arrival and recalled standing on top of the roof and seeing the strange absence of clouds in the distance. The blue sky had seemed like a beacon of hope.

'Yup, I remember.'

'That gap is always there. It's the one place in Ireland – probably the one place in the world – where it doesn't rain. It's still dry there; there's no flood at all.'

'But where is it?'

'It's the Phoenix Park,' said Donal, who had finished laying the play-mat out on the bench. The green felt took up most of the tabletop. On the underside of the felt, Arthur knew, was a printed street-view for playing with toy cars. But the back of the mat was facing up. It was bare except for a jagged shape drawn in permanent marker. It looked like a very rudimentary pear – rounded at one end, pointed at the other – and was spread across the majority of the mat.

'And this,' said Orla, as Donal tapped a finger on the shape, 'is our map of the park.'

'There are a few problems,' said Ash, walking around the makeshift map. 'First, it's one of the biggest city parks in Europe.'

'It's twice the size of New York's Central Park,' added Donal somewhat proudly. 'And larger than all of London's city-centre parks put together!'

Ash pulled a matchbox out of the plastic bag and showed it to Arthur.

'This represents the building we're in now.' She put it down next to the map; it was dwarfed in comparison to

236

the pear shape. 'It's to scale so it'll give you an idea of how huge the park actually is.'

'OK,' Arthur said, 'I get it. Big park. What else?'

Ash traced her finger along the permanent-marker outline. 'There's an eleven-kilometre wall running around the full length of the park. It's high enough to keep the water out. And a pair of Wolfsguard are posted every hundred yards just inside the wall, some in human form, some in wolf. Because of their sharpened wolf senses, it would be impossible for even one person to sneak past them.'

'Great!' said Arthur sarcastically. 'So where's Loki in all of this?'

She took a painted wooden brick out of the bag and put it on the north-eastern section of the map.

'He's right here,' she told him. 'In Áras an Uachtaráin.'

'The president's house?' Arthur had seen the home of the Irish president – known as Áras an Uachtaráin – several times in books and on the TV news. It was a beautiful, white, eighteenth-century building, with four tall Ionic columns in front of the entranceway. As well as being where the president lived, it was also a house of great historical significance. Governments had met there, ministers received their Seals of Office there and the president welcomed foreign dignitaries there. He

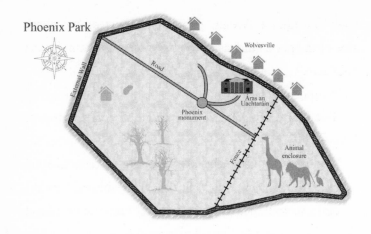

shuddered at the thought of Loki making the place his home.

She nodded grimly.

'So, what, Loki thinks of himself as the president now?'

'Not quite. More like an emperor. According to the Wolfsguard notes, he calls the Áras his palace. Also, that's where he's holding his personal prisoners.'

'My dad, your family, our friends,' Arthur murmured. He looked at the map more closely, taking in the size of it. The Áras was close to the north-eastern border so he pointed there. 'Why don't we cross through that way? It looks close enough that we could just sneak up to the Áras.'

'Two problems,' said Donal. He tapped the northern

wall. 'Blackhorse Avenue runs along most of the north side of the park. And, as in the park itself, the rain doesn't fall there.'

'Sounds perfect to me.'

'But Blackhouse Avenue is now unofficially known as Wolvesville.'

'The wolves live in the houses there,' Orla told him. 'They just took them. It's their base; probably because it's so close to their leader. It's not only impossible to get through Wolvesville, but it's also insane to try.'

'Brilliant,' muttered Arthur. 'OK. What else? You said there were two problems.'

'There are,' said Orla. She took a toy lion out of the bag and plonked it down on the map, somewhere between the Áras and the eastern wall. 'This here is the zoo.'

'So? We just go around it.' Arthur had visited the zoo on a few occasions. It was like a park within the park, walled off with high security fences.

'When Loki took over the park months ago, the animals got out,' explained Ash, taking out more toy zebras and monkeys from the bag. 'We think one of the guards let them out because in their wolf forms they like to hunt. Anyway, it seems that Loki wasn't too pleased by this because he made them catch the animals again. It turns out the World Serpent has quite an appetite for exotic animals and Loki wanted his precious child to always have a fresh supply.

'But the animals were too wild at this stage and the Wolfsguard were either too lazy or too stupid to herd them back into the zoo. So they just built a fence across a large chunk of the park, sealing off the eastern end.' She put the extra animals down, covering the spot she'd just mentioned.

Arthur saw the problem now. If they did somehow manage to break into the park at all via the eastern boundary, they'd have to avoid getting killed by a stray tiger or lion. So the north- and east-facing walls were out. But if they went across the western or southern walls, they'd have a lot of ground to cover before they reached the Áras and would have a much higher risk of getting caught by the Wolfsguard. He studied the few options on the map. It would be impossible to pass all those hundreds of acres without some sort of–

'Distraction,' he muttered.

The others looked at him quizzically.

'If we have to go in from one of these directions,' he said, gesturing to where he meant, 'we'll need a distraction to give us enough time to reach the Áras.'

'You're right,' said Ash, 'but what?'

Arthur looked at the small group around him and

then back at the map. For a few minutes there was silence as they all puzzled over what to do.

'That's it,' he shouted suddenly.

'What?' Ash half leapt out of her skin at the abrupt exclamation.

'I have an idea.' He bent over the map and started telling them his plan.

'OK,' he said. 'We'll need two teams …'

Later, Arthur lay on his mattress, going over the plan in his head.

After they had talked through the plan in detail – twice – they came to the agreement that it was their best option.

'It's not just our best option,' said Ash, 'it's our only option.'

'So when will we do this?' Egg-head spoke up for the first time.

'How does tomorrow morning sound?'

They all nodded. They secretly knew that the longer they waited, the more likely they would make excuses to themselves to drop out.

'Who's in the smaller group?' asked Orla, running a hand through her dreads.

'That's me and Ash,' said Arthur before anyone else could answer either way. He looked at Ash. 'If you want to?'

'Yeah.' She nodded slowly. 'Arthur and I are the small group. The rest of you are in the main group.' Then, as an afterthought, she added, 'If any of you want to back out, now's the time. No one will think any less of you.' They all stared resolutely back at her, none of them speaking.

'All right then,' she said eventually. 'We should get some sleep now. Meet back here at dawn.'

It was gloomy in the gaol now; the sun was setting outside and only faint green light was seeping its way in through the skylight. As they all felt their way back to their cells, Arthur and Ash walked upstairs together. They stood on the first-floor gangway, looking at each other in the dull light.

'Do you think it'll work?' Ash asked.

Arthur shrugged. 'Like you said: it's our only choice. I wish we had all the time in the world to come up with something better, to convince more people to help, to find some – or any – weapons, but you saw for yourself, Ash: time's running out.'

She nodded, somewhat sadly, and then turned towards her cell. 'Goodnight, Arthur.'

''Night, Ash.'

He headed up to the second floor – taking great care when leaping over the chasm left by the broken section – and lay down on his mattress. The setting sun was shining right through the small window, illuminating the room more now than it had during the day. He was suddenly – and inexplicably – filled with hope. He had to believe that they'd have no trouble breaking into the park, and hope that they'd defeat Loki once and for all, hope that the world would be set right again. And, most of all, hope that at the end of it he would find his dad and his mum again.

Out of habit, his fingers went to the ribbon around his right wrist. He stroked the smooth silk, remembering how fascinated he was by it whenever he held his mother's hand. He could still picture the scene: walking through the town with his mum as she made her way to the shops. Once there he would often pick up a packet of fun-size chocolate bars and dump them in the shopping trolley hoping she wouldn't notice, but she always did, although she never seemed to mind. And all the time he'd keep holding on to her hand.

He thought of how powerful the ribbon called Gleipnir really was. How it had bound Fenrir the wolf, how it had bound Hel, how it had bound him to reality. Just then something moved against his arm. He opened his eyes to see that one of the stray ends of the ribbon was dancing all by itself, standing like a charmed snake and stroking against his left wrist. He held up both his arms and imagined the ribbon coiling from his right wrist around the fingers on his left hand. Then, as if Gleipnir had plucked the command right from his mind, it did just that. It wound its way past his little finger, in and out until it reached the thumb. The whole thing was actually getting longer as it went. Arthur pulled his left hand away and the ribbon receded.

Something stirred in him then: the kernel of an idea, the seed of a plan.

He pictured in his mind's eye – and then his real eye – the ribbon winding itself around his left wrist. When it had made one full loop, it turned back onto itself and the loose end sealed itself to make Gleipnir an unbreakable whole.

Arthur tried to pull his arms apart, but the ribbon was much too strong and the binding around his left wrist was too securely fastened. For a moment Arthur panicked, unsure how to release his arm. Then the pendant on his chest started to glow. He could feel it. But this time the sensation was different from every other occasion when this had happened. Whenever Loki was nearby, the pendant became hot and it radiated frantically like a warning alarm. But now the bronze exuded a gentle warmth and when he looked down at it he could see that it was glowing with more of a pale ivy colour than the neon-green brought on by danger. It was calming. It told him to relax and it told him, deep inside, how to break free. It had almost destroyed Hel to break Fenrir's bindings. But Arthur now realised that Gleipnir was like a magical pair of handcuffs. And what Hel didn't realise was that there was no way to pick that lock. You needed to hold the key: you needed to be the one who had locked it.

Arthur shut his eye and imagined the ribbon uncoiling itself from his arm. He could see it letting him go, returning to its original length on his right wrist. And, in the darkness behind his eyelids, he could feel it happening.

When he looked again the ribbon was back to normal as if nothing had happened, and the pendant had ceased glowing. Things were looking up. Arthur now had a secret weapon.

CHAPTER SIXTEEN

The sun was just rising when they reconvened downstairs, and the vast central room of the gaol was awash with the eerie pale-green light. Arthur came downstairs to find that he was the last one to arrive. He had his rucksack over his shoulder, complete with the hammer and a couple of other items that might come in handy. He'd found a wetsuit left outside his room when he woke, with a note from Ash suggesting he put it on. It was red with dynamic green stripes down the side and he was wearing it now. It was so clingy that he felt exposed in it, but he was relieved to see that all the others were in their swimming costumes too and were not paying him any attention. Ash looked up at him as his feet clanged on the iron steps. She was wearing the jacket she always did over a black-and-white-striped wetsuit.

She also had the long stick he'd seen on the first day tied to her back.

'All set?' she asked as he joined the group.

'All set.'

She looked at the rest of the small gathering. Most of them tried to put on a brave face but the apprehension they were feeling still showed through.

'We'll be on our way now,' she told them. 'You lot should leave in half an hour or so. That way we'll both arrive at our target positions at roughly the same time.'

'Are you sure you want to be the ones to go in?' Orla asked.

'I think we have to be,' said Ash with a smile.

'All right then. Good luck.'

The rest of them wished Arthur and Ash well as they walked out into the corridor on their own. Arthur murmured to Ash as the door closed behind them, 'Are you sure they'll turn up? They looked pretty nervous.'

'I haven't known any of them for very long, Arthur, but I've trusted them all with my life. They won't let us down,' she replied, 'especially with Orla and Donal to lead them.'

It was darker in the corridor than it had been on the day Arthur had arrived and he stumbled forward, almost tripping up twice. Ash took his hand in the gloom and put it on her shoulder.

'Follow me,' she whispered.

Soon they were in the stone stairwell, making their way up to the attic room. Ash went first, climbing onto the stack of old mattresses and pulling herself up through the trapdoor. Arthur followed her. The city spanned out around them, much the same as the last time he'd stood on the rooftop. He looked at the gap in the clouds again, but this time a shiver crept up his spine because he knew what lay there.

Ash was already halfway down the outer ladder by the time he started to follow. The jet skis were waiting in the corner by the trees. Ash hopped onto the one closest and took the driver's position while Arthur clambered on behind her. She revved the engine and, after a bit of awkward manoeuvring in order to face the right direction, sped through the gap.

The city beyond the gaol walls was as quiet as they had expected. No birds called from the skies, no car horns honked, no babies cried, no people lived their lives. Dublin was dead and the only sound at this funeral was the roar of their engine.

The night before, Egg-head had given them the best route to the park. It was an intricate map of side streets and laneways that he'd drawn in crayon on a scrap of paper which Ash now held before her on the handle as she steered. Arthur noticed that she rarely referenced the map at all though. She told him she hadn't been able to sleep with anticipation the night before and had memorised the whole thing.

They could smell the smoke before they saw the fire. They caught a glimpse of the blaze as they cut through the water and Ash strayed off their route to get a closer look. The top floors of one of the apartment complexes that rose above the flood were ablaze. Tongues of fire licked out of glassless window frames, searing wooden doorways and collapsing ceilings and floors. The fire had mostly burnt out at one end of the complex and was more intense at the far end; it was clear that it had been set on fire hours ago. There was no sign of life among any of the burning buildings, either human or wolf. Arthur, with his arms wrapped around Ash's waist for stability, felt her bristle at the sight of the fiery homes. Her back stiffened and her shoulders set, as if the sight was making her more determined. He squeezed her tighter and, without a word passing between them, Ash set off once more, heading for their final destination.

For the rest of the journey, Arthur went over the strategy in his head, trying to find any weak points. The plan required that he and Ash would enter at the western side of the Phoenix Park, away from the zoo enclosure.

They would wait outside while Donal and Orla's team broke in over the eastern wall, which was largely unguarded thanks to the wild animals roaming freely there. Their team would then cause the diversion that would allow Arthur and Ash to enter the park and make it to the Áras unseen. The whole plan hinged on the guards at the western wall leaving their posts to investigate what was happening at the other end of the park.

As they drew nearer to the park, Ash slowed the jet ski to a crawl so that the engine would make as little noise as possible. Eventually, at the end of a particularly narrow alleyway, she turned it off altogether. She turned back to Arthur. 'We're about three hundred yards from the western wall here,' she told him in hushed tones. 'We should swim the rest of the way so they don't hear us coming.'

Arthur nodded silently and they both slid into the water. He looked up at the gap in the clouds, almost directly overhead now. The sky was a clear, azure blue. He could even feel a slight breeze coming through the opening. It was a fresh spring morning beyond the clouds.

They swam out of the laneway and towards the high wall ahead of them. Only the top layer of bricks was visible above the flood-line. They reached the wall and, careful not to make any extra noise, gripped the lip of the bricks and pulled themselves up for a closer look. They peeped over the edge of the barricade into the park. As Ash had said, the ground was dry under the cloud gap and the grass was a healthy shade of emerald. There was nothing to be seen but vast fields, broken up intermittently by tight clumps of trees. A pair of guards stood in the distance to the right beside the wall, and another pair was very close by on the left-hand side. They were wearing black overalls, flak jackets and the kind of helmets a SWAT team would wear: tight on the back with curved visors in front. The guards leant lazily against the bricks, crossbows slung idly over their shoulders. Clearly they weren't expecting any trouble. Arthur could hear the distant hum of their voices but wasn't able to make out what they were saying.

Ash ducked back down behind the wall and looked at her watch. The second group had agreed to set off their distraction at eight o'clock sharp; it was now seven forty-seven. Just over ten minutes to go. She showed her watch to Arthur, and the two of them settled back into the water, kicking slowly and quietly to keep themselves afloat and praying that the distraction would work.

Donal slid over the wall first and dropped silently to the ground on the other side. He landed a few feet inside one end of the fence that was as high as the wall and stretched across the east end of the park, sealing in the animals. They had left the speedboat at the main entrance to the park, now long sealed up, and he was dripping wet from the swim over. A penguin sunning itself on a nearby park bench looked at him briefly, then lost interest and shut its eyes once more. He spotted a giraffe's head poking through some treetops in the distance, pulling leaves off and chewing. He peered through the sight of the tranquilliser gun in his hand: no sign of any predators, thankfully.

'Come on,' he said, just loud enough for Orla to hear. She pulled herself lithely over the wall and landed next to him.

The barricade keeping the animals from the rest of the park was constructed from twenty-foot long segments of chain-link fence. Each section was fastened to the next with three pairs of nuts and bolts: one at the top, one at the base and one in the middle. Although Orla didn't see any sign of electrical wires running through the fence, the first thing she did was to take a three-inch nail out of her pocket. She had brought it from the gaol for just this eventuality. She tossed the nail at the wires and watched it bounce off and land on the grass without raising so much as a spark.

Donal looked at his watch: it was twenty minutes to eight, they were bang on time. He nodded to Orla and, together, they started to run along the inside of the fence. When they had gone as far as either one of them would risk – just over a third of the way along the barrier and in line with the road that cut through the centre of the park – Orla took an adjustable wrench from her other pocket and went to work on the fence, while Donal covered her with the tranquilliser gun propped against his shoulder. She clambered up the fence first, loosening the top bolt. It had been secured tightly but, with a couple of thumps from the side of her fist, the nut came free and she quickly unscrewed it and dropped it to the ground. She repeated the deed on the next two bolts and then the three on the other side. As soon as she was done, she pushed the loose fence segment over – it landed on the grass with a soft *fwosh*ing sound – and together they moved along to the next one, back in the direction they'd come. She managed to get three more segments down before Donal told her it was time to make a move.

With their job done they raced back to the wall. Orla climbed back over first. Donal had one last look at the park and then followed. As they swam in the direction of the speedboat, they both prayed that Arthur and Ash were in position.

The rest of Team 2, except for the boy Arthur knew only as Egg-head, who was keeping an eye on the boat, were also in position on the top of the outer wall. They looked in amazement at the animals roaming freely in the park below. A small herd of antelope grazed in a field next to a flamingo and other exotic birds flocked on a knoll in the distance. A small pride of lions snored loudly in the shade of a tree close by. None of them noticed the group of human invaders crouching there. But they soon would. The team spread silently and carefully along the wall. As soon as it turned eight o'clock – and Egg-head had signalled to them that Donal and Orla were safely on their way back – they nodded to each other before letting loose with whatever fog horns, flares and other noise-makers they had been able to lay their hands on, making enough noise to spook a couple of hundred wild animals.

'Say again,' said one of the guards. Despite the helmet and

the distance, Arthur could hear the disbelief in his voice. Ash was looking at him with widened eyes and gestured to the left. They pulled themselves silently along the wall, trying to get closer before peeking over the edge. One of the Wolfsguard was pressing a button on the side of his helmet but they couldn't hear what was being said on the other end of the radio.

The guard grunted irritably and released the button. 'Bleedin' idiots need our help over there,' he said to his partner, gesturing towards the far end of the park. 'Seems they've managed to let the zoo animals escape.'

Arthur and Ash looked at each other again, hopeful smiles creeping over their faces. It was working, the plan was actually working! Team 2 had sent the remaining zoo animals stampeding into the park. With all the animals free again, the Wolfsguard near the animal enclosure had called for back-up. Now they had to hope that the guards on the western wall would be overcome by their wolf instincts and leave their positions to join in the hunt.

'Let's go,' the first guard continued.

The other guard, however, was not so convinced and stayed leaning against the wall.

'It's their mess – let them clean it up. Why should we go chasing around after animals they let out? Besides, we're not supposed to leave our posts.'

'Great,' muttered Arthur. 'We get the one conscientious wolf in the pack!'

'Come on, would ya!' urged the first guard. 'It's not like you're gonna get a promotion for standin' around here. Anyways, think of the thrill of the hunt! Don't ya feel like sinkin' yer teeth into one of them cantaloupe things?'

These words seemed to convince his partner. 'I think you mean an antelope. But you do make a good point. And it has been a long night: we deserve a treat. Fine, let's go.' But before he did, he jabbed a finger at the other guard's chest. 'But if we get into trouble, and we're forced to write one of those bleedin' reports, I'm blaming you,' he grumbled.

'Yeah, yeah, whatever. Now let's go – we'll miss the big cats!'

There was a flash of green light around both of them and for a moment they blazed too brightly to look at. When the glow dissipated, the guards were gone and their uniforms were in heaps on the grass. Two grey wolves howled at the sky before breaking into a sprint across the expansive, empty fields towards the animal enclosure and away from Ash and Arthur. They looked down the wall and could see the rest of the guards had likewise transformed and were now streaking towards the other end of the park.

Ash gasped like she couldn't believe their luck. Arthur felt exactly the same way and knew that he was grinning like an idiot. They quickly heaved themselves into a sitting position on top of the wall then scrambled down the other side and landed in the park. As soon as they hit the ground, Ash fell to her knees and ran her fingers through the long grass. After a moment of doing that, she caught Arthur watching her inquisitively and her cheeks blushed a bright shade of pink.

'It's so long since I felt grass,' she explained, getting to her feet. 'It's stupid, I know.'

'It's not stupid,' he said. 'Not at all. But we'd better get on with it; we don't know how long those guards will stay away.'

They went over to the pile of abandoned clothes. The two guards had been much taller than Ash and Arthur, but they had agreed when talking the plan over that blending in was the key. Arthur picked up one of the pairs of overalls the wolves had been wearing and appraised the size.

'I think this is the smaller pair,' he said. 'You can have it.'

'I'm exactly the same size as you!' Ash snorted, but took the overalls anyway.

They pulled on the discarded uniforms over their

wetsuits as fast as they could, turning up the excess material of the legs and arms. The dampness of the wetsuits made the overalls stick to them, so they didn't look quite so loose. The flak jackets the wolves had been wearing were surprisingly heavy and far too baggy, but they pulled them on nonetheless and tightened them as much as possible with the Velcro straps. One positive Arthur noticed when he looked at Ash was that they had the pleasing effect of bulking up their frames. The disguises probably wouldn't stand up to close scrutiny, but they would do from a distance.

The steel-toed boots were far too big and would have flopped around on their feet noticeably. Luckily, they had brought some similar boots Ash had found on a looting raid with them in Arthur's bag. They didn't have the steel tips but were a lot less conspicuous than wearing the size elevens. Lastly, they fitted the helmets over their heads. The visors of the helmets completely covered the face and – as Arthur realised when he pulled on his helmet – were tinted to minimise the glare of the sun. The edges of the glass were magnified so if you tilted your head in a certain direction, it had a telescopic effect. Straps on the rear of the helmets ensured that they didn't wobble about too much on Arthur or Ash's head.

'What do you think?' Arthur asked Ash when she

came back from hiding her own jacket behind a thicket of brambles at the base of the wall. Speaking inside the helmet gave him a weird sensation; his voice echoed and it was like hearing himself back on an audio recorder. And it stank of sweat and dog hair.

'I think that once no one takes a close look at us, we should get away with it.' Her voice, too, sounded muffled behind her helmet. Arthur wondered how the Wolfsguard got any work done at all, it was so difficult to communicate. 'Are you going to bring the backpack with you?'

He clutched the strap over his shoulder protectively. 'If anyone asks, I'll just say I found it somewhere in the park,' he said. 'But don't you think that stick looks suspicious?'

She was holding her long baton in her hand. It was as tall as her and gave the impression that it was just an elongated walking stick.

'I'll say the same as you. Anyway if someone is close enough to talk to us, I think we'll have bigger problems,' she said, just as unwilling to part with her weapon as Arthur was with his.

'OK then. Let's go.'

They set off in the direction the wolves had run, towards Áras an Uachtaráin and Loki.

After fifteen minutes of walking, they saw the deer. They had started off across an expanse of green but were quickly forced to turn northwards when the field turned out to be so marshy that they kept sinking into the ground. The northern route was easier – and would take them to the main road that cut through the park, Arthur knew – but the grass here was much higher, making it difficult to walk and impossible to run. Though the air was cooler here than it had been outside in the city – probably due to the ventilation of the break in the clouds, Arthur thought – the sun beamed right down on them, boiling them inside their black uniforms.

They passed the herd of deer grazing in an adjacent field. At first, Arthur was surprised that the escaped animals had made it this far so quickly.

'They're not from the zoo,' Ash said when he shared his thoughts with her. 'Deer are native to the park. They're all over the place.'

A stag with impossibly tall antlers looked in their direction, his huge brown eyes staring them down. He stayed in that position for what seemed like forever, standing to attention like a statue, before galloping away. The rest of the herd followed briskly. Arthur stood and watched them go, wondering if they understood what was happening in their park.

They journeyed on, rarely speaking. Arthur's hammer started to weigh heavily on his shoulder and he could have sworn it was pulling his rucksack down more than usual. Even Ash was getting sick of having to raise her stick high enough to clear the long grasses. It was tiring work and Arthur began to wish they'd thought to bring some food or at least some water with them. They found a brambly bush at the edge of a tiny clump of trees, with dark purple berries growing on it. He was sorely tempted to pick a handful of berries and swallow them, but neither he nor Ash knew if they were poisonous and so decided against it. He'd never be able to face Loki with food poisoning. He might end up vomiting all over the Father of Lies. As Arthur chuckled to himself at the thought of it, Ash asked him what was so funny.

'Just imagine!' he said when he'd told her. 'Loki's standing there and, all of a sudden, I projectile vomit all over him. Right into his face. All this purple and green stuff. And it just keeps on going!'

Ash giggled along. 'There'd probably be loads of carrots in there too!'

'Even though I haven't eaten carrots in weeks!'

As they joked the grass started to get shorter and easier to walk across. Ash pointed out a house to their left: a boxy, grey structure with ivy climbing over the front. The bright-blue door was swinging open in the slight breeze and Arthur guessed the place had been abandoned. They kept going. Moments later, something in the distance caught Arthur's eye.

A lake.

'Let's take a break there,' he suggested, pointing a gloved finger. 'The trees around it will give us some cover.'

'Good idea. I can't believe how parched I am, considering we haven't gone that far! I guess maybe we should have taken off the wetsuits.'

It wasn't the most impressive lake Arthur had ever seen. It was somewhere between a pond and a lake, with an overgrown island off to one side. But, judging by the blackness of the water, it seemed to be deeper than he'd assumed at first glance. The two of them slumped to the ground beside the lake and pulled off their helmets. They were both drenched in sweat, their hair a mess, their cheeks and necks red and blotchy from exertion.

Arthur looked at the water. It seemed clear enough. No algae or fungus grew around the edge so it was probably safe enough to sip. Given the choice and the time, he would have felt happier boiling any impurities out of the water, but he had neither. He took off his backpack, then went and knelt by the water. Ash did likewise.

'Weird,' she muttered.

'What?' He joined his two hands in a little cup and dipped them into the lake.

'The ground all over the park has been bone dry. But here, around the lake, it's soaking.'

As water filled his cupped hands, Arthur looked around. She was right; the ground was wet for about six feet around the edge of the lake, maybe more. He started to wonder how that could have happened when he saw the answer for himself.

Something was in the lake.

Something monstrous.

Something headed their way.

The World Serpent.

CHAPTER SEVENTEEN

'Move back!' Arthur shouted to Ash, but it was too late. The Jormungand soared out of the lake and straight into the sky. A wave of water crashed into them, sending them toppling backwards. Ash watched in awed terror as the serpent swooped high into the sky then turned and plummeted back to the ground, landing just metres from them. A forked tongue flicked out at her.

She swore loudly; it was the first time Arthur had ever heard her curse.

The serpent looked exactly the same as it had the first time Arthur had come into contact with it. It was about a hundred feet in length and its body was approximately seven feet in diameter at its widest point, narrowing down to a sharpened tail at the end. Scales as large as Arthur's head covered the huge body, shimmering shades of red and green. It had a wing on either side of its frame – great, leathery, ribbed things with a span as wide as the serpent was long. They were flapping slowly now as the creature stared at them. It was perched on four tiny legs that ended in clawed feet and Arthur recalled again the comparison with a T-Rex he had made on their first encounter. Three ridged fins ran along the serpent's head. Its mouth was partly open and Arthur could see the razor-sharp teeth that protruded from its jaws, capable of ripping a man in two. Its eyes were golden slits that watched them closely.

'OK,' said Arthur in a hushed voice. 'Just stay calm.'

'Stay calm! How can I stay calm with that thing looking at us?' Ash shot back, keeping her eyes fixed on the serpent.

'It might think we're just some Wolfsguard. It might not hurt us.'

'I don't think it's that easily fooled. Why else would it be foaming at the mouth?'

Ash was right; bubbles of spit fizzed at the corners of its mouth. This didn't look good. The serpent was flicking its tongue in and out, as if getting a taste for its prey.

'All right then,' said Arthur. 'On the count of three, we get up and run for it. OK?'

'Outrun something that can fly?'

'Do you have a better idea?' snapped Arthur, a little

exasperated. He didn't look directly at Ash but could see her shaking her head out of the side of his eye.

'OK then. One … two …'

Just then, the Jormungand opened its great mouth. A screech burst out of its throat. It was like nails scratching on blackboards, teeth biting into ice and chairs squeaking on tiled floors all rolled into one. They could feel the blast of the soundwave hit them in the face and could see the uvula wobbling violently at the back of the beast's throat.

Arthur turned to Ash and screamed, '*Run!*'

They scrambled to their feet as quickly as they could, and scattering chunks of wet earth behind them, started racing over the grass away from the serpent. The Jormungand snorted and took up the pursuit. Arthur didn't dare look around; he kept his eyes focused on the space ahead of them and he concentrated on making his legs move faster, faster, faster, as his bag thumped painfully against his back. He could hear the serpent coming up behind them, its claws pounding into the ground as it ran. Faster, thought Arthur, faster!

'There!' cried Ash veering to the right. She was heading for a small grove of elm trees at the edge of the field. Arthur turned after her, chancing a glance around at the serpent as he did.

Its legs were too short and its body too massive to

keep up with them. Arthur was about to breathe a sigh of relief when the serpent seemed to realise this. It stopped, spread its wings and flapped them strongly, sending gusts of air that washed over Arthur and Ash as they ran. Slowly it lifted itself a few feet off the ground, beating harder and harder until it raised its great bulk into the air. Although this gave Arthur and Ash a good lead on the beast, once airborne it was able to glide rapidly towards them, beating its wings strongly to gather speed. Ash started to look around to see what was happening, but Arthur stopped her.

'Keep going! Just keep going!!'

His thighs were burning and he felt the beginnings of a cramp in his left calf, but Arthur kept on running. He didn't move his eyes from the clump of trees ahead. The branches were mostly bare, ready and waiting for spring growth. The grass started to get longer again as they approached the trees, but they didn't stop, they didn't falter, they just ran and ran.

As they sped between the trunks, Arthur felt a whoosh of air buffet him. The Jormungand had been forced to turn sharply to avoid slamming into the trees. Once they reached the densest part of the grove, Arthur and Ash stopped running. They bent over to catch their breath and turned back to watch the Jormungand. It had landed again and was glaring at them from beyond the first tree; seeing its prey just out of reach, it roared in frustration. It was too large to fit between the trees, which were packed closely together.

Arthur stood to his full height again, trembling all over. He looked at Ash.

'What now?' she said between gasps.

He shrugged, rubbing the oncoming cramp out of his calf. Suddenly the branches overhead clattered violently, like they'd been caught in a high wind. They looked back at the World Serpent to see it shaking its head, dazed. Then it took a few steps back from the trees before running right into them. The beast was attempting to reach them by battering its way through the trees. After just two blows, a handful of trees at the edge of the grove had already been half pulled up by their roots. A third blow would fell them. Arthur watched as the serpent took a few more steps back for its run-up and then turned to Ash.

'If it keeps going like this, it'll have knocked all these trees down in minutes. We have to do something!'

The trees at the edge of the grove collapsed to the ground with heavy thuds. The serpent screeched triumphantly; only four or five trees stood between them and it now.

'Look!' cried Ash, pointing over Arthur's shoulder.

Just beyond the clump of trees, behind the serpent, stood a stag. Arthur couldn't be sure it was the one they'd seen earlier, but part of him felt that it had to be. It stood straight and powerful, its antlers cutting a striking silhouette against the bright sky, its deep-brown eyes watching them.

The deer grunted loudly – a sound Arthur recognised from nature documentaries. The Jormungand turned its head and stared at the creature. The stag made the huffing sound again, as if challenging the serpent, then bolted off in the opposite direction. The Jormungand swivelled around on its tiny legs, distracted from its original quarry, and started off across the field, chasing its new prey.

Arthur gripped Ash's shoulders urgently. 'We need to move.'

'But where–?'

'The house we passed a few minutes ago.'

'What about Loki? The Áras?'

'We can't do anything about Loki if the serpent kills us.' This was no time for conversation – the Jormungand could come back any second – so Arthur tore off in the direction of the house. Ash was only a millisecond behind.

As they ran back across the field, there was no sign of the Jormungand. They could hear rustling and roars which seemed to be coming from a nearby chunk of scrubland, but it seemed far enough away for them to relax a bit. Arthur's calf was still tight so he was glad not to have to sprint as fast as they had only moments before. They were more than halfway across the field and could see the rooftop of the house when–

Roar!

The bellow came from behind them. They stopped and turned to see the Jormungand standing at the far edge of the thicket, screeching up at the sky. They could see fresh blood dripping from its jaws. It spat something onto the ground. The stag that had saved them, limp and lifeless, its body ripped to gory shreds. Arthur and Ash were transfixed with horror as the serpent put one leg on the stag's body, tore half the carcass away and gulped it down. Then it swung its head around and settled its gaze on them once more.

Without another word, Arthur and Ash started running again and the World Serpent quickly resumed its pursuit, soaring on its great wings a few feet above the ground. Arthur could feel his legs shuddering as he moved, the muscles and ligaments wrenching from the effort. Nausea churned his stomach, telling him to stop or throw up.

But the Jormungand's flapping was growing ever closer.

We'll never make it, he told himself, we'll never make it.

He wanted it to be over; he wanted to give up.

But he couldn't.

He thought of his friends, of Ash, of her family, of his family.

He thought of the world.

He couldn't give up.

A tarmac road led up to the house and they headed towards it. A few more seconds; just a few more seconds till they reached the front door.

Keep going, keep going.

Just a few more seconds.

Arthur's feet touched the tarmac.

And Ash fell.

She tripped on a little hillock of earth and cried out as she crashed to her knees. Arthur turned, just in time to see the Jormungand slam down and loom over her. Before he could react the beast had dug its jaws into the earth around Ash, snapped them shut and swallowed her whole.

Time seemed to stop for Arthur. He was rooted to the spot as a wave of terror, grief and rage rose in him. The Jormungand's screeching broke him out of the trance. He turned and sprinted the rest of the way to the house, his feet beating on the tarmac while angry and frustrated tears blurred his vision.

The World Serpent – temporarily sated by its second meal in as many minutes – waited a few moments before chasing after him. By the time it did move, Arthur was up the steps leading to the grey house. He fell through the door and kicked it shut behind him.

And then he curled into a ball and cried. Fitful, exhausted, breathless tears.

She was gone. Ash was gone. Dead. Swallowed by the Jormungand.

And he was trapped.

By the time he heard the serpent's claws scratching on the tarmac outside, his head ached from crying. He whimpered as the beast pulled itself up the steps to the door. It screeched that terrible shriek, shaking the door on its hinges and shaking Arthur into action.

He leapt to his feet. He wouldn't just give up. Ash wouldn't have wanted that. She would have wanted him to keep going, to fight, to save her family.

He looked around properly for the first time. He was in the entrance hall and a staircase led upstairs directly in front of him. Whatever the building was intended for originally, it had obviously been used as offices in recent years. It was a large old house with high ceilings and narrow windows. He raced up the staircase, the wooden steps creaking with each footfall. Behind him, the Jormungand crashed into the doorway. But the old door was stronger than it looked and barely shuddered at the blow.

At the top of the stairs Arthur found himself on a long, narrow landing that ran back to the front of the house. There were doors on both sides and a window at the far end, covered with a muslin blind. He ran to it and ripped down the blind. It was an ancient double-hung window with two sliding panes, one on top and one below. The glossy white paint on the frames was thick with old layers. He grabbed the bottom of the lower pane and tried to push it up. It resisted, stiff with age, but a couple of side-fisted punches soon loosened it. He slid it all the way to the top and locked it in place, then leaned out the window.

The World Serpent was right below him, lining up to race at the door again. When it did, the force of the blow shook the windowsill Arthur was leaning on. The Jormungand stepped back once more, taking a moment before battering again.

As Arthur stared at the monster he experienced a sudden blurring in his vision. Suddenly he could see the serpent for what it really was—

The sea serpent flops around on the steps leading up to the doorway. It is about one foot long, with no wings, no legs, no mutations and it misses the water: it misses its home.

⬚⬚⬚⬚⬚

Arthur blinked and looked down again. The Jormungand was still there, the gigantic and monstrous beast it always was. It was getting ready to bash the door again and if Arthur was going to act, now would be the time. He really didn't know what he was doing, but some instinct was driving him. At least, he assured himself, if I'm on the beast's back it can't eat me.

Well, I hope not anyway.

He climbed onto the windowsill and swung his legs over the edge. He had to crouch in order to fit himself underneath the upper pane. He looked down at the World Serpent, directly below his feet, and tried to estimate the distance. It was an eight-, maybe nine-foot drop. Not safe, but no more life-threatening than waiting in the house.

He shut his eyes and pushed himself out of the window.

And he landed right on the Jormungand's back.

The serpent reared upwards, screeching. Arthur turned himself around to get a grip of the fins along the beast's

274

head. Suddenly, the Jormungand's wings spread out. Arthur held on tighter, anticipating what was about to happen.

The serpent leapt into the air. Its wings beat fiercely pulling it higher and higher. Arthur felt his legs slipping from around the Jormungand's body. He shifted his weight forward as much as he could and clasped the fin tightly, spreading his legs apart as far as possible and gripping with them to balance on the serpent's neck.

As the beast climbed further into the sky, Arthur gazed with wonder at the world below. He could see zoo animals stampeding in the distance and wolves trying and failing to round them up. He could see the rooftop of the Áras through a gap in the trees. He could see the flooded city beyond the park walls, hopeless and lifeless. Then they soared through the gap in the clouds and, for as far as he could see, the sky was blue.

It was blue. Blue and healthy and wonderful.

Soon they were flying so high that his ears popped, while oxygen was getting so thin that his breathing became ragged; his straining lungs pulled shallow breaths in and out rapidly. Then, without warning, the serpent bucked its entire body violently. Arthur lost his grip on the fin and found himself sliding down the creature's back, down towards the ground. As he went, his arms scrabbled about, looking for purchase but finding none. As he reached the slimmer part near the tail, he threw his arms around the serpent's body, squeezing as tightly as he could.

All of a sudden, the serpent swerved down towards the ground. They burst back through the cloud cover, the earth rapidly rising to meet them. And then something caught Arthur's eye.

Most of the Jormungand's scales were green or red or a mixture of the two. And all the scales were shiny, glistening in daylight like glitter on a Christmas card. Except now Arthur noticed a small area of scales on the serpent's back that weren't glossy at all. Parts of them were dull and black: diseased-looking. But this wasn't any ordinary infection – the blackness formed symbols and shapes, lines and criss-crosses. Arthur thought back to the dream where he had seen Loki create the Jormungand. The god had plucked an ordinary sea serpent out of the water and then traced runes on its back with his own blood. The marks he could see were those runes – the infection of Loki. Suddenly the pendant flared against his chest. And, just like that, Arthur figured out how to stop the World Serpent permanently.

The Jormungand pulled out of its dive sharply just before it hit the ground. Arthur couldn't hold on any more and slipped off the beast's back, hitting the ground hard and tumbling along it. When he finally came to a stop he sat up, momentarily dazed, and rubbed his head. They were back near the lake and the serpent was coming his way.

Arthur got to his feet. The beast soared straight at him, opening its jaws to roar its victory.

'Here goes,' he said to himself, crossing his fingers and toes for good luck.

He ran straight at the beast and threw himself into the mouth of the World Serpent.

It was so dark that Arthur wasn't sure if he was alive or not. And if he was dead then this had to be hell because the stench was so awful. It was like boiled cabbages strained through dirty football socks and topped off with a generous seasoning of dog poo. After being swallowed, he had felt constricted, as something slimy pressed in on him from all angles. Then that tightening gave way and he landed somewhere with a splash.

Arthur reached out into the gloom, feeling the warm and moist softness of the serpent's stomach lining. Then his hand rubbed off something else and he recoiled in shock. His fingers felt it out again tentatively; it was more solid than the first surface, mostly dry and wrapped in … fabric!

'Ash!' he said loudly, grasping the fabric and shaking the shoulder he'd found.

There was no response.

'Ash! *Ash!*' He shook her more urgently. 'Please be alive.'

Suddenly, almost so faint he thought his ears were lying to him–

'Hmm?'

'Ash! Ash, wake up!'

'Ar … Arthur?'

'Yeah, yeah, it's me!' Although he couldn't see her, he pulled the shoulder towards him and then wrapped his arms around the body that followed, squeezing tightly. 'Are you hurt?'

'Hurt? I don't think so. What happened, where …?' Her voice trailed off groggily.

'Well … I don't know how to say this but … we're inside the serpent's belly.'

'*What?*'

Arthur found a flashlight clipped to the Wolfsguard's flak jacket. He switched it on, momentarily blinding them both. When their eyes had adjusted to the brightness, they peered around.

They were surrounded on all sides by red fleshy tissue: the stomach sack. Ash pushed a hand against the lining. It was partly translucent and they could make out the tightening muscles beyond. It was almost elastic to touch and she knew it was impossibly strong without even testing it. Despite how large the serpent was, they were still cramped tightly together. The remnants of some the Jormungand's less digestible diet over the last few weeks were squeezed in beside them, including the empty uniform of one of the Wolfsguard and even an old, twisted bicycle. Ash grimaced when she realised she was lying on top of the remains of the stag and pushed herself off it, only to find herself standing in a black, foul-smelling soup.

'Ugh!' she moaned in disgust.

'Watch out!' warned Arthur. 'That's stomach acid. Bile. Don't stand in it for too long or your feet will start to burn.'

She leapt on top of the old bicycle and regarded Arthur.

'I kind of remember the serpent swallowing me,' she said. 'I thought I was done for. I guess I passed out. It got you too?'

'Not quite.'

'Then how—?'

'That's not important right now. We don't have much

279

time. I don't know how much air is in here but I'm guessing very little. I'm getting us out of here.'

'How?'

He pointed over their heads, through the stomach lining, to the serpent's strong back muscles. Right above them the flesh was an unhealthy dark green, seeping pus and ooze into the rest of the body.

'See that?' Arthur said. 'That is Loki's infection. It's what turned the serpent into a monster.'

'*Eew.*'

'Eew exactly. I'm betting that the scales are too tough to treat from the outside. And anyway, everyone knows that the best way to treat an infection is to deliver the medicine straight to the source.'

'You're going to give the serpent an injection?'

'Not quite,' he said, taking the pendant from around his neck and reaching up towards the infection. His hand pushed against the side of the stomach, stretching it enough so that he could almost reach the infected spot – almost but not quite. Ash pushed her way next to him and reached her own arm up, pushing with him through the elastic tissue.

They were inches from it …

Centimetres …

Millimetres …

And then …

The pendant touched the infection.

There was a bright flash of green light around Arthur and Ash, and for a moment they were totally blinded. When their sight came back, they found themselves standing in the same position, arms raised, pendant in hand. But they were back in the field near the lake, safe and sound.

And covered in a thin, stinking layer of stomach slime.

'Where's the Jormungand?' Ash said, lowering her arm to pick a glob of mucus from her shoulder and flick it away.

'There it is.' Arthur pointed through the grass. The serpent was there, no more than one foot long, flopping about on dry land. It was back in its original form, finally free of Loki's infection.

'Wow,' murmured Ash.

Arthur gently picked the serpent up in his two hands. He walked to the lake and then let it slide into the water. They watched in silence as the creature happily swam away.

'I could see the truth,' Arthur muttered, half to himself.

'Huh?'

'I saw the serpent as it really was, just for a split second.' He turned to Ash. 'Like how I saw the tree splitting. The

281

Norns told me that I'd be able to see the truth like Odin. Because of my eye.'

'So what does that mean?'

'I don't know. But if it helped us defeat the Jormungand then maybe, just maybe, we have a fighting chance after all.'

'No.'

The word escaped Loki's lips involuntarily, little more than an exhaled breath.

He had felt it, a loss deep inside him. It was like forgetting a treasured memory, only much more painful – and much more primal – than that. A part of him was gone. Not simply dead, but gone. And it left a gap in his soul that he knew would never be filled again.

'You!' he barked at the Wolfsguard closest to his throne. 'Summon my granddaughter. Bring me Drysi.'

Chapter Eighteen

After scraping most of the slime off, Arthur and Ash returned to the lake and washed their hands and faces. Ash retrieved her stick from where it had fallen when the Jormungand had first appeared and Arthur picked up his backpack. Then they both lifted their helmets and put them back on. As uncomfortable as wearing the heavy helmets was, Arthur was glad to be undercover once more. They resumed their journey towards Áras an Uachtaráin.

The sun was hotter than it had been and within minutes they were boiling again. The going got easier, though, when they reached the main road. The thoroughfare was a straight line of neat, smooth tarmac slicing right through the centre of the park. Although it left them exposed to view, both Arthur and Ash felt it was worth the risk to get to their destination more quickly and they hoped their disguises would be enough to stop anyone looking at them too closely. The road was wide enough for two lanes of traffic, with space to park cars on either side. Although today, of course, there were no vehicles in sight. A slim structure stood out on the flat horizon, the sunlight reflecting off the white stone column. It was right ahead of them, slap bang in the middle of the road. Arthur couldn't make out the statue on top of the plinth but Ash was familiar with it.

'That's the phoenix,' she told him. 'You know – the bird that rose out of the ashes?'

'Hmm …' he said thoughtfully. 'How far do you reckon?'

'A kilometre, probably less. Then the Áras is just around the corner.'

They walked down the remainder of the deserted road in silence, both deep in thought. With their destination in sight, now was their last chance to turn around, to give up, to run away.

Arthur's mind turned to Loki. Each step took him nearer to the god and, even though the pendant was silent, he could feel the Father of Lies' closeness in his bones. What would he do when they came face to face? How would he stop him? Could Arthur actually kill someone – even Loki – if he had to? The Norns had warned him that killing a god was a terrible thing, no matter who that god was. Could Arthur do what Odin hadn't? Could he end Loki's life?

Yes, he thought. I could. If I was forced to it, I could. But the question is, should I?

'Nervous?' Ash asked in a croaky voice after a while.

Arthur didn't answer her. He just took her hand and walked on in stolid silence.

The phoenix statue loomed larger. It was on the centre of a roundabout in the middle of a six-way crossroads. The second turn-off to the left led to the Áras, Arthur remembered from Ash's plan, and to Loki. They were heading slightly uphill and couldn't see the main road beyond the roundabout. But when they reached the crest of the slope, they both gasped.

Members of the Wolfsguard were everywhere, charging about, barking orders at each other. Some were in their wolf shapes, but most were back in their human forms. In the distance a high, intimidating fence cut straight across the road and into the trees on either side. Wolves were snarling and barking at the wild animals on the other side of the boundary, warning them to stay back, while members of the guard in human form were securing a large hole in the barrier. They were hastily erecting new segments of the chain-link fence to close the gap.

'They've managed to get the stampede under control then,' murmured Ash.

Arthur looked at her and realised he was still gripping her hand. He let it fall, wary of being spotted. He somehow doubted that the Wolfsguard went around holding each other's hands. He stood for a moment gazing up at the phoenix. The carved bird was soaring out of stone flames, reaching for the skies. He tried to take inspiration from it, but the closer he got to Loki, the more he wondered would he rise triumphant again or go down in flames.

He looked back at the mayhem ahead of them and braced himself.

'Ready?' he said.

'As I'll ever be.'

'Stay calm,' he whispered inside his helmet to no one in particular. 'Just stay calm.'

Suddenly a pair of guards surged up from the first turn to the left, carrying a roll of fencing between them.

'Outta the way!' shouted one.

Arthur's heart thudded against his ribs as he waited for their inevitable discovery. But the guards clearly hadn't looked closely at them; they were too focused on getting to the fence to notice the ill-fitting uniforms and small stature of the two supposed guards. Arthur didn't mind: it proved that they would pass muster if no one looked too keenly.

With hearts still beating frantically, they took a moment to watch the guards hurry towards the fence. Most of the animals seemed to have moved away from it, finally chased off by the wolves. Only a couple of wild cats and a monkey lingered by the boundary. A lion was roaring in response to the wolves' snarling, clawing at the wired fence. A couple of the guards were thrusting electrified prods through the gaps at the lion, shocking him any time he got too close for comfort, although this only seemed to enrage him further. The panther was much quieter, striding backwards and forwards along a section of the fence and watching each guard. A chimp swung from a nearby tree, pulling acorns off the branches and shooting them through the gaps. One soared right down a barking wolf's throat, blocking its air passage. After a few seconds of violent hacking, the wolf coughed the acorn back up and it landed on the ground covered in white mucus.

'Quick,' muttered Arthur behind his helmet as soon as his heart rate dropped. 'This way.'

They scurried off to their left, up a long straight road that led through a wide, white gate. They quickly came to a crossroads. The road they were on, stretched on in front of them, then curved right some distance ahead. The road that cut across it ran in a straight line from left to right.

'Do you think we should head straight on or go right? Both roads seem to lead to the Áras,' said Arthur.

'That's right,' said Ash. 'According to the map, the road in front leads round to a couple of sheds and garages, which I would bet are being used by the Wolfsguard now. But the way to the right will take us straight to the front of the house.'

'Great,' muttered Arthur. 'We can knock on the front door and see if they invite us in for tea!' But he agreed that it was best to avoid the Wolfsguard as much as possible, and so he followed Ash as she took the road to the right.

The avenue leading to the front of the Áras was lined with trees and they walked close to the edge of the road so they could hide if necessary. A plaque stood in front of each tree, detailing when it had been planted and by what foreign dignitary. It was quieter down here, but Arthur and Ash weren't the only ones walking the road. They spotted a group of guards coming towards them and quickly ducked into the cover of some bushes, waiting for them to pass. Despite the fact that their disguises had gotten them overlooked so far, Arthur didn't want to risk any closer examination by the wolves and he hoped the guards, who were deep in conversation, had not noticed them or their sudden disappearance.

As the group came nearer, Arthur and Ash could hear their conversation. The guard in front, who was carrying a rolled-up piece of fencing tucked under one arm and had a barrel of a chest, was talking.

'… nearly under control now anyways, but still!'

'I can't believe I missed all the fun,' whined another, lighter-framed guard.

'Aye,' said a third. 'Typical that it happens on my shift off.' He turned to the first one. 'So didja get de bloody kids who released them?'

'Yeah, we got 'em. Of course we got 'em. We chased after 'em. Led us right to dere hideaway! Turns out dere's a hundred kids hidden there. Straight to de camps for dem!'

The gaol! Arthur sensed Ash stiffening next to him. He was glad they'd hidden in the bushes now. If they had risked passing the guards, the wolves might have noticed their reactions. He thought of all of Ash's rebels being captured by the Wolfsguard, squeezed into boats and brought to the camps, taken away from their little hidden home to endless days and nights of pain, of hunger, of torture.

The group of guards passed right by the bush but didn't so much as glance in its direction.

'Arthur–' Ash gasped as soon as they were out of earshot.

'I know.'

'Arthur, the gaol.'

'Come on then,' he said, trying to sound braver than he felt and helping her out of the bushes. 'The only way to help them now is to stop Loki once and for all.'

They stepped out from behind the bushes and resumed their journey in the direction of the Áras, keeping close to the tree cover all the while.

Ash walked a few steps ahead of Arthur, her arms wrapped around her comfortingly with her stick clenched tightly in one hand. She hadn't said anything since they had left the guards behind. Neither had Arthur. He felt bad for the people at the gaol, he really did. But he knew that they didn't have time to mourn. The element of surprise was key. They'd lost enough time dealing with the Jormungand and in order to have any chance of saving everyone they had to keep going. He looked at her shoulders, hunched over as she stared at the grass, walking quietly forward.

Arthur glanced behind and in front of them. There

was no one in view. Taking a chance, he caught up to her, grabbed her by the arm, turned her around and pulled her against him, closing his arms around her tenderly. She rested her visor on his shoulder and he felt the convulsions shudder through her as the tears poured out.

'We have to keep going,' he said in a gentle tone. 'You know this. We can't stop.'

'Mm-hmm,' she said, snuffling and pulling back from him. He gripped her shoulders and looked into her eyes.

'We can do this, Ash.'

'Mm-hmm.'

'We can.'

'I know.'

Arthur nodded, then let go of her and they resumed their journey. Soon the great structure of the Áras appeared between the trees on their left.

Arthur had seen pictures of the president's home and had a clear vision of how it should look. He imagined the long central building and the main entrance flanked by four columns beneath a central pediment. The walls would be painted a pristine white, the surrounding gardens and lawns would be neatly trimmed and impeccably kept, and the Irish tricolour would flap proudly in the wind over the entrance. But this wasn't what met them as they reached the avenue leading up to the front door. The Áras itself had been painted a lurid neon green. The paintwork was uneven and the shade shifted all over where layers had been poorly applied. Words as high as Arthur were scrawled in red across the left-hand side of the building: 'Long Live Loki'. A mural as tall as the structure itself balanced it out on the other side. It depicted a grinning Loki in crimson washes, wearing a crown and giving two cheesy thumbs-up like a gameshow host. Stone steps led up to the front door but were partly covered by a temporary wooden ramp. The lawn in front of the Áras was a mess. All the flowers and plants had been ripped out by the roots and were strewn about the place, shredded to bits and ground into the muddy earth. The fountain in the centre of the lawn was spitting out green sludge and the flag over the pediment was also green, with one word inked onto it in bold red letters: 'Loki'.

'Oh–' Ash began.

'Look!' Arthur cut her off.

The tarmac driveway in front of the Áras was occupied by somewhere between fifty and a hundred members of the Wolfsguard. They were lined up in three straight rows facing the building and standing to attention, with feet and arms by their sides and batons or crossbows slung over their shoulders. From their stance, they were obviously waiting for something or someone.

Arthur and Ash were right at the edge of the tree cover now. There was nothing between them and the Áras but the lines of the Wolfsguard. They hunched down behind one of two thick trees that flanked the entrance to the gardens, peering cautiously around it to see what was happening.

'What do you think's going on?' Arthur whispered.

'Shh,' said Ash, nodding forward. 'The door.'

He turned in time to see the front door of the Áras swing open. The guards all clicked their boots at the sound, standing even straighter as somebody stepped out.

'Hail, General!' the guards barked as one.

Arthur couldn't believe what he was seeing.

Not only was the general Drysi, but she was walking!

She was wearing a black uniform similar to that of the guards. Her flak jacket was trimmed with bright-green edging and she wore crimson high-heeled boots that thunked against the wooden ramp as she made her way down to the drive. A sword in a scabbard was strapped to her waist and hanging down by her legs. She stopped in the middle of the tarmac, facing them all.

'At ease!' she said in a booming, stern voice. 'Now listen well. We have intruders!'

There wasn't as much as a murmur of surprise among the well-trained soldiers.

'And I don't just mean the intruders who caused that stampede,' Drysi went on. 'The Jormungand has fallen and the culprits are somewhere in the park. Most likely they are on their way here.'

Drysi swivelled and marched to one end of the first row. She turned and strode along the line.

'We are the Wolfsguard, sole defenders of the mayhem and destruction that Emperor Loki creates.'

She trailed a finger along each guard's chest as she passed, straightening flashlights on flak jackets or wiping smears off visors.

'Our single purpose in life is to serve him. To do what he needs us to do. And what he needs us to do is ensure we are strong enough, powerful enough, organised enough and ordered enough. Order. That is the motto of the Wolfsguard. *Order within Chaos.*'

She reached the second row and moved through the ranks, continuing her inspection, her movement crunching the gravel.

'We must be Order so that Loki can be Chaos. If we are chaotic and fail in our responsibilities, do you have any idea what will happen?'

She stopped then, halfway through the second row and right in the middle of them all.

'Do you know?' She paused, waiting for an answer, but

the Wolfsguard remained silent, as if they knew better than to interrupt her. 'Well, allow me to educate you. If *we* weren't ordered, *humans* would become ordered. They would rise. They would be the ones causing the mayhem. They would attempt to stop our great leader.'

She walked through the ranks again, her voice softening.

'Of course, they could never stop him. But they would try. They would think themselves brave and strong. When they're not. They're weak. And we need order to keep them weak.

'Look what happened today. Order fell. Some lazy guards allowed a few children to cause all that chaos. But we regained order and then look what happened. The animals are locked up securely, as are the children. All the children. That victory came from …'

She came to the edge of the line and clacked her heels together defiantly.

'… order.'

Drysi strode quickly around in front of the troops once more.

'So you will ensure that order is maintained. Go out and find these new intruders. Find them for your fallen brother, the World Serpent. Find them for the chaos they have caused. Find them for Wolf-father Loki. And when you find them, bring them directly to me.' She smiled to herself, an expression that sent shivers down Arthur's spine. 'I want to deal with them myself.' Her eyes flickered towards the end of the avenue and, for a brief moment, Ash was certain they had fallen on her. 'Dismissed!'

The rows of guards turned as one to the right and marched off while Drysi strode quickly back up the ramp towards the Áras. Once the sound of the soldiers had receded into the distance, Arthur and Ash crept out from their hiding place.

No one was left in front of the Áras now.

'There are no wolves guarding the front entrance,' mumbled Ash. 'That's a little strange. Surely Loki would have someone on guard at the front of his palace, especially if he knows we're here. My spidey-senses are tingling. It looks like a trap.'

'Probably is,' agreed Arthur.

'So we go around the back? Find another way in?'

'No. We go through the front door.'

'But didn't you see the way she looked right at us? Like she knew we were here?'

'Of course I did. It's possible she could sense us.'

'And despite that you still want to go through the front door?'

'If we've lost the element of surprise it doesn't matter

any more. We're here. I came here to see Loki – and to defeat Loki – and that's what I'm going to do.'

'What about her, though? The lovely general? She could be waiting for us inside with a bunch of guards.'

'You've forgotten something, Ash. They've lost the element of surprise too. We know there's a trap. We know she's waiting for us just beyond that door. Anyway, Drysi's a puppy-dog. We can take her and any guards she has with her. Don't forget we have this.' He pulled the hammer out of his bag and dropped the backpack on the ground. 'It's more than a match for a few of Loki's wolves.'

He offered a hand to Ash. 'You coming?'

'I guess so,' she said, taking his hand, squeezing it once and dropping it again.

They walked up the deserted avenue, eyes darting left and right searching for any signs of movement, and took the steps up to the front door. Arthur tried the handle. It clicked open without a problem. He nodded to Ash, who grasped her stick protectively in front of her. Raising his hammer, Arthur pushed the door slowly inwards.

The corridor they were faced with was painted white, with thick Celtic-knot carpeting on the ground. Huge modern paintings hung on either side of the long corridor, with real crystal chandeliers hanging from the plasterwork ceiling. The corridor was empty, except for Drysi, who was striding towards the far end of the hallway, her back to them.

Arthur and Ash stepped inside and quietly pushed the door shut behind them.

'Well, well,' said Drysi at the click of the door, stopping but not turning. 'Arthur Quinn and Ash Barry. I thought that was you.'

CHAPTER NINETEEN

Drysi turned to face them, a broad smile pasted across her face. She was alone – no guards in sight.

Arthur and Ash twisted the helmets off and let them fall from their hands. They flumped onto the soft rug and rolled away silently before landing on the surrounding wooden floor with a hollow noise. Arthur was glad to be out of the constricting headgear: he wiped the sweat from his brow while Ash pulled some loose strands of hair out of her eyes.

'How did you know it was us?' Arthur asked, trying to appear as unperturbed as Drysi seemed.

'I was expecting you. And us wolves have a very good sense of smell, you know,' said Drysi. 'Even under all that dreadful stench, I still recognised your scents. Arthur, you smell of boy and cheese pizzas and something else I can't quite put my finger on. Maybe it's anger, maybe it's fear. It could just be sadness and longing. And Ash, you smell like your mother's baking, although I know it's been a long time since you've had that. Yes, your mother's baking. And there's something else there too. Something I don't recognise. An urge to fight, perhaps. Yes, you smell of fight.'

'You think you know me,' said Ash, still bristling at the mention of her mother.

'I do know you. I lived with you. I was your pet puppy.' Drysi's nose turned up at the memory. 'But that was in another time, another world. Which makes me wonder, how can you be here, Arthur?'

If Drysi remembers my reality, Arthur wondered, does that mean Loki and Hel do too?

'I have a few tricks up my sleeve,' Arthur told her, smiling. Literally, he thought, feeling the ribbon tucked under his right cuff. He moved forward and Drysi stepped back.

'I'm here to see Loki.'

'Hmm. Well, that's not going to happen, Arthur.' Drysi turned suddenly and walked away from them, moving out of sight down a perpendicular corridor.

'Wait! Come back!' Arthur called after her, but she gave no response. They could hear her steps drawing further away. They looked at each other, confused by the girl's actions.

300

'Should we follow her?' whispered Ash.

'I guess so. She might lead us to Loki. Let's go.'

They walked forward, cautiously turning the corner that Drysi had disappeared around, and found themselves in another hallway. It was almost identical to the first corridor but, instead of paintings on the walls, moulded stucco plasterworks portrayed scenes from Greek mythology. Half-naked men and women watched silently from panels along the wall. Marble plinths stood all along the left side of the hallway, with brass busts of past Irish presidents fixed to each one. Arthur recognised the more famous heads of state. Drysi had stopped further down the corridor and was facing them again. She was holding the most recent bust in her arms, along with its marble plinth, cradled like a baby, as if it weighed almost nothing.

'I don't know how you survived, Arthur, but I'm going to do something Wolf-father Loki has never managed,' she said. 'I'm going to kill you, once and for all.' In a sudden blur of movement she launched her weapon at Arthur. He barely had time to register the last president's calmly smiling face soaring towards his head before the plinth smashed into him and blackness took hold.

301

Ash dropped to Arthur's side. The bust had hit his head, knocking him out cold, and the plinth had fallen on top of him, trapping him underneath. A trickle of sticky blood oozed from a gash over his eye-patch. She strained to lift the plinth but was only able to raise it a few millimetres off his ribs before she heard footsteps running down the hallway.

Drysi was racing towards her, sword drawn, the blade glinting sharply in the chandelier light. Ash didn't have time to free Arthur so she laid the plinth carefully back down on him. Then, in one swift and practised motion, she picked up her staff and propelled herself up and forward, right at Drysi.

Drysi swung her blade as she ran, aiming straight for Ash's face, but blade met stick and was blocked just in time. Splinters flew from the staff, as the sword hacked a chunk out of it. Drysi took a step back and swung the sword lazily by her side, grinning menacingly at Ash.

'You expect to defeat me with a wooden stick?' She laughed.

'No, I don't. But a wooden stick with a reinforced steel core maybe.' She held it up for Drysi to see the undamaged steel pole through the gouge in the staff. The girl snarled viciously before slashing her blade through the air once more.

Ash met the sword swipe for swipe, keeping her eyes fixed on Drysi. Surprising the wolf-girl with her ability to fight, she drove her back down the corridor, away from Arthur, almost to the far end. She watched for the telltale change in posture that would let her anticipate Drysi's next move. A shift in her weight to her front foot told Ash that she was going to try an undercut; a slight straightening of her arm revealed that she was going to jab straight forward. Knowing where Drysi was going to attack next wasn't the problem; the problem lay in the other girl's unnatural strength and speed. Ash had hoped that she could divert one of Drysi's attacks long enough to land a blow on her head and knock her out. However, those attacks were coming so thick and fast that she never had a chance and, she realised with horror, she was slowly, inexorably being forced backwards. The power of Drysi's blows shuddered right up the staff into Ash's arms, vibrating the joints in her shoulders. The staff itself was a ragged mess. Whole chunks of wood had been sliced away by the sword and even the steel core – which Ash had thought would be unbreakable – was showing signs of wear, with dents appearing all over. Several times she was actually pushed backwards by the weight of the impact. She prayed each time that the unconscious Arthur, or even a ripple in the carpet, wouldn't catch her feet and trip her up. If she fell, she knew, she'd be done for. Truly and properly done for.

But still she fought. From the moment she'd found the staff in the attic in Kilmainham, she'd known she could put it to good use. She had practised for hours by herself in her cell, discovering a skill she hadn't been aware she possessed. She had Donal and some of the others come at her with their own makeshift swords or broomsticks, several at once, and she was able to fend them all off easily. She didn't know where this talent had come from, but she was glad she had it regardless. Nonetheless, facing off against a few untrained kids was a lot different to clashing with someone of Drysi's strength.

As she battled Drysi, a weird sense of déjà vu came over her. All of a sudden she could remember herself training in what appeared to be a Viking village, and a real Viking was there, instructing her. He looked like he should be dead – his skin was leathery and stretched – but he was still teaching her. She snapped out of the memory just as Drysi's sword rang off the staff again, pushing her backwards.

And that was when she tripped.

His head was throbbing when his eyes fluttered open. A chandelier hung directly above him, spinning rapidly, whirling up and down, side to side. The clang of metal against metal was coming from some place nearby, setting his teeth on edge. He tried to sit up but found he couldn't move. He reached his hand to his head, hoping to massage away the ache. His fingertips sank into something sticky. Blood, he realised with growing apprehension. Where am I? What's going on? I remember a head and–

Drysi! Drysi threw a bust at him. Arthur looked down at his chest, craning his neck to do so. The plinth was still lying on top of him, pushing down hard and, he now realised, making it hard to breathe. His hammer was lying by his right side. Beyond his feet, he could see Ash and Drysi battling near the other end of the corridor. One had an iron sword that looked like it could slice a man in two; the other had a wooden staff, falling to pieces as he watched.

He placed his palms flat against the plinth and pushed. The marble barely budged. He took a deep breath (or as deep as he could with the marble weighing so heavily on his chest), braced himself and heaved up a second time with all his might. The marble shifted fractionally, just a few millimetres, but enough to allow him to wiggle himself sideways until he managed to slide clear. As soon as he was out from underneath the plinth, he let it drop heavily to the floor. The rug was so thick there was hardly a sound – certainly nothing that could be heard over the ringing of the sword fight.

Still breathless and feeling woozy, he got to his knees and watched the fight. Drysi cut an intimidating figure, her sword swinging left and right, but Ash was doing surprisingly well. Then Ash seemed to be momentarily distracted and Drysi–

–is in a wheelchair, still swinging her sword. She is exactly as Arthur remembers her: a frustrated, angry girl with damaged legs. She lands another blow that–

–sent Ash tumbling backwards to the floor, the staff flying out of her grasp.

Arthur started breathing heavily. 'I know,' he said to himself. Hearing his own voice helped; it reminded him why he was here, what he had to do. 'I know the truth about her.' He had to help Ash, but first on his list of priorities was getting to his feet. One of his hands grasped the handle of the hammer and braced its head against the rug; he used it to slowly push himself upright. But as soon as he was standing, his head spun and his knees crumpled, incapable of taking his weight.

Ash, meanwhile, having rolled to the side to avoid a nasty downward cut by Drysi, was now on all fours, half crawling, half running from the girl. Drysi was striding after her, cackling as she approached. As Drysi lunged with her blade once more, Ash twisted, grabbing a chair that was sitting against a wall and throwing it between them. Drysi's blade plunged through the upholstery on the back of the chair. The general of the Wolfsguard swung her blade sideways, the force causing the chair to clatter away, then turned her attention back to Ash.

Ash, meanwhile, looked around desperately. She spotted two pieces of furniture further down the corridor – a large wooden chest and a coffee table across from it. Pushing herself to her feet, she raced towards them and forced her body into the tight space behind the chest, reached over the top and started fiddling with the latch on the front. It was stiff with age but, if she could just get it open, the chest lid was sturdy enough that it might give her sufficient cover from Drysi's weapon.

Drysi passed the last president and was now directly in

front of the chest. She pulled her elbow back and jabbed the sword forward. A dull *thunk* sounded as the blade dug into the wooden lid. The tip ground to a halt an inch before Ash's eyes as she pressed herself back against the wall. She quickly slammed the lid shut and the sword was wrenched from Drysi's strong grip, wedged in the hard wood of the chest. Drysi growled furiously, reached down and threw the chest aside; it flew down the perpendicular corridor.

As Ash started to scramble away, Drysi kicked out, catching Ash hard in the ribs and knocking her to the side. Ash screamed and was sure she had heard something crack inside her. Drysi lashed out again but, despite the pain, Ash grabbed her foot and yanked as hard as she could, sending the girl off-balance and crashing onto her back. The crimson boot came off in Ash's hand. She dropped it aside and tried pushing herself upright, but the pain in her side was too great and she dropped back to the floor like a rag doll. Drysi, meanwhile, was up again and moving in for another assault.

'*Drysi!*'

Arthur was on his feet. His legs were splayed wide, a stance designed to keep him stable. He was wavering slightly, still dazed and possibly concussed. His hammer was clutched tightly in his right hand, hanging down by his side. Beads of sweat popped out on his brow, mingling with the blood from the gash, turning it pink.

'Leave her alone, Drysi!' he said in a voice that tried – and failed – to hide how nauseous he was feeling.

'And why should I do that?' sneered the girl, standing mere feet from Ash, who was still sitting on the floor holding her ribs.

'*Why wouldn't you?*' Arthur spat back. He had to stop for a beat to catch his breath. 'Why would you continue to fight when it's so clear Loki doesn't care for you?'

Drysi's face flared a deep red. 'Don't you dare speak about the Wolf-father that way! He saved me after the tower; he looked after me when everyone – my father included – abandoned me. Don't say he doesn't care for me!'

'No, Drysi. He doesn't.'

Drysi screamed with rage and then, faster than the eye could see, she picked up a crystal vase from the coffee table and launched it at Arthur. He could feel his right arm moving by itself, pulled up by the hammer. The vase exploded upon impact and priceless crystal rained all about him. The hammer absorbed the force of the blow easily and he let it fall by his side once more.

'He let me walk again!' she ranted at him. 'He gave me back my legs!'

'No,' Arthur said sadly, shaking his head. 'That's not true. It's not true at all.'

Without warning, she was charging at him, her face contorted in fury, her hair streaming behind her. Arthur felt like a matador and she was the bull. He wanted to move aside. But he stood his ground. This was the only way she might listen to him. She grabbed him by the collar and, without so much as breaking a sweat, lifted him off the ground. His feet dangled inches above the carpet.

'Could I do this if he hadn't fixed me?' she snorted triumphantly. 'You dare speak of him like this?'

'I dare,' he said as calmly as he could manage under the circumstances.

'Then you die!'

'Listen to me, Drysi, *listen*!' He put his free hand around one of hers. 'He didn't heal you. He probably could have but he didn't. He just let you think you were healed. It's a trick, just another trick. He uses people. That's all he does. That's all he ever does! Once he no longer needs you, the magic will fail. You'll see the trick for what it is.'

'Lies!'

'It's the truth! I bet he barely speaks to you now that he has what he wants. I bet you hardly ever see him. You thought it would be better with Loki in charge, but it's not, is it? You're useful to him. You keep his army under control. You do his bidding. But he's practically forgotten about you, Drysi. If he wins – if he truly wins – he'll discard you. But this time, without Fenrir, you really will be alone.'

Arthur just had time to glimpse the wetness in her eyes before she threw him backwards. He slammed into a wall, destroying some of the stucco, and slid to the ground. In two great strides, Drysi was on him again, her hands curled into fists, ready to pummel him.

He shielded himself with his arms and shouted up at her. 'Drysi, look at your foot, look at your foot!!'

She stopped abruptly when she saw what he was seeing. Her bare, bootless foot was covered in ragged little cuts. Shards of crystal stood out along the side of her foot where she'd walked over the pieces of the broken vase. She lifted it and saw that even more punctured the sole. Some of the gashes were so deep that blood poured liberally from them, seeping into the carpet beneath her. She stepped away from Arthur, her mouth gaping in shocked silence.

'If you were truly healed,' he said sadly, 'if it wasn't all a trick, you'd feel that. But you don't, do you?'

They looked at each other quietly. Drysi was shaking her head. It was such a subtle motion that Arthur barely noticed it. Her cheeks were glistening with tears now and the redness drained from her face, replaced by a pallid, sickly yellow.

'Why–?' was all Drysi could utter before a green light burst from her chest.

'How are you?'

'I just need to rest a few minutes,' said Arthur, collapsing onto an antique sofa. 'What about you?'

'I think she broke a rib or two,' Ash said, using one hand to lower herself down carefully next to him, the other clasped to her side. 'But I can move at least.'

They looked at Drysi. After the green light had dissipated, she had appeared back in her wheelchair, slumped over and unconscious. Arthur had wheeled her into an empty room adjacent to the corridor. There was butter-yellow wallpaper patterned with gold on the walls, more thick carpeting on the floor and more antique furniture than Arthur had ever seen in one place. A broad white marble fireplace punctuated one wall and there was even more stucco work on the ceiling, covered in gold leaf.

'How did you know?' asked Ash, keeping her eyes on the still-unconscious Drysi. 'About her?'

'In the same way I knew about the World Serpent. I

suddenly saw the truth of the situation. I saw her as she really was,' he tapped his eye-patch, 'and I knew what I had to do.'

Just then, Drysi's head bobbed up. Her eyes opened, looked around to take in the new surroundings and noticed the wheelchair. Realisation set in.

'You did this,' she cried, not daring to look at them and opting to study the carpet instead.

'No, we didn't,' said Arthur. 'And you know we didn't.'

'Why?' She looked up at him. 'Why did he do this to me?'

'He needed you for the time being. He needed the order you brought to the army to maintain his chaos.'

'But why wouldn't he heal me properly? He has the power to do so.'

'Loki is a god of mayhem, of chaos, of mischief. Why do you think he's known as the Father of Lies? He prefers tricks to actually helping someone. He prefers illusions to actually caring about someone, even his own children. He would never have healed you. He just gave you a temporary trick. And now that you've seen through that trick, the spell is broken.'

'I can't believe he used me like that,' Drysi said, mostly to herself. 'I betrayed my own father to help him. I would have done anything for him.'

'I'm sorry, Drysi,' said Arthur, leaning forward and reaching for her hands. She yanked them away and clasped them tightly on her lap.

'We both are,' added Ash.

Drysi blinked her eyes and turned away from them, staring at the ceiling until the tears stopped. Minutes passed in silence as she studied the stucco. Eventually she said, 'See that plasterwork up there?' Arthur and Ash followed her gaze. Among all the floral patterns and curlicues were four depictions of different animals.

'They show some of Aesop's fables,' Drysi went on. 'Look at the one with the stork and the fox.' Arthur followed her pointed finger. The stucco showed a fox sipping water from a bowl, while a stork stood by, dipping its long beak in the pan. Drysi told them the fable.

'There was this fox, a wily trickster fox. And he had a pan of water. He invited the stork to drink from the pan but she couldn't. She couldn't sip the water because the pan was too shallow for her beak. The fox had all the water and laughed at the trick he had played. He'd won.' Drysi pointed to another part of the plasterwork, which also showed the fox and the stork but in a different position.

'So a few days later, the stork invited the fox to drink some of her water. She had it in a long bottle and was able to sip up the water easily with her slender beak. But the fox's tongue couldn't reach the water so he went thirsty. The stork had tricked the fox.'

Drysi looked right at Arthur. 'That's what you'll have to do,' she said. 'You'll have to trick the fox. It's the only way to stop him.'

'Where can we find him?'

'Go back out to the corridor and go through the door at the end. Then head upstairs. You'll find yourselves in another long corridor. He'll be through the very last door. He always has Hel there by his side. She's been unconscious since working the spell on you, Arthur. And … and he keeps the prisoners there as well.'

'Drysi, thank you.'

She turned away from them.

'Just … just trick the fox.'

CHAPTER TWENTY

The upstairs corridor was longer and narrower than the downstairs one, forcing them to walk in single file. The rugs were as lush as everywhere else in the Áras, the walls painted pristinely white and the ceiling a complex mass of stucco curlicues. Doors lined either side of the hallway, all covered in an ivory gloss that matched the walls. Arthur went first, keeping his eye fixed on the door dead ahead. It was just like all the others save for the brass plaque hanging on it that read in flowing calligraphy 'Throne Room'.

They'd left Drysi in the golden room on the ground level, still in shock over Loki's trick. Ash was leaning on her staff for support – almost totally stripped of wood by now. The cut over Arthur's eye-patch had stopped bleeding, but a large purple and green bruise was flourishing around it. He stopped a stride away from the door and turned to Ash. She put her free hand on his shoulder and squeezed. He looked at the door again and could see his reflection in the plaque. His face was drawn and even more exhausted-looking than he felt.

He turned to her and raised his eyebrows weakly, too tired to speak.

She smiled feebly back and shrugged: as good a 'let's go' as he was likely to get.

Arthur gripped the handle and turned.

He had expected a room around the same size as the one where they'd left Drysi. But this was not what he was met with.

Inside was a cavernous hall with a vaulted ceiling that reached so high he felt a wave of vertigo just gazing up at it. Brass chandeliers hung down, filled with candles burning with huge flames. The walls were sandstone, windowless but with long tapestries adorning them at every available spot. They depicted Loki in a variety of heroic poses: riding the Jormungand, battling a giantess, wrestling a bear, standing topless at the edge of the Grand Canyon with the sunlight gleaming behind him and a plaid bandana tied on his head. The floor was covered in a mosaic of tiny marble tiles, arranged to portray Loki's massive grinning face.

The hall had been alive with noise when Arthur had pushed the door open but now, as they stood on the threshold, the silence was so sudden and so thick he would be able to hear a pin drop.

Members of the Wolfsguard stood on either side inside the door and one slammed it shut as soon as Arthur and Ash stepped into the room then returned to his position. But it was the other occupants of the room that had Arthur and Ash staring. To the left was a gigantic domed cage hanging between the chandeliers. It was like an oversized birdcage, complete with a pan of water, a tubular feeder full of seeds and nuts and a hanging iron bar for the birds to roost on. As soon as Arthur and Ash had appeared in the doorway, the gigantic birds had flown off the roost and flocked to the base of the cage, squawking agitatedly at Arthur and Ash. These weren't ordinary parrots or budgies, however. They were Loki's prisoners. Arthur spotted his dad there, with a bright yellow beak replacing the lower part of his face, wings for arms and claws for feet. Everything else – the torso, the legs, the clothes and, worst of all, the eyes – were Joe's. Ash's family were there too and the Lavender siblings and even Fenrir – all transformed into man-sized birds. Arthur heard Ash gasp next to him.

'Dad …?' he croaked. The birds all cawed piercingly in response.

'*Silence!*' ordered a hundred voices together.

The hall was laid out for a banquet, with several large round tables arranged throughout the room. Each table was covered with a white tablecloth, golden cutlery and candelabras. A wild boar, spitted and roasted with an apple wedged in its mouth, was on the centre of each table. The diners were sitting on gilt-covered chairs, watching Arthur and Ash carefully. There were men and women, boys and girls, all of them in their finest garments and all of them with Loki's sneering face.

The birds quietened when the hundred Lokis shouted.

Beyond the banquet, next to a golden throne near the opposite wall, was Hel. Her arms and legs were splayed and she hovered a few feet above the ground, held suspended in a spherical, glowing green vortex. Her eyes were shut and Arthur knew by looking at her that she was unconscious; Drysi had told them the truth. Despite her resting state, there was no softness in her features; her face was still the twisted and craggy thing he'd seen in the graveyard.

I have to get to her, he thought. That's what I have to do.

'Hello, Arthur,' said the hundred Lokis in one voice. 'What a pleasant surprise!'

Arthur didn't respond. He walked forward, heading straight for Hel.

'Arthur, wait!' called Ash, running after him.

'It's OK,' he whispered to her. 'You stay here.'

'But the Lokis—'

'They're just tricks, illusions.'

He turned and kept walking in the direction of the banquet.

'Don't we scare you, Arthur?' the voices said together.

'Not any more.' He weaved between the tables. The Lokis looked up at him with those grinning expressions.

Suddenly, one of the Loki-women in front of him stood up. It was strange to see the Father of Lies in a billowing ball-gown – a sight that would have sent Arthur into a fit of laughter under normal circumstances – but he had no time to appreciate the get-up before being punched backwards. He soared onto the nearest table. The boar toppled away from him and onto the tiled floor. The Lokis around the table all stood up and grabbed for Arthur, twenty hands all reaching forward to pull him apart.

Two hundred clawing fingers scrabbling at him.

And all the voices repeating his name as one.

'Arthur. Arthur. Arthur.'

Before their fingers could even reach his neck, he had the pendant out. He flung it at the nearest Loki face and, with a blinding flash of green, they were all gone.

Arthur climbed down from the table, retrieved the

pendant and looked around. Only one Loki remained – the real one. He was sitting on the throne next to Hel's weird vortex, his fingers tapping impatiently on the golden wolf armrests. He was wearing the pinstriped suit he'd been so fond of in Arthur's world and a golden antler-shaped crown, with emerald gems embedded all over. He watched Arthur closely, a wry smile fixed on his face.

Slowly, deliberately Loki started clapping his hands. The sound echoed against the stone walls. He stepped off the throne and walked in Arthur's direction.

'I feel like I should congratulate you,' he said.

'For what?' Arthur took a step back, bristling.

'For still being alive, to begin with, and for making it here … to this reality. I don't know how you managed it, but you did. Who helped you?'

'Nobody.'

'Somebody did. Somebody gave the world the dream about Hel to help you. Didn't work, though, did it? You didn't find her soon enough. And then somebody brought you back to reality, despite Hel's best efforts. As you can see, it took quite a lot out of her. Somebody's been helping you all along. So I'll ask you again. Who?'

The Norns! Arthur realised suddenly. They must have planted the dream. He kept his facial features even, hoping he wouldn't give anything away to Loki.

'Not going to tell me?' he said when he saw Arthur's fixed expression. 'No matter. As you will see I kept an insurance policy for just this sort of eventuality.'

With one loud clap, there was another blinding flash of green. When Arthur could see again, the prisoners were no longer in the cage, nor were they still bird-people. But they weren't normal either – their mouths had been sealed shut. Where their lips should have been was just smooth flesh, as if they had never had mouths to begin with. They were all in stocks, bent over with their heads and hands poking through the tight holes. They tried to pull themselves back out but a padlock on each stock held them firmly in place. Above them, a giant curved blade swung over and back from the ceiling. With each swing, it descended an inch closer to their necks.

'*No!*' screamed Ash, rushing to pull at the padlocks. 'Let them go! *Let them go!*'

'I might set them free if Arthur tells me who's been helping him,' said Loki, keeping his eyes trained on him.

Arthur whipped around to face him. 'Fight me,' he fumed.

'What?' For the first time, Loki seemed genuinely surprised.

'I said fight me. If you beat me, I'll tell you who's been helping me. But you have to free them first.'

'Why should I?'

'Because they're worth nothing to you. What you really want to know is who's been helping me. If you know that, you can stop them and then you'll have won. For good. But if you kill our families, you'll never find out. Never!'

'Arthur, no!' Ash shouted.

Loki stared at Arthur as if considering his offer and all the while the pendulum-blade continued to fall. In a few more minutes it would slice through the prisoners' necks.

Arthur ignored Ash and said to Loki, 'It'll be a fair fight. At least on my part.' He held up the hammer and pendant in one hand and then threw them behind him. They landed next to the pair of guards.

'Heh,' said Loki. 'I like the odds. Guards, take those things out of my sight!'

As the guards did his bidding, Ash ran to Arthur and grabbed him by the shoulders.

'Arthur, he'll kill you!'

'Trust me, Ash, just trust me.'

'But–'

She was cut off when he gave her the smallest of winks.

Arthur looked past her at Loki. 'You have to free them first. That's part of the deal.'

The god rolled his eyes. 'Fine!' He unhooked a full hoop of keys from his belt and flung them at Ash. They slipped out of her grip as she tried to catch them, but she hurriedly snatched them from the floor and ran back to the stocks.

'I've been looking forward to this for a long time, Arthur,' said Loki.

'You're not the only one,' Arthur replied. And without another second passing, without another swing of the pendulum, without another beat of his heart, the boy ran at the god.

The edge of the blade glinted on each rotation as it swung ever closer to the prisoners' fragile necks. Ash ran right to the nearest stock, which held a man she didn't recognise. His hairline was receding but he had the same jawline as Arthur so she guessed this must be his dad, Joe. She rattled the hoop of keys, looking through them, trying to work out which was the right one for this padlock. There were dozens of keys, of various lengths, colours and designs. Joe thrust his head about in the stock as much as he could, his eyes wide, and grunted in the back of his throat as if to get her attention. She looked at him quizzically as he nodded in the direction of the padlock and then back at the keys.

'I'm trying my best,' she said.

He shook his head as if to indicate that wasn't what he was trying to say. He squinted furiously at the lock, forcing Ash to take a close look. It was a thick and heavy brass construction with the keyhole in the front. After examining it for a few seconds, she came to understand what Joe was trying to say. If the padlock was old and brass, then the key probably matched it.

Ash looked at the hoop again and counted eight tarnished brass keys just like the lock. She chose one at random and tried twisting it in the hole. She was met with resistance. Keeping one finger wrapped around that key so she wouldn't lose track, she tried the next brass one. Again, the same tight resistance. She held onto it, put the third key in the hole and turned. The padlock clicked open. She knocked it to the ground. Joe immediately pushed upwards and the top fell sideways. As soon as he stepped away from the stocks, the flesh above his chin split open into a mouth once more. One down, seven to go. Ash moved to the next stock and started the process all over again.

As he ran at Loki, Arthur grabbed for the nearest thing

at hand: a dinner plate from one of the tables. The meal was half eaten and most of the food was still stuck to it as he Frisbeed it right at the Father of Lies' face. Loki put an arm up and the plate exploded against his elbow, throwing some brown-coloured sauce into his eyes, momentarily blinding him. When he had scraped it away he looked around, but Arthur was nowhere to be seen. He was about to call out to him when he noticed the boy's legs disappearing under one of the tables beside him.

Arthur didn't know if his plan would work. He wasn't even sure it was a proper plan. There was certainly no strategy involved, despite the confidence he'd shown only seconds before. His goal was simple – to reach Hel. If he managed that, then he might be able to wake her up. Or, rather, he hoped he'd be able to wake his mother up. She was the only one with the power to make things right again.

Suddenly Loki was standing over him. He had the table in one hand, lifting it high. Arthur saw the fingers let go just in time to roll out of the way, as the table smashed back down onto the hard tiles, its legs collapsing and its top crashing to the floor, sending splinters and cutlery flying everywhere. The god threw back his head and laughed crazily, while Arthur threw himself under another table.

'Oh, I am having fun,' said Loki, gleefully eyeing his prey. 'Ready for round two?'

Ash was reaching the halfway point. After freeing Joe, she got Stace out, who held her in a tight embrace. Following a few too many seconds of it, Ash pushed her away and moved on to the next stock. The first key she tried on the next padlock turned instantly and a tall, powerful-looking man with bushy black hair and a beard reared out of his stocks. He was probably Fenrir, Ash guessed, remembering the story Arthur had told her about the other reality. Next to him was the only girl she didn't recognise, but she knew her name – Ellie Lavender.

Those already freed went to work on the rest of the stocks, pushing and pulling at the padlocks, trying to break them. But Ash knew it wouldn't be as easy as that; Loki's magic would ensure that only her keys could free them. The pendulous blade was dangerously close now and Ash could see dark smudges of dried blood on its edge. Finally, with a click, Ellie's lock opened and Ash moved on to her mom, keeping one finger on the used keys as ever.

With a flick of Loki's wrist, the second table was flung aside. But Arthur was already moving. While Loki was throwing the table, Arthur grabbed the edge of a tablecloth from the nearby wreckage and hurled it over the god. He tackled Loki and the two of them sprawled to the floor. As the god roared with frustration and tried to wrestle the tablecloth away, Arthur had already pushed himself to his feet and fixed his attention back on Hel. He turned towards the throne once more, but found himself tugged back violently as Loki shot an arm out from under the tablecloth, grabbing his ankle. Losing his footing, Arthur fell forward towards the hard floor and only avoided serious head trauma by throwing out his hands at the last instant. He struggled to break the god's grip, kicking desperately while using his arms to try and scrabble forwards. But the tablecloth was melting from the god and he was able to reach out and grab Arthur with both arms now. He flipped the boy over and pulled him so close to his face that Arthur could smell boar meat on his breath.

'Oh, Arthur, don't you know we're not playing "chase",' he spat. 'We're playing "pummel-Arthur-Quinn-to-a-bloody-pulp"!'

The last prisoner in the line of stocks was Max. By the time Ash reached him, the blade was so low she had to duck for fear it would cut her and she could feel the disturbance of it in the air. She'd been ignoring the noise of Loki and Arthur's battle as much as possible, concentrating instead on freeing the prisoners. But then, without warning, a single agonising, piercing scream broke through her focus. The keys slipped from her hand and clattered onto the tiles.

'*No!*' she cried in anguish, picking them back up. She couldn't remember which keys she'd used. There had only been one more brass key, which would surely have opened Max's padlock. But now she had to go through all eight again. And the blade was swinging so low that the very swish of it was deafening and the hair on Max's head stirred as it passed.

Suddenly Fenrir stepped to the side of the stocks, reached up and grabbed the blade in two massive fists as it reached the end of its arc. Using all his strength he managed to force the blade to a stop as it descended – but only just – and the steel sliced through the flesh of his palm as he held it steady. Ash looked up at him gratefully – any extra seconds would help – but his face was red with exertion and she could see the blade shuddering in his grasp as if it was desperate to continue its pendulous plummet. She realised he couldn't hold it for long.

She turned back to the lock. They were almost out of time.

Loki smacked one hand hard across Arthur's cheek, his needle-sharp nails tearing deep into the flesh. Not only could Arthur feel the slivers of skin ripping: he could hear them. The sound was almost as bad as the pain itself, and he screamed in agony. He didn't want to do it, didn't want to show any weakness in front of Loki, didn't want to give him the pleasure. But he couldn't help it. The scream burst from his lungs involuntarily.

The Father of Lies laughed. 'Now, this game is *way* more fun!'

He stood and flung the boy high into the air. Arthur felt like a rag doll being tossed about and he could almost touch one of the chandeliers before he started to fall, hurtling back towards the hard floor, spinning dizzyingly. The tiles rose to meet him rapidly and he could see his terrible fate coming; he'd smash into the ground and either be instantly paralysed or instantly dead. Then, as he plummeted down, Loki casually pulled back his arm and thrust it forward, catching Arthur in the stomach and sending him soaring across the hall.

The last key! Ash had tried all the others before she heard the reassuring click of the lock. Fenrir was gritting his teeth as he strained to keep the blade in place and a trickle of dark blood ran down between his fingers. The blade was so low that they couldn't throw the top part of the stocks open fully, but she managed to lift it part way and Max squeezed his head and hands through the gap. As soon as he fell free, landing on his backside with a thump, the stocks and the blade disappeared with a green flash.

Ash turned in time to see Loki approaching Arthur. The boy was slumped against the side wall, his eyelids fluttering rapidly as if caught in a dream – or a nightmare. Without giving it a moment's thought, she rushed into the narrowing gap between her friend and the god, and faced Loki.

He stopped and smirked maliciously at her.

'Do you really think you can save him, Ash?'

'Not alone, she can't.'

Whoever had spoken laid a hand on her shoulder. She

looked around to see Joe standing there, glaring at Loki. Max appeared to take her left hand and Ellie took her right. Then Ex, Stace, Fenrir and her parents clustered in behind her, hiding Arthur from the Father of Lies.

Loki's grin grew wider.

'All right,' he said, taking a step back. 'We'll do it your way.' He clapped his hands.

Instantly, the throne room vanished. The walls, the tiled floor, the chandeliers, the banquet tables, even the massive throne itself, all crumbled and floated away like ash. They were standing in the middle of a battlefield. Grey, churned earth stretched away in every direction with rubble, broken weapons and discarded army uniforms strewn all over. There were blackened and burnt trees in one direction, rolling mounds of mud in another. The sky was a matching charcoal, black clouds on the horizon threatening rain. There was no sign of life anywhere, no buildings peppering the landscape, no soldiers to fight whatever war had wrought such destruction.

Except that we're the soldiers, thought Ash, as she looked around. We're the ones who have to fight.

Even the atmosphere was lifeless; there was a church-like silence, waiting to be broken at any second. Hel was still floating in her vortex, a few hundred yards away.

'He's gone,' murmured Ellie.

Instinctively, Ash whipped around to check on Arthur, but he was still there and still unconscious. Ellie hadn't meant him. She had meant Loki. Loki was gone.

As if on cue, they heard a buzzing in the distance. It was barely audible at first but deep enough for Ash to identify it as an engine. She'd come to recognise the sound after months of keeping her ears pricked for similar noises in the flooded Dublin. It was an engine. And it was getting closer.

'There,' said the tall boy, who had to be Ex Lavender, pointing a long finger towards the horizon.

A dark smudge hovered over the battlefield, getting nearer and larger with each passing second.

'Run,' said Ash, her voice lower than she intended.

'What?' someone asked; her mother, she thought.

'I said *run!*'

She turned on the spot, planning to grab Arthur and drag him if necessary, but Joe was already there. He hitched his arms under the boy, cradling him like a baby, and then they both turned and followed the others, who were sprinting for cover behind a small hillock in front of them. The approaching plane started firing as they scrambled over the uneven terrain, sending a barrage of bullets into the ground behind them.

Ash didn't need to turn to know who the pilot was.

They were up and over the mound of earth just as the plane spat out one last *rat-a-tat* and swooped upwards. They could hear the god howling with laughter as he passed overhead. They went sliding down the far side of the hillock and into a trench that was partially sheltered by a wooden roof protruding from the side. Two inches of brown water sat at the bottom of the ditch. It was so icy that they shuddered the instant they hit it, but nevertheless they all hunched low and close together to get as much cover as possible. Ash took a chance and peered out from under the overhang to steal a look at the plane as it turned.

It was like something from those World War II films that her dad insisted on watching every Sunday afternoon. It had a pair of slim wings and a propeller on the nose that cut through the air. The single pilot could be seen through the cockpit dome: Loki, in full World War II pilot gear, including a leather helmet, large goggles and a brightly coloured, jaunty-looking silk scarf wrapped around his neck. He had even grown a twirling moustache that ended on either side of his nose in a question mark. An oversized machine gun protruded from each wing of the plane.

As Loki turned the aircraft around for a second onslaught, Arthur groaned in Joe's arms.

She turned to him. 'You're awake!'

'What happened?' he managed to croak out.

'Long story short, we're in the middle of a battlefield and Loki's firing at us from what appears to be a World War II Spitfire.'

'Just another day at the office then,' he murmured. When he saw who was holding him, he gave his father a tight embrace.

'I'll get us out of this,' he whispered.

Joe seemed uncertain. 'OK,' he said, 'but who are you?'

Although he understood that Joe couldn't know who he was, this remark stung more than Arthur had expected. He quickly wriggled out of Joe's grasp and turned to Ash, hiding his devastated expression from his father.

'Is Hel here?' he asked. 'If I can get to Hel, I think I can bring an end to this.'

'Well, I have good news and bad news for you then. The good news is she's here. The bad news is she's halfway across the battlefield.' She hooked a thumb out of the trench in the direction she'd seen the woman. By the rising sound of Loki's engine, he was closing in quickly for another assault.

Arthur looked in the direction of the sound and then urgently back to Ash.

'You have to distract him,' he said. 'All of you. Keep his attention on you. I need to reach Hel.'

'Arthur, you can't–'

335

'I have to, Ash. It's the only way we can stop Loki. I'm sure of it.' He looked at the others – and at Joe in particular. 'You don't know me. You once did, just not any more. But you have to trust me. Distract Loki. Do whatever it takes. Just buy me enough time to get to her. And then hopefully this will all be over.'

'I say we just hide here,' said Mr Barry quietly. 'Wait out the storm.'

'No,' said Joe, staring at Arthur. 'I trust this boy. We should help him. We need a distraction but we don't have any weapons and we barely have any cover.'

Ex dug his hand into the soggy earth and came back out with a fistful of muck. He felt the heft of it in his palm and showed the rest of them. Then he nodded in the direction of the plane. The others looked dubiously at him, but since no one offered any better ideas, the kids followed his lead, then the parents and finally Fenrir.

The plane was almost upon them once more.

Joe, holding his own pile of mud, nodded at the boy he didn't know was his son. As Arthur nodded back, he was sure he saw a glimmer of recognition in his father's eyes.

Loki chose that exact second to open fire on the trench. Even from the depths of the ditch, they could all feel the vibration of the hundreds of bullets gouging into the earth and they crouched even lower into the sludge, hoping that the wooden roof would protect them. The plane swooped low over the trench with the machine guns aiming two lines of shots at them.

As it passed over them Joe was first on his feet. He raced to the top of the hillock, swung back his arm like a pitcher in a baseball game and launched the mud pie at the fast-retreating plane as hard as he could. The clump of brown goo fell well short, but this didn't stop the rest of them joining in.

Arthur took his chance and scaled the side of the trench, heading in the direction that Ash had indicated. Glancing around quickly, he saw the full expanse of the battlefield for the first time – and Hel's floating green vortex in the distance. He raced off across the field, praying the distraction would work.

Loki hadn't noticed the mud pies, but the movement of his targets had attracted his attention as he turned the plane as sharply as possible to come around for another assault. He threw the plane forward, more bloodthirsty than ever.

While the others reached for more fistfuls of mud, Fenrir felt the weight of the stone he had found. It was about the size of a golf ball, jagged on one side, smooth on the other. He had dug his fist deep in the mud to find such a treasure and he hadn't thrown it on the first strike, waiting instead for just the right moment. And it was coming – any second now. The wolf-man squeezed the moisture out of the mud in his fingers and compacted the sticky mess into a more solid ball. A thousand years of hunting as both man and wolf had sharpened Fenrir's instincts and reflexes to fine points. He knew exactly when to loose an arrow or spear, as he knew when to pounce. And, feeling the rough edge of the rock, he knew that the moment to attack was rapidly approaching. Loki drove the plane even lower and it was now soaring no more than twenty feet above the ground towards them. The god's cockiness would be his undoing, thought Fenrir.

And …

Now!

Fenrir's stone left his hand in a blur. It hit the cockpit glass head on, shattering the windscreen. Loki, taken by surprise, threw the plane into a sudden climb. The aircraft then dived into a loop-the-loop and it was here – while momentarily upside-down – that the god spotted the tiny figure of the boy racing across the battlefield.

Loki gave an angry hiss and swooped the plane after Arthur.

Bullets bit at the boy's ankles as he ran, churning through the marshy earth.

The plane sped up, finding fuel in Loki's magic.

Hel, as peaceful as ever, hung in the air.

And then–

Arthur tripped.

His foot caught on a dead tree root that was hidden under the mud.

He went down.

Close to Hel.

But not close enough.

The shooting suddenly stopped and the noise of the plane disappeared. Loki's laugh filled the battlefield as he strolled towards Arthur. The boy turned from the sound and looked up at Hel. He'd landed mere feet from the vortex but didn't have the strength to move towards it now. The woman still had her eyes shut and her face was still contorted evilly.

'Mum,' he rasped with the little breath he had left in his body. 'Mum … help me. Please, Mum, it's Arthur. *Please.*'

And he remembered being the little boy who fell off his bike.

And he remembered calling his mammy for help.

And he remembered her coming to his aid and comforting him, caring for him, wrapping him in her arms and promising she would always look after him, always keep him safe.

'Help me, Mummy!' mocked Loki, picking Arthur up off the ground. 'You think she can help you? She couldn't even help herself! She's no match for my Hel. She—'

'Loki,' said a voice. Arthur and Loki turned their heads together. The vortex was gone and the woman was standing on the battlefield now, facing them, her eyelids open. Her skin was smooth and beautiful, her eyes caring, her lips carrying the echo of a smile.

'Hel,' uttered Loki. 'You've come back to me.'

'I am not Hel,' the woman said. Her voice had a deep, magical resonance to it, as if they were hearing it from another world. 'I am Rhona Hilda Quinn, wife of Joe, mother of Arthur. I am the baby that you took, the child you infected, the girl saved by Fenrir. I am not Hel.'

Loki dropped Arthur and stepped towards the woman.

'Hel,' he said, hands stretched out peacefully towards her. 'My daughter. You are in there still. Come out to me. You are more powerful than the vessel.'

Arthur watched in horror as his mother's face twisted into Hel's contorted and diseased features.

'Father,' she said, 'I have returned.'

'Finish him then,' Loki said, a smile forming on his face. He waved an arm in the direction of the freed prisoners, who were now running towards them across the battlefield. 'Finish them all this time!'

Hel raised a finger and pointed to where Arthur was huddling on the ground. His lip started to quiver as he stared at his mother, a sure sign that tears were on their way. Hel's hand started to tremble and suddenly her face softened once more as Rhona took over. The pointed finger shot towards Loki.

'No,' exclaimed Rhona. 'He's … he's …' she stuttered, her face twisting and smoothing, her skin undulating, the muscles forming and reforming. Arthur was disturbed as he watched her transform from Hel to Rhona and back again, over and over.

Hel and Rhona; Rhona and Hel.

The face was good one second and evil the next.

His mother and his destroyer.

And all the while a tormented sound burst forth from the woman's throat.

Until …

Finally …

The face settled.

And Hel turned to Arthur.

She smiled wickedly then pointed her finger at him.

He closed his good eye in resignation. He'd lost. They'd lost. Time to die.

'I love you, Mum,' Arthur whispered, bracing himself for whatever was going to come.

Whatever blackness, whatever void, whatever end.

But nothing happened.

'*No!*' cried Loki. Arthur's eye shot open again. Rhona was pointing at the god now, her expression filled with determination.

'Mum?' Arthur scrambled to his feet.

'It's me, Arthur. It's really me.' She kept her eyes focused on Loki as she spoke. 'I'm pushing Hel out of my life for good. But before I lose her powers, I have one thing left to do.'

Arthur looked from his mother to Loki and knew straight away what she meant.

'You can't kill him!' he cried. 'The Norns said! It's a terrible thing! If you kill him, part of you will be gone! You could die!'

'But if I don't, we all will.'

'Listen to the boy, He– … Rhona,' said Loki, suddenly nervous.

'Mum, don't do it! Please!'

'I'm doing it for you, Arthur.' She glanced at him briefly, keeping her finger pointed at the Father of Lies. 'I love you, son.'

He saw it in her eyes then. The green energy building, about to blow Loki out of existence. He wanted to let it happen; he wanted to see Loki meet justice finally. But he couldn't. He remembered what the Norns had said and he couldn't bear to be without his mother again. Once was enough to lose her.

Arthur ran at Loki, summoning a strength he didn't know he had. In the distance, he heard Ash call his name and, out of the corner of his eye, he saw the green pulse burst out of his mother's fingertip, shooting right at Loki.

Arthur slammed into the god just as the lightning bolt crashed against his chest, wrapping his arms around him, clasping his wrist against Loki tightly. With a surge of brightness, they were gone.

Both of them.

CHAPTER TWENTY-ONE

In Asgard, the realm of the gods, the whole world is still. Silence has spread across the land. Birds wait in their nests, foxes huddle in their dens, gods cower in their halls. The wind and storms that have besieged them all for months, rattling their bones, pulling trees from their roots and tearing Asgard apart, have finally come to a sudden and shocking end. Some of the older gods who have held witness at similar – although not as devastating – tempests insist that this calmness is merely the eye of the storm. They are certain, they tell the younger gods, whose egos are not so large as to ignore the advice, that this peace can be broken. It is held in a delicate balance, like the weighting of a scale, and a tip in either direction could end the squall forever or plunge them into a deeper, harsher storm that will rip creation apart in minutes. And

though it is not always in the habit of gods to be correct –
especially the gods of Asgard, who most frequently think
with their bellies and their warring fists – this time they
are right. The calm is a sign that the tempest will either
end or flourish. It all depends on the actions in the next
few minutes of two figures lying by the Well of Urd.

Arthur Quinn sits up first. He can feel the dull
throb of wounds and aches all over but he ignores them,
pushing them to the back of his mind. There are more
pressing matters at hand than a bleeding forehead. He
can feel the craggy ground of Asgard under his fingertips
and hears the pounding sound of the waterfall rushing
into the nearby well. He looks over and sees the Father of
Lies lying by his side, half propped up against a boulder,
eyes shut, tongue lolling out. Arthur's own hand is next
to his. The stray end of Gleipnir flutters in a non-existent
breeze and touches off the god's fingers. A single flake
of snow drifts down onto the ground by their hands. It
worked, Arthur thinks to himself, pulling the hand away.
Just by touching the ribbon, Loki was saved, as Arthur
had been saved before.

He gets to his feet, sliding slightly on the dusty
ground. He steadies himself against the boulder and looks
around, then walks a few steps towards the pool. Though
the water still falls into the well, there is no sign of the

Norns. More snow falls, alighting on the ground and on his shoulders. It is only when he notices the flakes settling on the water that he realises it's not snow. A fleck lands on the tip of his nose and he picks it off with a fingertip. It is a pale steely colour and doesn't melt to his touch like it should. He rubs it between two fingers and watches as it smudges them with dirt. It's ash.

Arthur looks at the sky as it rains ash over Asgard. The dark clouds are still there, though the ash isn't falling from them. It's fluttering down from the tree at the top of the cliff, Yggdrasill. There isn't much left of the tree now. The half that survived the lightning strike is black with disease and rot. Small flames burn along the split and the branches have almost totally disintegrated. All that is left of Yggdrasill is half the trunk, and even that is crumbling and decomposing into ash and embers.

'*Arrrw?*' asks a moan from behind him. He turns in time to see Loki's eyes open. They look about him, at first with confusion but then with growing relief. They find Arthur on the barren landscape and fix on him.

'I'm back here?' he says, taking in his surroundings, his voice hoarse and croaking. 'No matter. I'll summon Bifrost in a minute to take me back to Midgard.' He looks at Arthur. 'You saved me.'

'No,' says Arthur. 'I saved her.'

Loki plants an arm around the boulder and pulls himself to his feet. He is momentarily shaky and leans back against the rock to steady himself.

'Hmm,' he says as a grin reaches from one ear to the other. 'You did, didn't you? But how, pray tell, did you manage that?'

Arthur holds up his wrist for Loki to see. There is no breeze to pick up the ribbon yet Loki sees it glimmering in the dull light.

'Is that Gleipnir?' he asks.

Arthur nods, keeping silent.

'Ah. I should have noticed it. I would have worked it out if I had.'

'You were too wrapped up in your own plans.'

'Ha! I suppose that is the problem with gods. Too wrapped up in ourselves to notice the rest of you. But you're not like the rest, are you, Arthur? You're not like the rest of mankind at all.'

Arthur doesn't reply. He slides his hands behind his back, and a finger and thumb start to work at the knot on the ribbon, loosening it. Loki pushes himself away from the rock and begins to pace.

'The last time I was here,' he starts, 'the gods betrayed me. They laughed at me. Like I was the trick and not the trickster. And then, when they discovered my plan for revenge, they banished me from this place. From my home. They bound me under the earth for what they thought was eternity – all that time spent in agonising torture. But they should have known that even that wasn't enough to stop me. Revenge is a very powerful motivator, Arthur. If you learn nothing else, learn that.'

As he paces, he gets closer to Arthur.

'But you, Arthur. You succeeded where the gods failed. Time and time again. You killed the Jormungand when they could only stun it. You found Fenrir after he escaped. You stopped a war. And even now, even though you shouldn't exist, you're still here! Standing before me. Nothing can stop you. But, as you've no doubt realised, nothing can stop me either.'

Loki comes to a standstill mere feet from the boy.

'Of course, it's to be expected, really. You are my grandson, technically. So I have a proposal for you. I haven't been a good grandfather to you. I haven't given you sticky Werther's Originals from my pocket and I haven't told you naughty jokes when your parents weren't listening and I haven't done all the other cutesy things granddads do in adverts on television.

'But despite all that I feel we have a bond, Arthur. True, I may not show it much – or at all. But I do care for you. I love you, as much as a god can love his meddling part-human grandchild. I know that really you're just going through a rebellious phase. Hormones are raging, you're probably finding hair in strange places and you just want a parental figure to act out against. Well, let me tell you something, Arthur. That doesn't have to be me.'

Arthur continues to listen, still fiddling with the knot of the ribbon out of sight.

'You are such a clever boy, Arthur. You tricked me. You even tricked your own mother into not destroying me. We could be great allies, Arthur. You and me. So what do you say? Huh? Let's join forces. Together we'll control all of creation. Together we'll do wondrous things. Together we'll be unstoppable. Totally unstoppable.'

'There's one problem, though,' Arthur speaks for the first time.

'Oh? And what's that?'

'You'd be unstoppably evil.'

Loki throws his head back and Arthur watches his pointed Adam's apple bob up and down as the god cackles loudly. Loki looks back at him, tears of joy streaming down his face.

'I take it that's a no then?' he asks between chuckles.

'That's a no,' Arthur confirms. He manages to get the ribbon off his wrist for the first time in almost a year. He palms it in his right hand, holding tight.

'Well, if you won't join me, you're against me. And I'm afraid, grandson or not, I'll have to put an end to your interfering. It's time to do things the old-fashioned way.' He clenches his hands by his sides, blue veins popping up along the skin, and takes a step towards Arthur. 'With my fists.'

Before Arthur can react, Loki hits him a blow that sends him spinning backwards. He tumbles to the ground and grinds to a halt on his front against the lip of the well. The little ring of stones around the edge of the water barely reaches as high as his shins. Loki leaps onto his back: a dead weight that forces something to snap excruciatingly loudly inside Arthur's body. For one terrible moment, as the pain washes through his back and chest, he is certain that his spine has been broken. But when he discovers that he can still move his legs and torso, he throws himself on his side, dislodging the god. Staggering away, he realises that the ache is pulsing from his left ribs.

Arthur is stumbling across the barren landscape when he hears Loki's rollicking laugh coming from behind him. Feet pound across the stony surface before a shoulder knocks into Arthur's spine. He cries out in agony and tumbles to the ground before he can so much as cushion the blow with his hands. His head slams into the rocky ground and the world spins.

The gash over his eye – which had partly scabbed over – gushes blood once more with the impact. He can feel the heat of the blood running down his face, over the eye-patch, and he can taste the metallic flavour on his lips.

Suddenly he is on his back and Loki is looming over him with a wicked sneer fixed on his face.

'No more talking,' he says through the smile. 'No more pleading. No one is here to save you.' He drops to his knees, one leg on either side of Arthur's chest. Loki wraps the long, bony fingers of each hand around Arthur's neck. 'This isn't as much fun as torturing you. But at least it's quick.'

The gripping fingers tighten around Arthur's throat, vice-like.

Arthur gasps as the flow of oxygen to his lungs is cut off.

He can't catch a breath.

Loki pushes his head back.

His neck is being slowly crushed and he can't catch a breath.

Ash, he's thinking. Dad, Mum, everyone.

He can't breathe. He can't breathe. He can't breathe.

And he's reaching up his hand.

His nose whistles as it tries to suck in oxygen.

And it's not enough.

It's not enough.

Ash, Dad, Mum, everyone.

Blackness darts around the side of his vision.

And Loki is smiling.

He's grinning.

He's laughing.

He's happier than he's ever been before.

He's finally squeezing the life out of Arthur.

And Arthur can feel it leaving him.

Ash, Dad, Mum, everyone.

And all Arthur can do is reach up his hand.

And he keeps reaching.

And he touches Loki's wrist.

And Arthur Quinn is about to die.

And.

And–

Water. There is water washing over him. It's so cold that it's almost burning; so cold and so unexpected that the shock causes Loki's hands to release his throat. Arthur sucks in a great gasp of air. He can breathe, he can breathe!

Loki rises to his feet and turns to look at the well. Arthur also lifts his head. This simple act sends pain shooting through his body. His ribs are still tender, his throat hurts with every breath and the fresh blood on his forehead continues to pulse out of him. But when he sees what Loki is looking at, he can't help but smile.

The Norns are standing in the well, staring right at Loki. Water is drying on the stones around him from where a wave has crashed over the rim of the well.

'You!' Loki is saying. 'It was you three. You have been helping him all along, haven't you?'

The Norns say nothing.

'*Answer me!* You have to answer me! You helped him, didn't you?' shouts Loki striding towards the rim of the well.

'We merely guided him,' says Urd, standing between her sisters.

'You can't do that!' Loki sounds like a petulant child to Arthur, who pulls himself into a sitting position. Every part of him still hurts, but he has to do it. He has to get moving. He looks at the ribbon still in his hand and he knows what to do.

'You can't do that!' Loki says again. 'You can't interfere in the deeds of gods and men.'

'We protect the tree,' says Verdandi. 'That is our most important purpose.'

Arthur is on his feet and he's shuffling towards the

boulders by the well. He's keeping his footsteps light, keeping his breaths shallow, keeping his one eye fixed on Loki's back. He reaches the rocks by the side of the well. Loki is still too focused on the Norns to notice him.

'So when the life of the tree is threatened,' says Skuld, 'we can act.'

'And you, Loki,' says Urd, 'you threatened the life of the tree.'

Arthur is walking around the boulder nearest the well when Loki spots him.

'You can't hide, Arthur Quinn!' he shouts at him. 'Get back over here! I need to kill you before I go back to Midgard.'

'No, Loki. You're going somewhere. But you're not going back to Midgard.'

'What *are* you talking about?' Loki jeers as he storms towards Arthur.

Arthur simply lays his hand on the boulder and then the god sees what he's been up to.

Gleipnir is coiled right around the rock, criss-crossing itself countless times so that the rock is held tightly in its grasp. There is no knot keeping it in place; the end is bound to the rest with magic, sealed forever. Loki's eyes follow the other end of the ribbon as it trails across the ground, between pebbles, over dust. Finally, his gaze follows it off the ground, as it rises towards him. He cries out in horror when he sees that the other end of the ribbon is wrapped around his wrist.

Arthur smiles. While Loki was preoccupied with strangling him, he had sealed it around the god's arm.

Loki tugs at it. His face turns beetroot red as he struggles to slide it off or snap it in two but, throughout the assault, Gleipnir stays firmly fixed around his arm.

Arthur has somehow, somewhere found the strength to slide the boulder up onto the lip of the well. It balances there, precariously. Like the eye of the storm, this could all end with a tip either way. Loki, still struggling to release himself from Gleipnir, turns his attention back to Arthur in time to catch the boy's smile.

'*Noooo!*' Loki screams, rushing towards him. But he's too late. Arthur throws all his remaining strength against the boulder.

It's as if time stops in that moment. The Norns turn to watch. Arthur stares. Loki can't take his terrified eyes off the boulder. It seems to take forever to grind over the lip before toppling down into the water with a slow-motion splash that barely even ripples the surface. Once it hits the water, it disappears from sight, sinking into the eternal depths of the well.

Loki watches as the ribbon grows taut above the

ground. He grasps it tightly, but this is a tug of war he can't win against the inexorable pull of gravity and Gleipnir simply slices through the soft flesh of his palm. He lets go with a cry and is dragged forward in the direction of the well. With a flash of light, he transforms into Joe.

'Arthur!' he pleads to the boy in his father's voice. 'You have to help me. I'm not really Loki. It was all a trick. I'm your dad! Let me go.' His feet scrape along the ground, struggling to find some purchase.

Arthur looks on with pity and shakes his head.

With another green flash, Joe becomes Rhona.

'I love you, Arthur,' she says. 'Even if you won't save me.'

'You're not fooling anyone, Loki,' Arthur says.

Loki transforms a third time. His feet keep sliding across the craggy ground, scrabbling frantically as he tries to pull himself back from the water's edge. He claws at the ribbon, doing his best to break free. But his best isn't good enough. Gleipnir is so strong that it shows no sign of being shredded by the rock lip around the well. In fact the reverse is happening. The ribbon is cutting a shallow dip in the stone itself. And all the while, Loki is pulled relentlessly on and on.

He has become Ash now, who is begging Arthur with pained eyes.

'You'll be sorry, Arthur,' she says. 'You'll realise that I really am Ash. Loki tricked you and now you're killing me.'

'Just give up,' Arthur sighs wearily. 'Can't you see it's over? You're nothing, Loki.'

And now Arthur remembers all that Loki has done to him, to his friends, to his family. As he recalls the pain, the hardship, the pure wickedness of every action, sudden red-hot anger rises in him.

'You're nothing, Loki!' he screams, his voice breaking on the higher register. 'You hear me? *Nothing!*'

The god is so shocked by Arthur's outburst that he instantly changes back to his own form. He falls to his knees and claws at the ground to try and slow his progress, but the ribbon keeps dragging him towards the well. As Loki's feet touch the water, he shrieks in anguish.

There is one flash of green after another as Loki becomes Ellie and Ex and Stace and Max and Morrissey and Fenrir and Donal and Orla and Drysi and Nurse Ann and even Ruairí and Deirdre and Luke Moran and everyone else Arthur has met in the past few months. All these faces plucked from Arthur's memories and meant to stir his sympathy. And finally, finally, Loki becomes Will. The boy with the platinum-blond hair and distinctive nose – the boy who betrayed Arthur – grips the edge of the lip. The rest of him is submerged in the water and Arthur can see that the muscles in his hands are white from the strain of trying stop himself being dragged completely under the water.

'Arthur ...' Will says. 'Help.'

'Goodbye, Loki.'

With one last burst of green light, Loki reappears. His face is an expression of torment, of dread, of fury. His hands grip tighter around the stones. But now three pairs of watery hands reach out from the cascade. They stroke his fingers, teasing them apart and away from the stones, making them slippery and slick.

He loses his grip.

And with one last look at Arthur, the Father of Lies, the trickster god, the god of mischief, the Lie-Smith, Loki, is gone.

CHAPTER TWENTY-TWO

It was the sunlight coming through the window that woke him.

He turned in his bed, still too tired to get up and hoping he'd fall back to sleep. It usually helped if he concentrated on the dream he'd just had, so in his mind's eye he visualised the well and the Norns' fingers and Loki sinking into a bottomless pit and–

Arthur sat bolt upright.

That wasn't a dream. It couldn't have been a dream. Could it …?

He'd been in Asgard one second and in his bed the next. He gingerly reached over to the locker, expecting his ribs to ache as he did so, but he didn't feel any pain. Picking up his phone, Arthur touched the screen and checked the time and date. It was 11:23 on a Sunday in early March.

Arthur flung back the bedcovers and swung his legs over the edge of the mattress. The pendant wasn't around his neck so he surveyed the room. It wasn't on the desk by the window either, where he always kept it. He fell to his knees; the only things under his bed were a stack of old *Beano*s, a burst basketball and a deserted spider-web. No hammer to be seen. There was no sign that what he'd experienced had been real. Had it all been a dream? The missing Viking weapons and lack of pain certainly seemed to indicate that this might be the case.

'It's not, though,' Arthur said to the room. 'I didn't imagine it all. That's the kind of thing that happens in lazy movies, not real life.'

He stood back up and looked around the room once more. There was still something he was missing, some little clue he hadn't noticed yet. The furniture was all in its correct place. His clothes were folded on the chair. He usually left them lying on the floor, but Joe sometimes tidied them up when he was sleeping, so nothing out of the ordinary there.

Finally, he saw what he was missing. There was nothing unusual in the room at all. What was unusual was the room itself. He was back in his Dublin bedroom, not the one in Kerry. He ran to the window and pulled open the curtains. Sure enough, the scene through the window was the one he'd gotten used to over the past few months. There was no sign of a flood; in fact, the ground was bone dry. The sky was a cloudless blue wonder and the sun gave off a fresh spring warmth that he could feel through the glass. People were coming and going around the estate, some walking dogs, some coming back from the shops with the newspaper and the makings of a Sunday morning fry-up. The Barry house was just as it had always been. There was no sign that any explosion had taken place and the family people carrier sat in the driveway as usual.

As he pulled back from the window in quiet, hopeful awe, he caught a glimpse of his own reflection. The black semicircle of the eye-patch was there still, looking like a hole in his head. He raised his fingers to touch it.

Standing there by the window, he caught the aroma of frying from downstairs. He threw his clothes on as quickly as he could, opting to take a shower after eating. His stomach was growling at him like he hadn't eaten in days.

Arthur raced downstairs and into the kitchen to find Joe standing over the cooker. He flicked the handle of the frying pan and a pancake flipped in mid-air before landing back in the pan and sizzling as Joe placed it back on the heat. Then he scooped sausages and bacon out of the other pan and stacked them on plates on the sideboard. The toaster spurted up some fresh slices just as Arthur spoke.

'Uh … morning, Dad.'

Joe jumped and he swivelled to look at his son. His surprise at the sound of Arthur's voice was instantly replaced with a warm smile. He ran to him and picked him up in a tight embrace.

'Morning, sleepy-head,' he said, setting him down to take a seat at the breakfast table. 'We were wondering when you'd ever wake up.'

'We?'

'Yeah. We.'

Just then, the door leading to the small back garden opened behind him. The woman coming in was wearing gardening gloves smudged with moist patches of earth. She was carrying a small watering can in one hand, along with a trowel, and had her hair tied in a loose ponytail looped through the back of a baseball cap.

'Mum?'

'Morning, Arthur.'

'*Mum!*' He kicked back his chair and was on his feet, sliding over the laminate floor in his socks. She had just enough time to set the gardening tools aside before Arthur knocked into her, sending them both into a spin.

He held her as tightly as he could. Part of him was afraid that if he did, she'd just disintegrate, that she wouldn't be there any more, that he had imagined her. Then she hugged him back and Arthur knew – he really knew – that she was real.

Eventually, Joe's voice brought them back to the kitchen.

'Your breakfasts will go cold, you two.'

Arthur and Rhona loosened their grips and looked into each other's faces.

'You're here,' Arthur murmured.

'I'm here.'

'You didn't die.'

'I never died. At least not in this reality. So at least that's a few uncomfortable conversations I won't have to have.'

'But how?'

Rhona went to the sink and ran her hands under the tap. Arthur sat at the table next to Joe, who was chomping down his food. Arthur held his cutlery but just kept staring at his mother.

'We don't know,' she answered as she wiped her hands dry and sat next to them. 'We just remember being on Loki's battlefield. And then I tried to stop him but you touched him.'

'Next thing we knew,' said Joe between chews, 'we were all back in our beds, you included. The flood was gone, the Wolfsguard were gone. The world was back to normal and no one remembers a thing about Loki.'

'But you do.'

'Only those who were at the battlefield seem to remember,' explained Rhona.

'And Ash and Max and–?'

'They all remember. And they're all fine.'

'I need to go see them!' Arthur started to get up from his seat.

'No, you don't,' said Rhona in a stern voice he remembered and loved well. 'Not yet anyway. I'll let everyone know you're awake and tell them to come over later. They've been looking forward to seeing you. But right now, you need to eat your breakfast. You've been asleep for the past three days.'

'I have?'

'Yup,' Joe said with a sausage suspended on the end of his fork. 'But your mum knew you'd wake up soon enough. She told us not to worry.'

'What happened, Arthur?' Rhona asked him. 'While you were sleeping. What happened with Loki?'

Both his parents looked at him expectantly, so he told them.

It took surprisingly little time to recount the vanquishing of a god and Arthur finished the story between bites of food. 'So Loki's gone. He can never return.' He hesitated, afraid to ask his mother the question that was gnawing at his gut. 'What about … Hel?'

'She's gone too,' said Rhona. 'She was a part of Loki, but she couldn't stay in control once you called to your mammy for help.' She smiled at him.

They ate the rest of the breakfast in silence, just glad to be in each other's company.

After three helpings of pancakes and allowing time for the food to be digested a bit (during which Joe explained that work at the Metro site was starting back up in a week and that it seemed as if he had never quit his job – most likely thanks to some grateful gods, Arthur figured), Arthur helped his parents clean up. Joe washed, his mum dried and he put away the dishes. Every time Rhona handed him another bowl or bunch of cutlery, they smiled at each other in silence. Afterwards, they retired to the living room and watched an old murder mystery that had just started on TV. It was set on a train and they'd seen it more than once down the years but, to Arthur, it was still the best feeling in the world: sitting there and sharing a lazy Sunday afternoon together. Finally, just as the moustachioed little detective was unmasking the killer, the doorbell rang.

Arthur rushed to answer it and was immediately swept up in a warm embrace that smelled of lilies. Mrs Barry nearly pulled him outside she was cuddling him so forcefully, repeating over and over how thankful they all were that he'd rescued them from that terrible man. Mr Barry, who was standing stoically behind her throughout, offered his hand to Arthur when she was done. This was more acknowledgement than Arthur had had from him in all the months they'd known each other.

When the adults were finished expressing undying gratitude, Mrs Barry and her husband stepped out of the way to let Arthur's friends through.

Four pairs of feet thundered across the threshold. Ash was in front, trailed closely by Max and the Lavender siblings. They ran straight into him, enclosing him in a group hug. Ex somehow managed to lift them all a few inches off the floor.

When they were done, Ash stood a few steps back from him and looked him up and down.

'You're alive. Really alive.'

'I guess so.' Arthur blushed. He really didn't know how

to take all the sudden praise. 'Thanks to all of us.'

'And Loki?'

But before Arthur could answer, Joe had appeared behind him and started bustling everyone into the kitchen. Arthur waited for them all to pass by him before shutting the door. As soon as he did, the bell rang a second time, an urgent *ding-a-ling-a-ling*.

Stace was standing there, looking pleased as punch to have her arm around a handsome boy close to her own age. Without saying a thing, she grabbed Arthur, covered the crown of his head in kisses and then planted a sticky lip-gloss mark on each cheek. She stepped away from him, blushing.

'I'm ... I'm just so grateful, Arthur,' she said in a breathless voice.

Embarrassed, Arthur flattened his hair where her kisses had disturbed it, shrugged nonchalantly and turned to her companion. He was a tall young man with broad shoulders, choppy hair the colour of hay and a flawless smile. Arthur was sure he'd never met the man before but something about his pale eyes told him that he should know him.

Stace's date put out his hand and said, in a deep and slightly accented voice, 'You saved us all, Arthur.'

Finally, the penny dropped.

367

'*Eirik?*'

There was no sign of the dark leathery skin that Arthur had grown used to in the Viking, and his cheeks and hands were fleshier than before but, staring into the young man's eyes, there was no denying that this was Eirik standing before him.

And he had spoken!

'But … how …' Arthur stuttered into silence.

'We woke up,' said Eirik, enunciating every sound clearly and evenly. No more grunts. 'Just like everyone else did. Only we had our lives back.' His fingers went self-consciously to his throat. 'Even our vocal cords.'

Stace hugged one of Eirik's toned arms.

'This is our third proper date,' she told Arthur.

He had a million questions he wanted to ask, not least of which was how Stace felt about her 'new' boyfriend having been dead for a millennium under the city, but he bit his tongue when his mother called him from the kitchen.

'Arthur! Come on! We're waiting for you!'

Stace and Eirik stepped into the house and hurried past him into the kitchen. He shut the door finally and went after them.

A banner hung in front of the kitchen cupboards. It was a birthday banner that Rhona had had printed up years ago. It used to read 'Happy Birthday, Arthur!', but someone had covered up the first two words and replaced them with handwritten words so the banner now read: 'Thanks for Saving the World from Certain Destruction, Arthur!' The breakfast table was covered in party food of every description: cupcakes, finger sandwiches, cookies, sausage rolls and bagel pizzas. And they all surrounded a three-tiered chocolate fudge cake in the middle.

A cheer rose from everyone in the kitchen as Arthur entered, startling him slightly.

'What's this for?' he asked when the cheering petered out.

'It's for you,' said Joe. 'We wouldn't be here today if it wasn't for you.'

'That's not true,' said Arthur. 'It wasn't just me. It was all of you. I couldn't have stopped Loki without you.'

'Now, Arthur,' said Mrs Barry, 'there's no need to be humble.'

'I'm not being humble,' he said. 'It's the truth. We stopped a god, we saved the world, but we did it together.' A few nods and smiles went round the kitchen. 'Now, let's have some cake!'

Another cheer.

The party went on into the evening and still Arthur hadn't had a chance to talk to Ash, Max, Ellie and Ex alone. Eventually, when the adults (and not-quite adults Stace and Eirik) were settling down to some coffee in the kitchen, Arthur and his friends sat on the porch steps and breathed a united sigh of relief. The sun was going down now, casting the estate into a fiery red.

'So …' Ash started, staring meaningfully at Arthur.

He proceeded to tell them all that had happened in Asgard and how he'd finally managed to trick Loki.

'The well is bottomless,' he finished. 'The rock and the ribbon will just keep dragging him down forever. He'll never find a way out.'

'That's perfect,' Ellie mused. 'He's trapped for all time.'

'So the Norns really did help you then?' asked Ash.

'Yeah. Back in the throne room, I figured out that they must have been sending me the dreams all along. And I guess they gave the world the dream about Hel to try and warn everyone about what was coming. But they were helping us long before then, centuries before.'

'How do you mean?'

'The Norns helped Fenrir escape from Asgard. I'd always wondered why, but I think I worked it out. When Fenrir was in Asgard, he really was a monster. But when he got to our world, he saw the good that mankind can do, so he actually became more human. Because of that, he hid Hel and then set my mum free.'

'If he'd never done that,' piped up Max, 'you'd never have been born!'

'And you were the only one who could stop Hel,' added Ellie.

'Exactly. The Norns sent Fenrir to our world to become more human. And I reminded my mother of her own humanity.'

'So even back then the Norns knew what was going to happen!' Ash exclaimed.

'They know everything. Speaking of Fenrir, whatever happened to him after the battlefield?'

'He phoned us the day after we woke up,' said Ash. 'He and Drysi woke up the same way, on his boat at the docks. They're happy now. She's accepted who she is. Now that they're free from the threat of Loki, they're going to travel the world together.'

'That's great!'

'When the Vikings woke up, most of them wanted to go back to Scandinavia,' explained Ellie. 'So Fenrir's offered to take them a few at a time.'

'I can't believe they're *actually* all alive!'

'Yeah. All of them,' said Ash. 'They look normal and they can talk now too. A couple of them have gotten jobs in the Viking Experience, believe it or not, as actors!'

'They're surprisingly chatty when you get to know them,' added Ex, which was the most he'd said all day.

'They still don't know much English but they're working on it,' said Ellie.

'So everything's as it should be,' said Arthur in wonderment.

'Everything,' agreed Ash. 'Except that.' She pointed at the eye-patch.

His fingers went straight to it.

'Actually, I quite like it,' he told them. 'It reminds me of what we went through.'

'A souvenir,' suggested Ellie.

'A battle scar,' corrected Arthur.

She laughed and looked at her watch. 'Oh. Is that the time?' She turned to her brother. 'We'd better be off.'

'So soon?' asked Arthur.

'Sorry. We've been staying at Ash's for the past few days but our parents are due back from their expedition soon. We need to pretend like we've had a boring few weeks. And we need to get back to home schooling.'

'You're not going to stay in Belmont?' Ash asked.

'No. We only enrolled to investigate you, Arthur. Plus we actually live on the other side of the city. Anyway, we like home school. It gives us more freedom for our … uh

'... extracurricular activities.' She winked at them and got to her feet.

Ellie put her hand out to Arthur but he shrugged it aside in place of a hug. Ex gave him a remarkably tender embrace when it was his turn.

'It's been great getting to know you, Arthur. And you, Ash. And Max,' said Ellie.

'Likewise,' said Arthur. 'Really, really great. But this isn't goodbye. You'll keep in touch and come visit us, right?'

'Of course we will.'

'Stay out of trouble,' said Ash.

'We can't make any promises,' laughed Ellie. 'You know that, Ash.'

They watched as the Lavender siblings walked across the green, around the corner and out of sight. As soon as they were gone, Max whipped his head around to Arthur.

'Wanna play some football?'

'Sure,' Arthur replied, laughing. 'Why don't you go get the ball!'

Max ran off as quickly as he could in the direction of his house in case Arthur changed his mind.

The trees of the Phoenix Park were black husks against the red-streaked evening sky. Families were walking dogs, couples were strolling hand in hand and joggers were pounding the footpaths. And none of them knew of the great deeds that one boy and his friends had carried out there in another time and another place.

A doe lapped from a lake in the northernmost half of the park. Something flashed before her eyes in the water, something dark and long and quick. But it didn't startle her. She sensed that it was no danger. And it wasn't.

The water snake that was once the World Serpent flitted through the water. It was home now and it was happy.

✿✿✿✿✿

The girl watched the sun be swallowed up by the North Sea. It was cold here – it was always cold – and her breaths puffed white in front of her face. But she didn't mind the cold. After the cold came the warmth, and that she liked. She would go inside shortly, into the cramped cabin with the Vikings, and have some of the hot chocolate that Bjorn so loved to make.

Somebody lent over and laid a blanket across her knees. Drysi looked behind her up into her father's dark eyes.

'It's beautiful, isn't it?' she said, indicating the sunset.

'It is,' said Fenrir, laying one hand on her shoulder. 'It really is.'

The man who was once the Fenris Wolf smiled to himself. He was home now and he was happy.

Chatter continued in the kitchen but Rhona barely listened to it any more. She looked at Joe, at the way his eyes shone when he talked, at his hands – calloused from years of guitar playing – at the little smile that he kept only for her when no one was looking.

She looked through the open door at her son and his friend on the porch. They were hardly moving and the setting sun cast them in a bronze light that put her in mind of statues.

The mother who was once Hell's Keeper refilled her mug of coffee. She was home now and she was happy.

When they heard Max burst through the Barrys' front door, Arthur smiled and turned to Ash. They looked at each other in silence. There was so much left unsaid between them and Arthur felt awkward. He couldn't explain it. He'd always felt so comfortable around her but now there was a nervous lump in his chest.

'Ash,' he said.

'Arthur,' she said.

'I like you.'

They said it together and laughed together.

Their hands met on the step. Arthur looked at the golden sky above them.

'It was a perfect day,' he muttered.

Ash leaned forward and kissed him once on the cheek.

'Now it is,' she said.

Epilogue

Loki falls.

That is his existence now. Falling.

His rage is so hot, so vicious that it could almost boil the water he falls through.

Falling. Constantly falling. The perfect prison.

Except for one thing. He is falling through the Well of Urd. The place where all knowledge that was, is and will be goes. And Loki ... well ... Loki is soaking it up. Loki is learning. As he falls.

And one day Loki hopes that he will learn that one, single, beautiful piece of information that tells him how to escape from the perfect prison.

One day.

Acknowledgements

When I was younger I would read authors' acknowledgements and wonder why they felt the need to thank so many people. After all, the author wrote the book. Were all these names really recognition-worthy?

Well now I know the answer. Yes.

First I'd like to thank my family for their bottomless well of support; my parents Ann and Luke, my brother Paul, and all my extended family. A special mention also goes to my cousin Ciara, who was a huge help when it came to my first few (terrifying!) book events.

To my friends: I appreciate every word of encouragement, every piece of advice, every copy bought and every Facebook share. And to Paul, Dee, Ruairí, Tag and Lou in particular: you didn't complain when I named sometimes unflattering characters after you. You didn't even complain whenever I would drift off mid-sentence because I suddenly had a solution to a particularly tricky plot point. So this book is dedicated to you.

The help and support I got from booksellers, librarians and teachers cannot be understated and if I was to list them all, you'd be holding a book twice as long as this. But I would like to take the opportunity to thank Jane Alger and all in UNESCO Dublin City of Literature for choosing my first book for their inaugural children's city read.

Three cheers to the wonderful gang at Children's Books Ireland and Inis Magazine. They do sterling work both for writers and readers of children's books and deserve all the kudos they get and more. Hip-hip! Hip-hip! Hip-hip! Hooray!

Massive thanks to all in RTÉ's Elev8 for helping me name one of Ash's rebels and, of course, to Orla Doyle for helping Arthur save the world!

Thank you to everyone at Mercier Press for taking a chance on me in the first place and for all the work they've done over the past three and a bit years. And I tip my hat especially to Wendy and the editorial team. Without their invaluable input, Arthur's adventures wouldn't be as exciting/scary/funny/gripping as they are.

I also wish to gratefully acknowledge the support of the Arts Council of Ireland.

Lastly, I turn to you – yes, YOU. I wrote the stories but I believe that the reader brings them to life. So, on behalf of Arthur, Ash, Loki and all the rest – *thank you!*

Alan Early

Dublin, 2013

Also Available

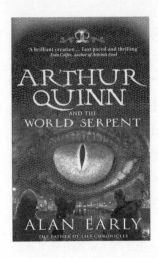

ARTHUR QUINN

AND THE

WORLD SERPENT

Part 1 of
the Father of Lies Chronicles

978 1 85635 827 9

Something monstrous is stirring under Dublin …

Arthur Quinn has problems. He has just moved to Dublin and started a new school, and now he's having crazy dreams about the Viking god Loki. But it soon becomes clear these are more than dreams – Arthur is actually having premonitions about a great evil that threatens the world.

With his new friends, Will and Ash, Arthur sets out to investigate what Loki is up to. Together they discover that under the streets of Dublin, buried in a secret chamber, is a creature that's been imprisoned for a thousand years, a creature that can and will destroy the world if Loki has anything to do with it.

Can Arthur Quinn defeat the Viking god of mischief?

www.mercierpress.ie

Also Available

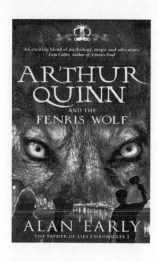

ARTHUR QUINN

AND THE

FENRIS WOLF

Part 2 of
the Father of Lies Chronicles

978 1 85635 998 6

Arthur Quinn thinks life is back to normal. Three months have passed since he and his friends defeated the Viking god Loki and saved the world, and everything has been quiet. But then Arthur starts having the dreams again: dreams of gods, dreams of magic, dreams of a wolf. It can mean only one thing. Loki is back and only Arthur can stop him.

With the clock ticking, Arthur and his friends find themselves in a race against time to track down the god and prevent him from putting his sinister plan in motion.

But what they don't know is that this time, Loki has help …

www.mercierpress.ie